ALSO BY RESHONDA TATE BILLINGSLEY
A Good Man Is Hard to Find
Say Amen, Again

ALSO BY VICTORIA CHRISTOPHER MURRAY
The Deal, the Dance, and the Devil
Sins of the Mother

SINNERS
& Saints

VICTORIA
CHRISTOPHER MURRAY
and

RESHONDA
TATE BILLINGSLEY

A TOUCHSTONE BOOK
PUBLISHED BY SIMON & SCHUSTER
NEW YORK   LONDON   TORONTO   SYNDEY   NEW DELHI

Touchstone
A Division of Simon & Schuster, Inc.
1230 Avenue of the Americas
New York, NY 10020

First Touchstone trade paperback edition January 2012

TOUCHSTONE and colophon are registered trademarks of Simon & Schuster, Inc.

For information about special discounts for bulk purchases, please contact Simon &
Schuster Special Sales at 1-866-506-1949 or business@simonandschuster.com.

The Simon & Schuster Speakers Bureau can bring authors to your live event. For more
information or to book an event contact the Simon & Schuster Speakers Bureau at
1-866-248-3049 or visit our website at www.simonspeakers.com.

Designed by Akasha Archer

Manufactured in the United States of America

10   9   8   7   6   5   4   3   2   1

Library of Congress Cataloging-in-Publication Data
Murray, Victoria Christopher,
    Sinners and saints / Victoria Christopher Murray and ReShonda Tate Billingsley.
        p. cm.
    "A Touchstone book."
    1. Bush, Jasmine Larson (Fictitious character)—Fiction. 2. African American
women—Fiction. I. Billingsley, ReShonda Tate. II. Title.
    PS3563.U795S59 2011
    813'.54—dc22   2011006867

ISBN 978-1-4516-0815-1
ISBN 978-1-4516-0817-5 (ebook)

A Note from
Victoria

This is the most difficult part of the writing process for me. Because now I have to talk about real people. My characters always do what I tell them to do (well, not always!). But real folks . . . whew; they get upset if you forget to mention their names. So in what has become my practice, I mention no one. If I love you, you already know it. If I like you, you know that, too. If I respect and admire you, I'm sure I've told you . . . and if I don't like you . . . well, I would never mention you anyway. So there, now I've covered everyone.

Now, on to those who could care less if they are mentioned or not. This has been by far the most fun I've had writing in the fourteen years that I've been blessed to do this. And it is completely because of ReShonda Tate Billingsley. Whew; Rachel worked nerves I didn't even know I had and ReShonda kept me on my toes. I took my game up because of her and I am so grateful that we fought for this project together. Thank you, ReShonda, for being such a great friend and writing partner. Can we just do this from now on? I am so glad that Trish Todd had the chance to edit this for us. Thank you, Trish, for believing in the project and for letting us know that you had a great time reading the story. Your edits stretched us and definitely made the story stronger. To Sulay Hernandez, I just didn't get enough time. But at least I get the chance to say thank you for coming to us at such a good time and for helping ReShonda and me to take this book up to a higher level. I had visions of you working with me on my next one hundred titles, but the best thing that came out of this connection is our friendship. To Shida Carr—there is only one word for you: The Best! Okay, that's two words, but you know what I mean. There is no one better in publicity. Period. Thank you for how you've helped build my career through the years. To the wonderful readers who stay with me year after year, novel after novel, we hope that you enjoy this one and will help ReShonda and me continue to pass the word. We write because of you!

And finally to my Lord and Savior, Jesus Christ. Whenever I think I'm too weary to walk this road anymore, you send a shining star. I just want to please you in all ways and I pray that my writing will continue to do just that. Thank you for guiding me as you see fit and for gifting me with a career that is my passion!

Peace,

Victoria

A Note from
ReShonda

As an avid reader, I was enthralled with the character Jasmine Larson Bush in Victoria Christopher Murray's Jasmine series. Not just because she was an intriguing, scandalous character, but because this little voice in my head kept saying, "Oh, I could *so* take that chick down."

That little voice belonged to one of my most popular characters—Rachel Jackson Adams from my Amen series. Rachel kept demanding that she and Jasmine meet.

That's why I was thrilled when Simon & Schuster gave us the go-ahead to make that meeting happen.

To say I loved writing this book with Victoria would be a serious understatement. This is the *most* fun I've ever had writing a book. Victoria is such a talented writer and I never knew what she would have Jasmine do next. That's the beauty of this collaboration. I'd write my chapter, and then sit back and wait to see how Miss Jasmine would work her way out of it. I literally would drop whatever I was doing when Victoria sent her chapters to me because I couldn't wait to see the story unfold.

I am thoroughly pleased with the result. So I hope you enjoy reading this book as much as we enjoyed writing it.

But before you get to reading about these two outrageous first ladies, please allow me a moment to thank those that made this journey possible. Of course, thank you, God, for your favor in allowing me to realize my writing dreams. Much love to my writing partner herself, Victoria Christopher Murray. You made this entire experience one I'll never forget.

To my family, who understood when I wanted to drop everything and write—my husband, Miron; mother, Nancy; sister, Tanisha; and my three beautiful kids. I appreciate your love and support. To my girl, Pat Tucker, thank you so much for not only allowing me to bounce scandalous scenarios off of you, but for always having my back.

As always, thanks to my agent, Sara Camilli, and to my team at Gallery Books: editor extraordinaire Brigitte Smith, my publicist Melissa Gramstad, and Louise Burke. Thank you to Trish Todd, Sulay Hernandez, and Shida Carr at Touchstone for all your hard work on shaping this into a final product that readers will love.

Thanks to the best literary assistant in the world! Kym Fisher, what would I do without you????

To my other literary friends, thanks for all of your support. You prove that we can all work together for a common goal—to get people reading: Nina Foxx, Kimberla Lawson Roby, Eric Jerome Dickey, Zane, Al Frazier, Dee Stewart, Tiffany Warren, Trice Hickman, Pat G'orge-Walker, J. D. Mason, and Rhonda McKnight.

Thank you to all the wonderful libraries, book clubs, churches, and schools that have supported my work. A big shout-out to my Facebook and Twitter families.

And finally thank you . . . yeah you, holding the book. Your support of this endeavor means the world to me. I hope you enjoy and we'd love to hear your feedback! Hit me up at www .reshondatatebillingsley.com.

Now . . . let's get ready to rumble!!

Much Love,
ReShonda

SINNERS
& Saints

Chapter
ONE

How in the world was Jasmine going to keep her promise to God now?

Two years ago, she had promised Him that if He saved her daughter when she was kidnapped, if He brought her home safely, then she was going to live a life devoted just to Him. Jasmine had vowed that with Jacqueline's return, she was going to live the life that God had for her as Hosea's wife, as Jacqueline and Zaya's mother. She wasn't going to want for anything more than what God had given her, because surely, He had supplied her with enough.

God had done His part.

And for the last two years, Jasmine had done her part, too.

She'd lived a low-key life, thrilled that her greatest dramas were debates about fashion choices every morning with her seven-year-old daughter.

But how was she supposed to keep her promise to God now? After what her husband had just told her?

"So, hold up," Jasmine said, slipping into the chair across from Hosea. "I thought you were just going to the convention as the keynote speaker."

Hosea nodded.

"So, explain this to me again."

With a sigh, Hosea folded the newspaper he'd been reading and placed it on the table. He stuffed his mouth with a forkful of pancake, chewed for a moment, then said, "The call came in from a friend of Pop's, Pastor Earl Griffith. He thinks I need to submit my resume."

"To be the head of the American Baptist Coalition?"

Hosea nodded.

"But we're not Baptist."

His eyes danced with his amusement. "Get out of here."

"You know what I mean," Jasmine said, waving one hand. "I just don't get it. Why would they call you?"

"*They* didn't call me. Only Pastor Griffith. Seems like there're a couple of men in the running, though according to Griffith, the front-runner is Pastor Adams, Lester Adams from the Southern region."

Jasmine frowned. "I've never heard of him."

"Out of Houston. But Pastor Griffith doesn't think Adams is the man. Seems that the last four presidents have been from the South and Griffith and a couple of other pastors on the board think that the Coalition needs someone from the North, someone more progressive, to really move the organization forward."

"And they think that can be you?"

"Not *they*, darlin'. I told you—Griffith called me."

"But you said there were others who agreed with him."

Hosea nodded. "Apparently, they don't have anyone from the North who they think can go up against Adams. I guess they think my name could win this."

"That makes sense to me."

"It doesn't matter how much sense it makes, darlin'. I told Pastor Griffith that I'm not interested."

As if she didn't hear any of Hosea's last words, Jasmine whispered, "Wow." Old thoughts, familiar desires came to her mind—of power and prestige and money. How much money would a president receive?

She didn't know a lot about the American Baptist Coalition, but she knew enough. Like the fact that they were the largest African American religious organization, and wielded major political clout. And as much as black folks loved religion, the head of the ABC would have a boatload of power—and so would his wife.

Talk about being the first lady!

"Jasmine?"

I'd be the first lady of like . . . the world!

"Jasmine?"

"Huh?" Her eyes were glassy with images of her future and it took her a moment to focus on Hosea.

His admonishment came before he even said a word. It was in the way his eyes narrowed and the way he'd already begun shaking his head. "Don't even think about it."

"What?"

"You know what. I'm not gonna do it," he said slowly, as if he was speaking to one of their children. "I'm gonna go to the convention and speak, just like they asked. But I'm not gonna run for that office. The little I know about Lester Adams, he's a good man. They'll be fine with him."

"How could he be the one if I've never even heard of him?"

"Like you know every pastor in the country."

"I'm not talking about knowing every pastor. I'm thinking that Pastor Griffith is right. The head of the ABC should be someone who's known and who can add to the Coalition. Think about what you bring as the pastor of one of the largest churches in the country. Then, there's your show." She nodded. "Pastor Griffith is right," she repeated. "It has to be you."

His head was still shaking. "No. I don't want the drama."

"Who said anything about drama?"

"Any type of election—political or religious—is always about drama." He stood and placed his plate in the sink. "And then there's you, my wonderful wife. As much as I love you, darlin', anytime you're involved in anything, drama makes its way into our lives. No, I don't want any part of it."

"So, you're just gonna let this huge opportunity pass us—I mean, pass you by?"

"Yup, because it's not an opportunity that interests me. The church, the show, and most importantly you and the children are enough for me." He leaned over and kissed her forehead. "Speaking of the church, I'm gonna get dressed and head over there. I have a meeting in a couple of hours."

"Okay," she said, dismissing him with words, though she'd already dismissed him in her mind. Jasmine stayed as Hosea left her alone in the kitchen.

You and the children are enough for me.

Until a few minutes ago, she would've agreed with her husband. But this conversation was a game changer.

Hosea was right—their lives were without drama, but it had gotten kind of boring. Every day it was the same thing—getting the children off to school, then working on the women's committees at the church, then coming home to meet the children, then helping Mrs. Sloss with dinner, then . . . then . . . then . . .

Not that she had complaints; she loved her life, her family. But she would still love everyone, and maybe even a little bit more if Hosea were the head of the ABC.

Oh, no. She wasn't going to sit back and let this opportunity pass Hosea. He needed this position, even if he didn't know it.

Standing, she moved toward their bedroom, the conniving wheels of her brain already churning. She stood outside the door of their master bathroom, listening to her husband praise God, the spray of the shower, his accompanying music.

"I trust you, Lord!" He sang the words to one of Donnie McClurkin's songs.

"Babe," she said, interrupting his praise time. "I'm gonna run over to Mae Frances's apartment, okay?"

"Don't you have a meeting at the church?"

"Yeah, but it's not till this afternoon and Mae Frances just called and she really needs me to help her with something." Jasmine paused. It had been a long time since she'd manipulated the truth to get something she wanted. But it wasn't like she was going back to being a total liar again—she just needed to get this done and after Hosea was in his rightful place, she'd go back to being on the side of righteousness.

"Oh, okay. Is Nama all right?" he asked, referring to Mae Frances by the name their children called the older woman.

"She's fine. You know Nama. I'll call Mrs. Whittingham and tell her that I may be a little late for my meeting."

By the time they said their good-byes and Jasmine grabbed her purse, she already had a plan. But she'd need some help, and Mae Frances, her friend who knew everyone from Al Sharpton to Al Capone and his offspring, was just the person to help her.

"Sorry, Pastor Adams," she said to herself as she rode down in the elevator. "Whoever you are, you can be the president of the ABC once Hosea and I are done—in, say, ten or twenty years."

She stepped outside of their Central Park South apartment building and into the New York springtime sun. Slapping on her designer glasses, she laughed out loud.

Oh, yeah, today was gonna be a really good day.

Chapter
TWO

W atch out, Michelle Obama!

Rachel Jackson Adams smiled in satisfaction as she surveyed her reflection in the bathroom mirror. She'd had to leave the prestigious American Baptist Coalition regional dinner and step inside the restroom to compose herself. After all, she was about to be the first lady of one of the most prestigious organizations in the country. She couldn't very well be acting a plumb fool because she was overcome with excitement. But Rachel had wanted to do a backflip, front flip, toe touch, cartwheel, and anything else she could think of to express her joy.

Rachel fluffed her honey brown curls, then lightly refreshed her MAC Oh Baby lip gloss. She had come such a long way. Her mother was probably dancing in her grave at the sight of Rachel as not only a first lady, but a soon-to-be prominent one at that. Rachel had worked hard to garner the respect of the parishioners at Zion Hill Missionary Baptist Church. She'd grown up in that church, so everyone knew her dirt—all of it—and it had taken God himself to get these people to respect her. And while Zion Hill had grown tremendously, it still wasn't considered a megachurch, and outside of Houston there were few who had even heard of it. As the first lady of the American Baptist Coalition, her status would go to a whole new level. Shoot, if she had to be first lady, she might as well be the *top* first lady.

Rachel savored the thought as she dropped her lip gloss back into her clutch and stepped back into the corridor.

"I was beginning to think you'd fallen in," her husband of eight years said before leaning in and lightly kissing Rachel on the cheek.

Lester Adams wasn't her true love—that title belonged to her thirteen-year-old son's father, Bobby Clark. But Lester was good *for* her. Her love for Lester was that agape love they talked about in First Corinthians. It brought out the best in her. Well, for the most part anyway. Life with Bobby had been filled with drama—Rachel admitted much of that was her own doing, but it was drama-filled nonetheless. And although Bobby still remained a part of Jordan's life, Rachel had finally gotten him out of her system and was focusing all of her attention on making her marriage work.

"What took you so long?" Lester asked, snapping Rachel out of her thoughts.

"Sorry," Rachel said with a slight smile, "but you know I'm about to be the preeminent first lady, so I had to make sure my makeup was on point." She tossed her hair back. "Come to think of it, I think I'll change my name to Lady Rachel so I can have the title to go along with the position."

Lester narrowed his eyes and glared at his wife. "Rachel," he began in that voice she hated—the one that he always used when he was chastising her.

"What?" Rachel shrugged, already getting defensive.

"I don't have the position yet," he said matter-of-factly. "The regional board just nominated me tonight. There's still a national election."

Rachel waved him off. "That's just a formality. Did you hear those election results? You beat Pastor Johnson seventy-three to twenty-five percent!"

Lester sighed. "Pastor Johnson also got his sixteen-year-old stepniece pregnant." As soon as Lester said it, he looked like he wished he could take the words back.

The smile immediately left Rachel's face. Lester was no saint himself. He'd had his own little pregnant-woman-on-the-side debacle. But thank God, they'd worked through that crisis.

"I'm just saying," Lester quickly continued, like he wanted to prevent Rachel's mind from traveling down that rocky memory lane, "Pastor Johnson wasn't that hard to beat. I still have to run against whomever they nominate from the North region, and rumor has it they're bringing out their top dog—Pastor Hosea Bush."

"That jack-legged TV preacher?" Rachel asked with a frown.

Lester shook his head. "Pastor Bush is not jack-legged. He's well established, comes from a highly respected family, and leads one of the largest churches in the country."

"*So?* He's. Not. You," Rachel said, reaching up and adjusting Lester's bow tie. Lester had been an extreme nerd when they were in high school—which is why Rachel had never given him the time of day. But he'd pursued her relentlessly and eventually had worn her down. He was willing to be a father to her two kids and he loved her unconditionally. So she agreed to give their relationship a try, but not before having him shave off that red mop of a hairstyle he wore and introducing him to Proactiv. She'd revamped his wardrobe, taught him how to have a little swagger, and now, even she had to admit, he had it going on. Not to mention the fact that he was an awesome preacher. "Lester, sweetheart," Rachel said, taking her husband's hands, "you heard that emcee tonight. For the past sixty years, the president of the ABC has been a Southerner. That's not about to change. I don't care how prominent this Rev. Tree is."

Lester let out a small chuckle. "Pastor *Bush,*" he corrected.

"Tree, Bush, Leave, whatever," she said, flicking her hand. "The bottom line is, that position is ours. God said so."

He laughed again. "Oh, God said so, huh?"

Rachel nodded emphatically. "He sure did. And if God said it, then it's so." She grinned widely.

"Look at my baby," Lester said proudly. "And to think, you threatened to divorce me for entering the ministry."

"Well, that's because I'd spent my life as a preacher's daughter. I wasn't trying to be a preacher's wife. But I've gotten the hang of it now."

"You do make a great first lady," Lester said, kissing her again. "And can I say it again—you look lovely in that dress."

"Thank you. And I'm going to make an even better first lady on a national level." She tightened the belt on her royal blue Diane von Furstenberg silk dress. Her attire tonight was just one indication of how far she'd come. Just a few years ago, she would've shown up to an event like this in the latest Baby Phat or Apple Bottoms style that she could find. And although she still loved her some Kimora Lee Simmons, she didn't have to wear it *everywhere*.

"Congratulations, Rev. Adams," an elderly man said as he walked past them.

Lester stopped and smiled. "Thank you, sir."

"I can't wait until you officially claim that presidency," the man said as he stepped on to the elevator.

"From your lips to God's ears," Lester replied as he waved good-bye.

Rachel waited for the elevator door to close. "See, everyone knows you're the man for the job. And I'm the woman that needs to be next to the man for the job."

"Since when did this kind of stuff excite you?"

Rachel's hands went to her hips. "Since I did my homework. Do you know that the last wife of the ABC president was invited everywhere? To White House dinners, commencement ceremonies, the Grammys—she even cohosted on *The View*!"

"But wasn't she a TV journalist anyway?"

Rachel frowned. Lester and all this negativity was about to work her nerves. "That's beside the point. Everyone knows the ABC president is one of the most powerful men in the country, so that means the ABC's president's wife would be one of the most powerful women."

"I'm just saying, don't get ahead of yourself."

"Whatever, Lester." Rachel rolled her eyes. She'd been euphoric since they announced he'd won the election an hour ago. Of course, she always knew he would, but hearing it confirmed was the icing on the cake.

As thoughts of hanging out with Michelle Obama danced in her head, Rachel once again smiled.

"Rachel, I see your mind working."

"Just trying to determine where I'll get my dress for your induction ceremony." Maybe she could get Kimora to design her something personally.

"Rachel—"

She put her finger to his lips. "Shhhh," she said, draping her arm through his. "Let's just savor the moment tonight. Let's go back in, mingle with the people, and enjoy ourselves. My dad and Brenda have the kids, so the night is all ours. Tomorrow, we'll talk about the national election." Rachel decided to just change the subject because she didn't care what Lester said, he *would* win the national election. And if this Reverend Bush proved to be a problem, well, Rachel might just have to revert to her old bag of tricks—just for a moment—to make sure that he wasn't a threat. She wasn't going to let anything, or anyone, stand in the way of claiming what was destined to be hers.

Chapter
THREE

Not even the deep breath she took could stop Jasmine's knees from knocking; this was really happening. She wiggled her butt against the wooden chair in the Langston Hughes Auditorium, but it was difficult to get comfortable, especially since she couldn't stop shaking.

"You all right, darlin'?" Hosea squeezed her hand.

She could only give him a nod before her glance wandered again to the men in front of the stage. Their heads were bowed together, their voices low. Jasmine strained, wanting to take in even a single syllable of what they were saying. But it was impossible to hear their whispers through the chatter of the two hundred or so participants in the room.

She pressed her knees together. It wasn't that she was nervous—this was all excitement. Because this was the day she'd been waiting for . . . the voting for the pastor who would represent the Northern region in the national election for president of the American Baptist Coalition. The region had actually postponed the election for more than three weeks under the guise of opening the ballot to more pastors. But though several had submitted their resumes, only Hosea's had been accepted to go up against the four other pastors whose names were already on the ballot.

Now, just weeks after Hosea had declared that he would never run for president of the esteemed organization, Jasmine, Hosea, the Senior Reverend Bush, and a host of friends from their church filled the first two rows of the auditorium waiting for what Pastor Griffith had called the inevitable.

And this was all happening because of her.

Just like with everything else in their lives, she had taken charge, knowing what was best for her husband, even when he didn't have a clue.

She hadn't done it alone, though—no, a task like this had taken big names, big guns. It had taken Mae Frances. And her connections.

For the last eight years, every time Jasmine needed to win, her friend had handled it, had worked it out, had brought the victory home. And this time was no different . . .

"I agree, Jasmine Larson," Mae Frances had said the morning Jasmine had barreled into her apartment, telling her that she needed her like never before. "This position would be wonderful for Preacher Man," she said, calling Hosea by the nickname she'd given him when they'd met all those years ago. "And"—she paused for a moment—"this will be great for you."

Not more than the beat of a second passed before Jasmine said, "And anything that's good for me will be good for you."

Mae Frances had reared back on the sofa that Hosea and Jasmine had given her, and released a hearty laugh. "You got that right. I always gets mine." She was still chuckling, but then turned to her serious get-down-to-business tone. "So, tell me what you know."

The two had moved to the mahogany dining room table, this piece of furniture a gift to Mae Frances from Hosea's father, Rev. Samuel Bush. And as Jasmine leaned forward and relayed to Mae Frances everything that Hosea had told her, Mae Frances took notes as if making things happen was her job.

"So, that's it?" Mae Frances asked when Jasmine stopped after two minutes.

Jasmine nodded. "I don't even know that pastor—Griffith. I never heard of him before this morning."

Mae Frances frowned a little. "I wonder if that's Earl Griffith out of Chicago."

Jasmine shook her head. Was there anyone her friend didn't know?

"I don't know where he's from," Jasmine said. "All I know is that he called and he wants Hosea to run . . . and I do, too. I want him to have that position . . . I need him to be the president."

"Whoa! Hold on, Jasmine Larson." Mae Frances held up her hands. "Calm down. You've been home being the good wife for the last couple of years and it shows. You talking like you've forgotten how to play this game."

Jasmine's frown asked her question.

"You're acting like you've already hit the home run. The old Jasmine would know that you can't get too far out in front—you've got to touch first, second, and third base before you can bring it home." Mae Frances continued, "So, back to the business of getting Preacher Man to be the leader of the—"

"Not the leader, the president."

"Whatever! You want him to be the head Negro in charge, right?"

Jasmine cringed at her friend's choice of words, but still, she nodded. No one had ever accused Mae Frances of being loaded with class. But no one could deny that for an assignment like this, there was only one person who could make it happen . . . and that was exactly what Mae Frances had done.

She had sent Jasmine home with no information, but no worries, either, and by the time Jasmine maneuvered the thirty or so blocks from the Upper East Side to Central Park South, Mae Frances's plan was already in motion.

It hadn't even been a half hour from when she left Mae Frances until she stepped into her apartment, but when Jasmine walked inside, Hosea had not yet left to go to his office in the church. He was still at home, pacing the length of their living

room, his cell phone pressed against his ear. With his eyebrows
bunched together, and his forehead creased with deep wrinkles,
Jasmine knew that the talk was serious—she knew it was about
the ABC.

"I hear you, Steve," Hosea said as Jasmine laid her purse on
the table.

Ah, she thought. So that's where Mae Frances had started.
She'd begun with Hosea's award-winning cable talk show. Steven
Hager was the executive producer of *Bring It On,* and because
of his and Hosea's efforts, the show enjoyed ratings that rivaled
some network programs. *Bring It On* was Hosea's cherished
project, his idea, his success. And Jasmine knew what Mae
Frances knew—that Hosea would do anything to help the show
thrive even more.

Jasmine peeked into the living room from the foyer and
waved to Hosea, letting him know that she had returned. But
he'd only nodded, distracted by his conversation. She pretended
to have her own distraction, glancing through yesterday's mail,
which she'd already sorted. But though her eyes were turned
away, her ears were at full attention.

"Yeah, it would be great for the show, but if I were going to
take a position like that, it would have to be for much more than
just good ratings," Hosea said, still pacing.

Then more silence, peppered every few seconds with Hosea
grunting, "Uh-huh, uh-huh." Then something on the other end
of the line made Hosea stop. Made his eyes widen. Made him sit
down . . . slowly.

Jasmine's heart pounded.

"You're kidding me?" he whispered. "Jeremiah Wright?"

Jasmine pressed her lips together, but it was still hard to
keep the scream inside. It pressed through her lips—a little
yelp—just enough to make Hosea look up and at her for just
a moment.

"Well, yeah," Hosea said. "If he thinks I should do it . . . if he
thinks I can bring something to the Coalition."

There was more silence, but at the mention of Jeremiah

Wright's name, Jasmine knew that Mae Frances had hit that home run. Hosea might say no to Pastor Griffith, and even no to her. But not to the man whom he considered a stand-up guy, a hero, a mentor, even though he'd never met him.

"Okay," Hosea said. "Yeah, definitely give Reverend Wright my number." His voice was filled with an excitement that Jasmine had not heard in a while. "I'll call Pastor Griffith back now."

Hosea hung up and turned to a nonchalant Jasmine. "You are not going to believe this."

"What?" she asked, her eyes still on the mail.

"Jeremiah Wright."

"Oh, did you speak to him?" When Hosea frowned, Jasmine realized that maybe she was being a bit too casual. So she added, "Really?" as if she were surprised.

It was enough to get Hosea back on track. "No, I didn't speak to him, but he called Steve over at the studio. He said he heard that the ABC was considering me and that he'd followed me and the show after all that we went through with Jacquie." He paused and sat down on the sofa. "He really wants me to run and represent the North in the national election."

"Babe, that's great!" This time, Jasmine didn't have to add anything to her voice. Her excitement was enough. "So, if Reverend Wright is taking an interest in this, then . . ."

She left the sentence open for Hosea to finish. "Then, I have to do it." He nodded. "I don't have any choice." Glancing at Jasmine, he smiled as he stood up. "I need to make another call. I'm going to call back Pastor Griffith."

Within an hour, Hosea had reneged on his promise to never run and had faxed his resume to Pastor Griffith. An hour after that, Hosea Bush's name was on the ballot to represent the Northern region.

From that point, it was a done deal. Three candidates who'd been in the running dropped out—very quietly, but quickly. Only a single pastor, Reverend Penn, remained. William Penn, a sixty-seven-year-old small-time pastor, was the leader of New

Hope Baptist in Springfield Gardens, Queens. New Hope was Pastor Penn's seventh church, and interestingly, he'd had as many wives, changing spouses every time he was moved to a new congregation for one reason (or scandal) or another.

But while the Northern board had been able to convince the other pastors to step away, no one had been able to persuade Reverend Penn to do the same.

"This is my rightful position," the reverend had complained when he found out that Hosea was now in the running. "I've been trying to be president for the last twenty-three years!" He'd whined and stomped his foot like a child, but no one listened—no one except for his thirty-eight-years-younger wife, a synthetic-hair-weave-wearing leggy blonde who'd left her porn career behind when she married the pastor.

When Jasmine had first heard that Reverend Penn refused to drop out, she'd had Mae Frances pull a dossier on the Penns. But then she'd met the pitiful couple and told Mae Frances to forget it. If justice didn't prevail, if Hosea couldn't beat this false prophet and his trick of a wife, then he didn't deserve this position.

"So, the votes are in."

The voice of Pastor Griffith dragged Jasmine away from the memories of the past weeks. She smiled at the pastor, and did her best to have only pure thoughts about the sexiest preacher that she'd ever seen. Pastor Griffith (yes, Earl Griffith; yes, a connection of Mae Frances's) may have been a man of the cloth from Chicago, but if he'd ever decided to walk away and onto the stage, any movie producer would gladly scoop him right up. Even though he was in his sixties, he had the suaveness of that back-in-the-day actor Billy Dee Williams, and the swagger of President Barack Obama. Jasmine was in love—or she would have been, had she not been married and loved Hosea so much.

As if he felt her stare, Pastor Griffith glanced over at Jasmine and granted her a small smile.

She sighed like a teenager.

"You okay, darlin'?"

Jasmine had to shake her head a little, to take her eyes off of Pastor Griffith. "What?" she said, turning to her husband. "Oh. Yeah. I'm fine." This time, she squeezed Hosea's hand, but turned her eyes back to Pastor Griffith.

It wasn't just his amazing looks that made Jasmine admire the man. It was the way he did business. As the Northern director, Pastor Griffith was in charge. So, he had changed the election date to give the membership time to read about, and get to know, Hosea. And then, he'd told her and Hosea that there wasn't a single thing to worry about.

"It's gonna go down the way I want it to go down," he'd said in his deep, melodic, Barry White voice.

Hosea hadn't been pleased, always wanting to do everything by the good book. But Jasmine had melted. Pastor Griffith's words, the way he handled things, were as pleasing as the sound of his voice.

Now Pastor Griffith cleared his throat, adjusted the microphone, and said, "By a vote of ninety-three to seven percent, Pastor Hosea Bush will represent the Northern region in the national election for president of the American Baptist Coalition."

The applause was strong and loud; there was hope in the cheers as so many saw Hosea Bush as their first real chance of victory in more than sixty years.

Hosea stood and hugged Jasmine. But while there was nothing but smiles all around as the entire City of Lights assembly congratulated Hosea, Jasmine's face was pinched with a scowl.

Ninety-three to seven? Who had the nerve to vote against Hosea?

"Well, congratulations, Pastor Bush."

Reverend Penn's scratchy voice infiltrated their celebration. "It was a hard-fought fight," the reverend said.

No, it wasn't. The only reason Jasmine kept that thought inside was because Pastor Griffith had stepped down from the podium to offer his own congratulations—and she needed him to know that she was a proper—the perfect—first lady.

"Thank you, Reverend Penn." Hosea responded with a slight bow, gracious, as always. "I hope that I'll have your support when we get to Los Angeles."

"Of course, of course," Reverend Penn said. Though his words were positive, his tone told them all that he wasn't going to do a damn thing.

"And you can count on my support, too." The reverend's wife swung her waist-long fake hair so hard over her shoulder that both Reverend Bush and Pastor Griffith, who were standing behind her, ducked. "We definitely want one of our own to win finally," she purred, with her lips and her chest poked out.

His wife sounded way more sincere than her husband, and Jasmine wondered if she would have been as affable in defeat. But then all good thoughts of the woman evaporated when Mrs. Penn licked her full, ruby-red-colored lips. With her eyes planted on Hosea, she said, "I'll do whatever I can to help you win, Pastor Bush. *Whatever!*"

Jasmine could almost feel Hosea hold his breath when she jumped in front of the ex–porn star. But he didn't have a thing to worry about. She wasn't going to act like a crazy fool—not in the Langston Hughes Auditorium. Not in front of all the people who were going to work to get her husband elected.

Jasmine simply reached for the woman's hand. "Thank you. Hosea and I are both looking forward to working with you." A smile was on Jasmine's face, but she held the woman's hand even after she stopped talking. Squeezed it a little, then stepped back. Her eyes stayed glued to Mrs. Penn. *Don't mess with me,* Jasmine told the woman telepathically.

From one man-stealer to another, the message was received. Mrs. Penn stumbled back, turned away, and scurried out of the room like she was being chased.

Hmph! Jasmine grinned; it was good to know that she still had it.

"Well," Pastor Griffith said, "I guess we all need to get home and do some packing."

"Yes, definitely," the senior Bush said. "We just have a week to get ready for Los Angeles."

And a week after that, I'll be first lady to every African American Christian in America. And Hosea will be president, too.

The victorious group edged up the aisle. But as everyone talked about their plans, Jasmine had no time to participate in the petty chatter. Her thoughts were on Mae Frances.

It was so unlike her friend to miss an occasion like this. And Hosea had been disappointed when Mae Frances had called that morning and told him that she wasn't feeling well. But that had been the lie that Jasmine and Mae Frances had conjured up. The truth was that her friend had stayed home because she had much work to do. Pastor Griffith had assured them that Hosea had this election——there was no need for any last-minute manipulations. So, Mae Frances had stayed home to move forward to phase two.

"Babe, I'm gonna go check on Mae Frances," Jasmine said, once they all stood outside.

"Oh. But Pops wants to take us out to dinner for a celebration."

"Yeah, I figured we'd head over to Sylvia's," Hosea's father added.

"I'm sorry, but I really want to make sure she's okay," Jasmine said, her face pinched with concern for their friend. "Being that she's home alone and everything."

"Yeah, you're right. Go on." Hosea kissed her. "I'll bring a plate home for you."

"That would be great," Jasmine said, already rushing to a cab that'd stopped in front of the group.

She blew Hosea a kiss before she gave the driver Mae Frances's address. Then she leaned back and closed her eyes.

Okay, they'd gotten to first base. Really, second and third base, too. Now Jasmine wanted to know how they were going to hit that grand-slam home run.

Jasmine couldn't wait to see her friend. She couldn't wait to find out what the plan was to make sure that Hosea won the national election.

She couldn't wait to hear how they were going to bring Pastor Lester Adams down!

Chapter
FOUR

Rachel, what in the world are you doing in there?" Lester's voice startled her and Rachel jumped like a kid caught with her hand in the cookie jar.

"Nothing," she said, quickly minimizing the screen on her computer.

"Uh-uh," Lester replied, walking over to Rachel. She was sitting behind the large mahogany desk in his home office. She'd risen early, hoping to get what she needed before Lester and the kids woke up.

"What, I can't use my husband's computer?" Rachel innocently asked.

"Not when you have a sixteen-hundred-dollar MacBook Pro and the latest edition of the iPad—both of which you just had to have," he said, leaning in to peer at the screen.

"Yes, but I needed to print something," she lied. Rachel wasn't above lying to her husband. But she really had tried to do better over the years. But this . . . this was an exception.

"Which is why we have a wireless printer," Lester said.

"The Internet is down for some reason. And I can't print anything from the Mac."

"Well, you've been in here for over an hour and that means you're up to something."

Rachel jumped up in front of her husband and seductively ran her hand up his shirt. "Why must you always think the worst of me?" she purred.

He smiled, removed her hand, gently pushed her aside,

and leaned back over to the computer. "Because I know my wife." He wiggled the mouse until the screen popped back up. " 'Prominent Pastor Wins Nomination,' " he read, before looking up at Rachel. "Why are you reading the article about Pastor Bush's win again?"

"Can't I read the online newspaper?" She tried to move back in front of him. "Now, if you don't mind . . ."

"Awww, Rachel," Lester moaned as he opened up another website that she'd minimized. His eyes scanned the screen. " 'Dirt Diggers. We find dirt on anyone.' Really, Rachel?"

Rachel stood next to him, her arms folded defiantly, her lips pursed.

"Do you want to explain to me why you're on a shady private investigative website?"

"No."

"Rachel . . ."

Rachel huffed as she pushed him aside and plopped back down in her high-back leather chair. "Because, Lester, I'm trying to help you out. Do you see all of this stuff that jack-legged preacher has accomplished?" she said, pointing to the computer screen. "A TV show, a megachurch, and you know his daddy is probably paying off everybody and their mama to make sure his son wins the position."

"First of all, stop calling him jack-legged. Pastor Bush is an upstanding man of God."

She turned up her lips.

"Secondly," Lester continued, "he just won the regional nomination. We still have the national election, an election we will win fair and square if we win it."

If? He was already going in with a negative attitude. "Nothing's fair in religious politics," Rachel spat.

"Thirdly," Lester added, ignoring Rachel's rant, "if it is God's will for me to have this position, then it's mine."

"Faith without works is dead," Rachel reminded him.

Lester smiled. "Don't go bending Bible verses to fit your agenda."

Rachel sighed in frustration. "Lester, I've been reading up on this Pastor Bush. He could give you a serious run for your money and I'm trying to make sure we don't have any problems next week at the national election."

"By digging up dirt?"

"Whatever works." Rachel shrugged.

"Really, Rachel, what kind of dirt do you think you will find on Reverend Bush that hasn't been found? Everyone knows about him shooting the man that kidnapped his daughter, and I would've done the same thing."

"Oh, I'm not digging up dirt on Reverend Bush," Rachel said nonchalantly. "I already tried that and came up with nothing."

"Then why are you on that website?" Lester asked.

Rachel grinned mischievously. "I'm digging up dirt on his wife."

"Jasmine Bush?" Lester asked incredulously. "What does she have to do with anything?"

Rachel spun around in her chair. "Oh, my God. That chick is a walking public-relations disaster." She excitedly tapped some keys and another website popped up. "Look at this Media Takeout story. They call her the scandalous first lady. And I talked with someone in Los Angeles who said she stole her best friend's husband, or something like that. I haven't been able to confirm the details, but I will."

Lester narrowed his eyes at his wife. "Should you really be casting stones about someone's past?"

Rachel glared at him. She couldn't believe he'd gone there. Yes, she'd had some drama in her life. She'd tried to sabotage Bobby's marriage by doing some pretty scandalous things herself, and to some extent she had been successful, but she was a child then. Nineteen. Anything that happened in life before twenty didn't count. And yes, she had lots of family drama—from a brother who had battled drugs and another brother who had had a huge down-low scandal. But David was clean, and Jonathan had made peace with his sexuality, so none of that should even be an issue. At least Rachel hoped it wasn't.

Lester must've known he was about to make her mad because he quickly softened his tone. "Babe, I'm only saying that we all make mistakes. And if Jasmine does have all of this stuff in her past, then it's not our job to go digging for it."

"So you don't think the people of the American Baptist Coalition deserve to know their potential first lady is a backstabbing, stripping, scheming skeezer?"

"You don't even know her, so how can you say that?"

"Whatever, Lester." Rachel turned back around to her computer. This was exactly why she didn't want him to know what she'd been in his office doing. He was so freakin' holier-than-thou sometimes, it made her sick. "You act like you don't want the position. You probably just want to stay here in Houston, stuffing all these people into this little bitty church."

"Zion Hill is hardly little," Lester said. "We have over three thousand members."

She spun around in her chair and pleaded with him. "But we could be so much bigger if you were president of the ABC. I mean, we could get our own TV show, kind of like a husband-and-wife team."

"You're not a minister."

She grinned widely. "That's the beauty of it all. I think our appeal would be that I'm a first lady who's keeping it real. You know, one that women could actually relate to." Rachel didn't bother telling Lester that she'd already run that idea by her friend Elise, who was a TV producer in Atlanta. Elise had thought the idea was great and couldn't wait to get started putting together a pilot. Then, on top of that, Elise was poised to be the next president of the National Association of Black Journalists, so she could open all kinds of doors for Rachel.

But Lester had to win the election first, which was just part of the reason why Rachel had to make sure he did. However, it was obvious that argument wouldn't get her very far, so she switched gears. "I'm just saying, think of all the good we could do for the community if you won."

"Oh, so now this is about the community?"

Rachel threw up her hands. Sometimes her husband's weak ways drove her mad. That's how Mary, that harlot who had caused them all that marital drama, had been able to manipulate her way into their lives. Because for all his strengths, Lester's biggest weakness was his fighting spirit.

"Rachel, I know what you're saying, but I'm asking you to just let it go. If it's for us, it's for us."

When Rachel had met Lester back in high school, he had been a pimply-faced, passive nerd. She wouldn't give him the time of day because as nice as he was, all the boys used to bully him, harass him, and do things like take his lunch money. Rachel couldn't stand a weak man. Lester was a long way from those high school days, but right now, that's what he reminded her of. He was willing to just sit back and let Hosea Bush take the ABC presidency from him. But she wasn't about to let that happen.

Rachel nodded, without saying another word. She was through talking. The election was in less than a week. They were heading to Los Angeles in two days and that left her little time to find what she needed to find.

Rachel shut off the computer, ignoring Lester's stare as she stood.

"Excuse me," she said, trying to go around him.

He gently grabbed her arm. "Are you mad at me?"

Rachel let out a small sigh. She was mad but she had to tell herself to suck it up. She knew that her husband was not a weak man anymore; he proved it all the time by the way he ran their church. If he was weak, they wouldn't even be in the church because when he'd announced that he'd been called to preach, she gave him an ultimatum—her or the pulpit. Lester had politely given her her walking papers. So he knew how to stand up for himself when he had to do it. It's just that he was a by-the-book man. His straightlaced nature actually balanced her over-the-top theatrics—most of the time, anyway. Knowing that, she decided this wasn't something she'd ever have his blessing on.

"No, sweetheart, I understand." She leaned in and pecked

him on the cheek. "I'm heading out. I need to pick up a few things for our trip."

"Okay. I'm just gonna stay here and work." He caressed her face. "I love you and I appreciate you trying to work this out, but it'll work itself out."

She nodded without responding. No need to prolong this dead-end conversation. She hadn't lied; she was going to pick up some things for the trip. Right after she stopped at Starbucks, logged back on to her laptop, and did some more digging. She had a gut feeling that there was more dirt to be found on Mrs. Jasmine Larson Bush and Rachel was determined to find it.

Chapter
FIVE

As the Boeing jet descended from thirty to twenty to ten thousand feet, the state of Jasmine's birth came into view. Her eyes took in the terrain below, flooding her with memories, mostly nightmares of her past—her lying, cheating, stripping, man-stealing days.

But all that was so far behind her; this was her triumphant return to the Golden State. To Jasmine, it felt like she were coming home as the most important first lady in the world.

No, Hosea hadn't yet won the election—it had only been a week since he'd won the right to represent the North. But according to Pastor Griffith, the only thing that stood between Hosea and the presidency of the American Baptist Coalition was one more week.

"When you return to New York on that charter flight next weekend," Pastor Griffith had told her last night, "your husband will be the newly elected bishop."

Jasmine had squirmed, unable to hold her excitement as she sat across from the pastor at Mae Frances's dining room table.

Just an hour before, Mae Frances had summoned Jasmine to her apartment. It had been difficult to get away—she'd had to tell Hosea that she was helping Mae Frances with last-minute packing, even as she and Hosea had their own to do. But she'd left instructions with Mrs. Sloss, their housekeeper, and made a promise to Hosea to be back in an hour. Then she'd dashed over

in a cab, telling the driver that she'd tip him a twenty if he got
her uptown in less than ten minutes.

The tip would be worth every penny just so she could get
to Mae Frances quickly. Because if her friend was ready to
share, that meant that schoolhouse, country pastor who had the
audacity to go up against Hosea was going down.

When she'd arrived on the Upper East Side, Jasmine hadn't
walked into the private meeting with her friend that she'd expected. Waiting with Mae Frances was the man Jasmine had met
just a week ago, and who, eight years ago, she would've had in
her bed by now—Pastor Earl Griffith.

The pastor looked even better than he had last week. He rose
from his chair and strutted toward her with so much swag in his
swagger that Jasmine had to take a deep breath. And when he
embraced her with his greeting, she'd wanted to hold on to him
for longer than the two seconds that was appropriate. Because
she was in love with her husband, she'd done the right thing and
stepped back. But she had inhaled deeply and taken his lavender-
and-sandalwood scent with her; she was pleased. Not only was
this man fine, but he was loaded with good taste. His cologne of
choice—Giorgio Armani.

"Earl flew in to bring me some of this information himself,"
Mae Frances explained as she held up a thick manila folder.

"Oh, okay," was all that Jasmine said as she thought about
what Mae Frances's words meant. Obviously, Pastor Griffith was
one of Mae Frances's connections—that was the only reason
he'd be here, right?

"So, you really think Hosea will be elected?" she asked Pastor
Griffith as the three sat at the dining room table.

"Oh, I know he will." The pastor clasped his hands together.
"Not only have we raised more money in the North for the Coalition than the South, which is a big indication of which region
will win, but Mae Frances has some information here"—he took
the folder from Mae Frances and held it above his head—"that
will help to bring Lester Adams, the main competition, down."
He slammed the folder back onto the table.

"Main competition? I thought this was just between that country bumpkin and Hosea."

"Oh, it is," Pastor Griffith had assured her. "For the most part. But there will be others who will throw their names into the hat; none that will matter, of course." He leaned forward, bringing his face just inches from her. "Trust me, sweetheart," he said, "Hosea is the new president."

Grabbing the folder back, Mae Frances said, "And here are some of the reasons why."

"Huh?" Jasmine muttered. She'd gotten stuck on the sweetheart part of the pastor's words, but she forced herself now to look at Mae Frances.

"My people didn't find too much on Lester Adams, except that he'd been arrested for attacking a woman who claimed that he'd fathered her child; this happened just a couple of years ago— while he and his wife were married."

"Married? Not separated or anything?" Jasmine asked, getting excited.

Mae Frances shook her head. "Married."

"Wow, that's good stuff."

Mae Frances waved her hand. "That's small stuff, because the charges were dropped. But now, his wife? She's a walking disaster zone." Mae Frances pulled out a photo and pushed it across the table to Jasmine. "Here's a picture of the reverend."

"You're kidding," she said, picking up the photograph with the tips of her fingers just in case ugly was contagious. "This is the pastor who is going up against my husband? How can anyone stand to look at him?" Jasmine squinted as she peered at the pock-faced man with a mop of red hair. "Dang, what does his wife look like? A mud duck?"

Pastor Griffith chuckled, but Mae Frances was all about business.

Mae Frances said, "That's what he *used* to look like; somebody done cleaned him up good." She passed another photo.

"Yeah, he does look a little better," Jasmine admitted. "But he still can't stand next to Hosea."

"Too bad it's not that kind of election," Mae Frances said, rolling her eyes as if she wanted Jasmine to focus. "And here's his wife."

Jasmine grabbed the photo, eager to see her real competition. Okay, Jasmine thought, so she wasn't so bad. Yeah, she was rough around the edges, but if you didn't know ghetto, you might miss it on this one. "She's young."

"Uh-huh," Mae Frances said.

"And she doesn't look sophisticated at all."

"Uh-huh."

"She won't be able to handle me."

"It's not her age or lack of sophistication that gives us the advantage," Mae Frances said. "If we have to use the pastor's wife to bring the pastor down, it won't be a problem. She's given us plenty of ammunition."

As Mae Frances reviewed the dossier with Jasmine, Pastor Griffith stood and strolled into Mae Frances's kitchen. Jasmine's eyes followed the man and two thoughts came to her mind: There should've been an eleventh commandment—that no man's butt should ever look that good. And the second was that he was pretty comfortable in Mae Frances's house. How close were these two? And how long had they known each other?

It took everything within her to break the lock her eyes had on Pastor Griffith's behind and turn back to Mae Frances.

"Okay, so this is what we know," Mae Frances said. "She may have been brought up in a middle-class home, but she's as low class as they come." Jasmine leaned forward to hear this news. "I'm telling you, Jasmine Larson, she almost makes you look like a Girl Scout."

Jasmine frowned. "What you tryin' to say, Mae Frances?" She'd been called lots of things, but ghetto wasn't one of them.

Her friend waved her hand. "I'm sayin' what I'm sayin'. Don't be getting your feelings hurt when we have so much to do. Focus. Now, the first thing we have that we can use is that this

Rachel chick slept with the best friend of the man she claimed she loved."

"Really?"

"And then, got pregnant by the friend."

"Dang," Jasmine said, making Mae Frances look at her with raised eyebrows. "What?" Jasmine asked.

"You ain't always been saved."

"I never slept with any of Hosea's friends," Jasmine huffed. And then, she felt something pull her eyes . . . up . . . and she looked into the eyes of the pastor.

Just for a moment, she'd forgotten that he was there and she wanted to slap her friend for saying those things in front of him. How was she supposed to make a good impression with Mae Frances talking about how she hadn't always been saved?

But it didn't seem like she had anything to worry about. Pastor Griffith seemed unfazed, perched against the counter, sipping water, his gaze on both of them, though it looked like his thoughts were beyond this room.

She cleared her throat, shifted a bit in her seat, and forced her attention back to Mae Frances.

"Anyway," her friend continued, "she's done everything from slashing tires, to having utilities turned off, to showing up at a wedding and fighting with the bride."

"Dang, she is worse than ghetto—she's country ghetto. Has she ever been arrested?"

"Yeah, she's been arrested, which will play into another plan I have. But the thing is, she's not the only one in that family with issues. Their father may have been a pastor, but all three of his children were running around like they were trying to get him kicked out of the pulpit. Besides Rachel's antics, one of her brothers is gay and the other one is a serious drug addict."

"And this is the first family of that hick church?"

"Maybe that's why it's a hick church. But their three thousand members seem to love them."

"Three thousand?" Jasmine laughed. City of Lights at Riverside

Church had four times that membership. "And they say everything is bigger in Texas. Please." Jasmine tossed the papers that Mae Frances had given her back onto the table, as if this information on the Adams family was irrelevant. "Okay, so she's ghetto, they have lots of family drama, but I don't see how any of this is gonna help us."

"Oh, it's gonna help us," Mae Frances said, glancing sideways at Pastor Griffith as if they'd talked about this before. "Plus, look at what all of this tells us about Rachel—she's young, hotheaded, and she can be manipulated."

"And if all of that fails," Pastor Griffith began as he strutted back to the table, "she can be set up to take a big fall. And with her history, everyone will believe anything that we set her up for."

"Oh, that's good. So what are we gonna do?" Jasmine said excitedly. It had been a while, but she'd taken down a lot of people in her time. She'd sent one man to jail, made another disappear from the city quickly; she'd stolen husbands and left women hysterical and alone. Oh, yes, this was her expertise. And the best thing was that this time, it wasn't about her—she wasn't doing it for any personal gain, she wasn't being selfish. She was doing this for Hosea and for the good of all African American Christians everywhere.

Pastor Griffith said, "Mae Frances has a fantastic idea on how we can make Rachel take a big fall, but I don't think it will come to that." He pushed Mae Frances's folder aside. "I think it's going to be as simple as knowing who's on the voting committee and getting to every single one of them. When they hear about Hosea and what he can do for the Coalition, they'd be crazy not to vote for him."

Pastor Griffith talked for the next twenty minutes about his plans, and he was so thorough that Jasmine wondered for a moment why he was so adamant about Hosea's election. But she pushed those thoughts aside and looked at Pastor Griffith as the blessing he truly was. If it hadn't been for him, Jasmine wouldn't be on the verge of such power. When Jasmine finally left, she was impressed, elated, and ready to go.

More than fifteen hours had passed. Now Jasmine leaned back in her seat seconds before the plane's tires skidded against the runway.

"That feels like a roller coaster," Jacqueline squealed in the seat behind her.

Jasmine smiled at the sound of her daughter's voice. And by his silence, she knew that her son was asleep.

When the plane rolled to a stop, Jasmine squeezed her husband's hand. "We're here."

With a grin, Hosea leaned over and kissed her cheek. "Just remember, darlin', we haven't won this yet."

"It's just a matter of days."

"We might not win at all."

"We will."

"I just don't want you to be disappointed if we don't."

"We're gonna win."

The strength of her conviction made him pause, made him frown. "Jasmine?"

She reeled in some of her enthusiasm. "I'm just saying that when they all get to know you, they're gonna love you as much as I do."

He chuckled. "Yeah, right. Just remember what I said. I want to win this straight up—no tricks."

"What kind of tricks could I have when I don't even know these people or anything about the Coalition?"

"Hmmmm . . . let's keep it that way, because like I told you, the Coalition will have the president that God wants it to have."

Yeah, yeah, yeah! Jasmine thought. She was thrilled when the airplane's doors opened; there was no time for Hosea to give her a long lecture about God. As if she didn't love the Lord. They both loved God—it was just that Hosea walked in his faith and she worked her faith.

It was a good thing she did—they wouldn't have half the life they had now if she hadn't combined faith and works. Hosea just didn't know—he'd come up because of her and she was about to shoot him into the stratosphere.

Taking Zaya from Mae Frances's arms, she followed Hosea. The two of them, the children, Mae Frances, and the rest of the New York delegation, which included the Senior Reverend Bush and Reverend Penn and his wife, were swept away by an entourage of ministers that Pastor Griffith had put together. The minutes moved in a whirlwind, and if this was the life that she could expect as the president's wife, then it couldn't come fast enough for Jasmine.

Already, they'd been flown across the country on a private jet and whisked into the hangar, before being escorted to three waiting limousines that would carry them all away.

Jasmine shivered as she stepped outside. Not from the temperature—it was April in Los Angeles. Her trembling was from her excitement. She was home.

She slapped on her sunglasses as Hosea strapped the children into the backseat of the first Town Car, but she kept her eyes on her husband since Reverend Penn's wife was standing so close to the car. Jasmine shook her head. She still couldn't believe that the Penns had been invited to fly on the chartered plane, as if they belonged with their group. What was worse was that it had been Hosea's idea to include them.

"Reverend Penn has tried to become president twenty-three times!" Hosea had said. "We need to show him respect."

"And how does letting him travel with us show him respect?" Jasmine had asked.

Hosea had just waved her words away, letting her know that it was a done deal—the Penns were going to be part of the Bush entourage.

But as Jasmine stood eyeing the reverend's wife, she had a feeling that Hosea had made a grave mistake. "I just don't trust that woman," Jasmine muttered to Mae Frances.

"Who?" She turned to see who Jasmine was staring at. Mae Frances sucked her teeth. "You don't need to worry about that

Debbie Does Dallas movie star. Hosea don't want to have nothin' to do with the likes of her. Who you need to be thinking about is right over there." She jutted her chin forward, pointing to the left.

And there he was. Just feet away . . . the man from the photo, Hosea's competition—Lester Adams.

Mae Frances had been right. Someone had cleaned the man up good, but even from this far away, Jasmine could tell that he was no match for her husband. Reverend Adams looked like a country boy for real, as he shuffled toward his car. And if the size of his entourage was any indication of what was to come, Pastor Adams needed to take the two men who stood on either side of him, turn around, get back on the bus, and go home.

Still, Jasmine wanted to get closer. If there was anything that she knew well, it was men. With her man-dar up, she would get a read on Lester Adams. Pastor Griffith had his own plans, but if Reverend Adams reacted to her in the right way, this election might be as simple as sending a prostitute into his hotel room.

She straightened the light wool of the designer pantsuit that her personal shopper had selected for this trip, tossed her curls over her shoulder, and sauntered toward the men. The sidekicks' eyes were already on her as she approached, though Reverend Adams was concentrating on a newspaper he held.

See? Country. He didn't even know when a beautiful woman was nearby.

But right when she was just inches away from the man, a tornado blew by—in the form of a woman wearing a beige pantsuit that was too light, so inappropriate for the month of April.

Barreling in front of her, the woman blocked Jasmine. With her arms folded, her lips poked out, and her attitude showing, she asked, "May I help you?" as if she had her own radar. As if she knew exactly when a woman was within feet of her husband.

Jasmine had to hold her laughter in. Rachel Adams. Oh, this was going to be easier than she thought. This heifer thought she was big and bad and bold. Well, Jasmine had something for her—the perfect way to introduce herself.

Jasmine's lips spread into the slowest of smiles. "Hello," she said, reaching for the woman's hand. "My name is Lady Jasmine—actually, Jasmine Cox Larson Bush, the new first lady of the American Baptist Coalition." She paused. "And excuse me, but who are you?"

Chapter
SIX

No, she didn't. Rachel had to take deep, slow breaths because it was obvious this old hag was delusional. She'd recognized Jasmine right away. The sultry way she slithered off the jet. The whole entourage, like she was M.C. Hammer. The way she slid those designer glasses on—just showing out.

Had it not been for Dirt Diggers, Rachel might actually have been intimidated. But the information she knew about Jasmine Cox Larson Bush empowered her.

A smile crept up on Rachel's face as she shook Jasmine's hand. "Jasmine?" she said, ignoring the first lady comment. *In her dreams.* "Rev. Bush's wife?"

Jasmine smiled confidently as she nodded. "The one and only."

Rachel feigned confusion. "I'm sorry. I thought Rev. Bush's wife was named Natasia."

Bingo! Jasmine's whole body tensed as she lost her smile. Rachel tried desperately to fight back a smirk. Hosea was practically a saint, but the private investigator had managed to find out about his ex-fiancée and former producer, Natasia Redding. The rumor mill said the two of them had had an affair. The PI couldn't confirm it, but judging from Jasmine's uneasy reaction, there was something to the story.

Jasmine looked like she was about to lose that fake air she had going on, but she composed herself and said, "No, it's Jasmine. Jasmine Bush. And again, you are?"

"Rachel Jackson Adams, first lady of Zion Hill Missionary Baptist Church in Houston."

"Oh"—Jasmine put a finger to her head like she was thinking—"I've never heard of it." She didn't give Rachel time to reply before saying, "Wherever did you get that adorable pantsuit? I thought I saw it in a commercial for Marshall's last year."

Jasmine's tone let Rachel know this was definitely not intended as a compliment. "No, if you must know, I got it from T.J.Maxx. Yours is lovely, too. Whose tithes paid for it?"

Lester stepped in before she could reply. "Lady Jasmine," he said, reaching around Rachel and extending his hand. "It is such a pleasure to meet you. I've heard wonderful things."

What was this Lady Jasmine crap? Rachel glared at her husband out of the corner of her eye as he took Jasmine's hand. He'd balked when she suggested she be called Lady Rachel. Oh, she would definitely be telling Lester about himself later.

Jasmine looked like she was breathing fire out of her nostrils before she finally smiled and said, "Reverend Adams. It's my pleasure."

Lester grinned like he'd won the Lotto as Hosea approached them. "And if it isn't the esteemed Reverend Hosea Bush." He vigorously shook his hand. "I am so honored. I'm a big fan of your show, *Bring it On*. Your messages are always on point. And the work that you do in your community is just phenomenal."

Oh, hell to the no, Rachel thought as her husband dang near salivated at the sight of Hosea. He was acting like he was meeting Barack Obama himself. It was just disgusting.

"Lester, darling, don't be so modest. You do a lot yourself," Rachel interjected.

Jasmine looked like she was eating the whole scene up. Hosea nodded. "Reverend Adams, your lovely wife is right. I hear you won the Southern coalition hands down."

"He did," Rachel said, draping her arm through her husband's. "But it's no surprise. I mean, you should see what he's done with our church. The membership has multiplied since he took over."

"Oh, that's right, to a whopping three thousand people,"

Jasmine said with a fake smile. "Honey, didn't City of Lights have three thousand members back in, what, '85?"

No, this heifer wasn't trying to downplay their membership rolls. Rachel dropped her arm and took a step forward. "Well, we believe in quality, not quantity," she said as nicely as possible. "And we try to keep our family-feel so that our members can truly be fed in the Word and not just be a number on a roster. Let me guess. City of Lights, Camera, Action has an ATM in the sanctuary?"

"Okay, ladies," Lester said, putting a hand on Rachel's forearm to calm her down.

Rachel and Jasmine stared at each other in a face-off. Sure, Jasmine may have had ten or thirty years on her, but Rachel wasn't about to let this broke-down Chaka Khan–looking woman punk her.

"Jasmine," Hosea said sternly.

"What?" Jasmine raised an eyebrow at her husband.

"Reverend Bush, let me apologize for my wife," Lester said, shooting Rachel the evil eye.

"Apologize for what?" Rachel snapped. The ghetto was seeping out. "Chaka here is the one that stepped off the plane in her designer duds like she's royalty, talking about she's the new first lady of the American Baptist Coalition."

"Chaka? Who is Chaka?" Jasmine asked.

" 'Cha-ka, Cha-ka. Chaka Khan, let me rock you—' " Rachel sang with an attitude.

"Rachel Adams," Lester admonished, cutting her off.

Rachel caught herself, rolled her eyes, and managed a tense smile. "I was just kidding with her. You know when you get old, you lose your sense of humor, so I was just trying to lighten the mood."

Lester looked horrified and Jasmine looked ready to pounce. Rachel was thrilled. She'd wiped that smug expression right off Jasmine's face.

"We'll see who has the last laugh," Jasmine said, not bothering to smile. She turned to her husband. "Hosea, sweetheart, we really should get going. Where are the cars?" she asked, turning around and noticing that the three Town Cars were gone.

Hosea sighed like he knew trouble was brewing. "I sent Mae Frances and the rest of the team on. The kids are extremely tired and Mrs. Sloss wanted to get them to the hotel so that they could rest before the reception tonight. We were supposed to have four cars and the other is on the way. They're about five minutes out."

"You're more than welcome to ride to the hotel with us," Lester said, trying to ease the obvious tension.

Thankfully, Hosea quickly nipped that idea. "No, no, the driver is on the way. Our plane did touch down a few minutes early."

"Oh, okay. Well, I guess we'll see you at the welcome reception tonight," Lester said. "Mrs. Bush." Lester nodded toward her.

Jasmine half nodded back. Lester looked at Rachel out of the corner of his eye. She knew he wanted her to say something. Fine. She huffed. "Rev. Bush, it was a pleasure. My apologies if I came off a little harsh. Sometimes people don't appreciate my attempts to break the ice."

Hosea smiled. "I'm sure my wife offers up her apologies as well." Jasmine folded her arms across her chest and didn't reply.

Rachel wasn't fazed. It's not like she was apologizing to that witch anyway. She spun and strutted to the car.

Lester stayed behind, no doubt continuing his apologies. Suddenly, an idea hit Rachel as she climbed in the backseat. She leaned forward to the driver. "Do you work for the same company as all the other cars that were out here?"

The portly gray-haired man nodded. "I do."

Rachel grinned widely, reached in her purse, and pulled out a fifty-dollar bill as she quickly told the man what she needed him to do.

"That was so absolutely uncalled for," Lester hissed as he climbed into the limo a few minutes later. "You'd better be glad Rev. Bush is a godly man and didn't get upset at the way you were acting."

She reached in her purse again and pulled out a tissue. "Here," she said, handing it to Lester.

"What's that for?" he asked.

"To wipe the drool from your mouth since you were all but licking the man's shoes," Rachel snapped as she tossed her purse on the seat.

"Rachel, that is ridiculous. Reverend Bush is a highly regarded minister. I'm just showing him his proper respect. Regardless of this whole competition thing, I'm going to give the man his respect."

Rachel ignored her husband. Respect was one thing. Utter adoration was another. Why couldn't Lester see that the Bushes thought they had this thing in the bag? It was obvious from Jasmine's whole demeanor that they believed they were better than she and Lester. And now that Rachel had met Jasmine, she knew that skank wouldn't be above fighting dirty. Good thing she'd beat her to the punch.

As the limo pulled away from the curb, Rachel glanced back at Hosea and Jasmine standing there waiting on their ride.

"Why are you sitting over there grinning?" Lester asked.

Rachel pulled her sunglasses out of her bag, Chanel knockoffs that looked just like Jasmine's, but probably cost half as much.

"No reason," she said, leaning back in the seat. Oh, how she wanted to tell her husband what she'd done. But his Donald Do-Good behind would make the driver turn around. No, she'd wait until they checked into the hotel before she let him know that she'd had their driver radio in and cancel the car service for Reverend and Mrs. Bush. She had already done the same for their hotel. Sure, they'd get it all worked out—eventually. But Miss Priss would probably act a fool, piss a few people off. And while they were trying to figure out what happened, she'd be in the lobby, mixing and mingling with folks, drumming up votes for her man. Rachel couldn't help but chuckle as she closed her eyes and repeated, "No reason, at all."

A taxi, Hosea," Jasmine huffed. "We are actually taking a taxi!"

As the yellow car edged away from the curb, Hosea settled back against the cracked pleather seat. "Darlin', you say that as if you don't take cabs."

"I don't."

"You were in one yesterday." He chuckled.

"That was in New York. No one who is anyone takes taxis in LA."

Hosea did what he always did. He shook his head a little, squeezed Jasmine's hand, then closed his eyes—without even one angry word.

Jasmine pushed out a long breath, trying to bring it down. It wasn't easy, though. It would have helped if Hosea had shared just a bit of her fury, instead of reacting like she was some kind of diva. Because truly, this was all so ridiculous.

She and Hosea had waited for more than thirty minutes before Hosea had called one of the handlers Pastor Griffith had assigned to them. Fifteen minutes after that, the call came back that there was some kind of mix-up. Their car had been canceled and it would be an hour before another one could be diverted to them; the car companies were all overbooked with the hundreds of convention attendees arriving today.

"So, what are we supposed to do?" Jasmine had asked, totally exasperated. It was bad enough that she'd stood on the curb outside Terminal 8, as if she were some common traveler. Now they'd have to wait even longer? She needed to get to the hotel, rest up, and change into the fabulous St. John dress that her shopper had selected for the welcome reception tonight.

"No, we're not gonna wait," Hosea had told her. Then he'd dragged her to the taxicab line, twelve passengers deep—they'd have to wait for the thirteenth car to show up.

It was just absurd that the next president of the American Baptist Coalition would arrive at the Millennium Biltmore in such a pedestrian way.

Someone was going to pay for this. Jasmine was going to let her dissatisfaction be known—in a totally appropriate fashion that was befitting of the new first lady, of course—to Pastor Griffith, as soon as she marched into that hotel.

But then, thoughts of taxicabs, Pastor Griffith, and inept handlers airlifted right out of her mind when the cab came to the red light. At the intersection of Airport Boulevard and her life of shame.

The taxi had stopped at the corner where she'd spent hours peeling off her clothes—and doing many other things—in the name of finishing her college education.

It surprised her—Foxtails, the pink-and-purple stucco building, was no longer there. She'd expected it to be standing for at least as long as she lived—the torturous reminder that she had not always been a first lady, and as Mae Frances liked to say, she had not always been saved.

She pressed her face closer to the window. On the land where the strip club used to be was a McDonald's, complete with a children's playground that backed up to where men had come from all over the county to get a look at her—Pepper Pulaski, the stripper who could quake her booty like it was part of the San Andreas Fault.

Foxtails had become McDonald's—somehow, that just didn't seem right.

With a single blink, she turned away and glanced over her shoulder. Hosea was still in meditation mode—his eyes closed, his chest rising slowly up, and then down. Good! There were only a few who knew about her life on that dark side, and thank God her husband was not one of them. As far as she knew, her secret life as a stripper had been revealed to only a few: her father-in-law, who'd worked with a private investigator many years before to dredge up that past; Mrs. Whittingham, the woman who'd used that past to torment and blackmail her; and Mae Frances, because Jasmine had needed someone to confide in and help her get out of the blackmailing situation.

So, with Foxtails completely demolished and only three people alive who knew of that dark period, Jasmine decided that she could truly leave that part of her life behind. She would no longer have any memories, no longer have any thoughts of her times at Foxtails—they would stay right here on this corner. All that mattered now was her future . . . well, Hosea's future, too. He had to be the one to win the election so that she could step into her rightful role.

Jasmine hated that the election was a week away. Why did they have to wait so long when truly, Hosea was going to stomp that country-fried-chicken preacher? Jasmine did feel a little sorry for Reverend Adams—but his bargain-basement wife? She didn't feel a dang thing for her. Not after what she'd pulled back at the airport.

Calling her Natasia! That trick actually had the nerve to call her by Hosea's crazy ex-fiancée's name. If Reverend Adams hadn't been standing right there, Jasmine would've knocked her right upside her head—the exact same way she'd done Natasia.

Well, maybe not exactly that way. All Jasmine had to do was sniff and she knew Rachel wasn't anything like Natasia—this one was straight hood and could probably handle herself in a fight.

Yeah, all of Rachel's power was from the neck down—there didn't seem to be too many brain cells alive and operating. It would be easy to outsmart this one. All Jasmine had to do was think and she'd have the advantage.

Finally, the taxi eased off the 110 Freeway and maneuvered through the streets of the new and improved downtown Los Angeles. She'd heard about all the changes in the area: old warehouses that had become expensive lofts, clean streets that were no longer home to the homeless. But what she saw was even better than she imagined. Of course, the Lakers had left the Forum in Inglewood many years before for the Staples Center, but downtown was much more than just a sports arena. From the restaurants and theaters and upscale shopping, the area that had become known as LA Live was bubbling with excitement, rivaling other city attractions like Beverly Hills, Hollywood, and Universal City.

By the time the cabdriver rolled to a stop in front of the Millennium Biltmore, Jasmine had no memories of her anger. She stepped from the car, then hooked her arm through Hosea's—the queen being escorted by her king.

She chuckled at that thought—maybe it was time to change her name. Lady Jasmine just seemed too small for her now. Queen Jasmine was far more appropriate.

Jasmine strutted into the splendor of the eighty-five-year-old grand hotel that had welcomed celebrities and dignitaries over the past decades. She and Hosea swept into the lobby, past the soaring columns and vaulted ceilings inspired by Roman architecture. A couple hundred people had gathered in the massive space, an informal meet and greet of the convention attendees before the official welcome reception.

The chatter swelled as the crowd took notice of Hosea and Jasmine.

"Pastor Bush," many called out.

The gathering parted as if they were making room for Moses himself, and they all invited the Bushes into their midst. There were smiles and greetings of welcome and best wishes. A few even broke out with impromptu applause.

Hosea's steps quickened against the marble floor, his eagerness to move past the attention apparent. But Jasmine gripped his arm a bit tighter, slowed him down, and basked in the adoration. She gifted the greeting pastors and their wives with her best smile and held her hand stiff in a wave as if she were strutting on the stage of the Mrs. America pageant.

Pastor Griffith found them when they were just steps away from the front desk. "I'm so sorry about the car service," he said, his eyes on Hosea. But when he added the next part, he turned to Jasmine. "I hope you'll let me make it up to you."

Her plan had been to tell him just how unhappy she was and just how embarrassing it'd been. But, with a slight nod of her head, she took the high road and told him that all was forgiven. She wanted the man who wielded so much power in the North to see that she was a woman who was full of grace.

"Here, let me get you checked in," Pastor Griffith said. "The plan was to have your keys waiting, but as you can see"—he turned and his hand swept across the lobby—"so many are already here. I've been working the room, getting all the necessary delegates on our side."

As she followed Pastor Griffith, Jasmine's eyes scanned the crowd. This was her domain—a luxurious space with a predominance of men. She studied the few women who were sprinkled throughout the gathering. Most were pastor's wives— their hats, tea-length skirts, and worn, tired expressions gave them away. But there were a few younger women who slipped through the maze of men, single and scoping.

You've got to be kidding me. Jasmine chuckled. She recognized their kind—she'd been a part of that club for too many years. Groupies, though she always hated that name. She'd never done anything in a group—except for maybe once or twice.

But these were groupies for sure. The question was, what were they doing here? In her hunting days, athletes, actors, even CEOs of major corporations had been the prey. These women were going after pastors? Get out. She laughed aloud. What were these new groupies called? Holy rollers?

Her laughter stopped, though, when she heard Pastor Griffith. "What do you mean the reservation was canceled?"

His tone was a bit condescending. Clearly he meant business, and Jasmine appreciated him even more. He was nothing like her gentle, we-are-all-equal-in-God's-eyes husband.

"I'm sorry, Pastor Griffith." The twentysomething woman

was trembling already. "But Mrs. Bush called earlier and canceled the suite. She said she didn't need it—that it was an extra one she was just holding on to."

With an attitude as massive as the lobby, Jasmine stepped up to the desk, nudging Hosea aside slightly. "I didn't call anyone," Jasmine said, her words staccato, her tone matching the man on the left, not her husband on the right.

"There must be some mistake." Now the woman behind the desk's voice quivered, as if she saw nothing but blame and punishment in her future.

"Obviously," Jasmine and Pastor Griffith said together.

Hosea spoke up. "No need to go back and forth. Like you said"—his voice was low and calm as he spoke to the nervous attendant—"this was a mistake and we'll just rectify it. Just give us back that suite."

The clerk's eyes moved away as if she was searching for a hideaway. "I'm sorry, but that suite isn't available anymore," she whispered.

"What?" This time, it was a three-person chorus.

"Because of the convention, we had a waiting list and that suite was given to someone already. It was gone within three minutes—after you canceled," she said, looking straight at Jasmine.

Jasmine had no intention of telling this woman again that she hadn't canceled a thing. Instead, she said, "Fine, whatever." She glanced at her watch. All she needed was to get to her room because it was going to take at least two hours to become fabulous. "Just give us another suite."

The woman shook her head and looked like she was going to burst into tears. "We don't have another suite. We don't even have another room. All six hundred rooms are taken."

"This. Cannot. Be!" Jasmine said, sounding a little too dramatic even to her own ears. "So, what are we supposed to do now?" she asked.

Gently, Hosea nudged Jasmine to the side. "Let me handle this, darlin'."

She stepped back only because she couldn't promise that she wouldn't start screaming. And while she wanted the limelight, she didn't want it this way, and she certainly didn't want it before she had a chance to freshen up and change her clothes.

She took a deep breath as she stepped aside for Hosea. Glancing down at her watch, she sighed deeply. Precious time was slipping away.

What in the world happened? First the taxi, now the hotel room. Something was going on.

Behind her, the crowd buzzed with chatter and laughter. It was business, but clearly a celebration, too, as bartenders moved through the crowd, refreshing what Jasmine assumed were all nonalcoholic drinks. She scanned the gathering of preachers and their wives, and then . . . she froze when she looked into the eyes of Rachel Adams.

Rachel was far across the vast lobby—dozens of bodies were between the two women. But Jasmine could clearly see Rachel's eyes, shining with amusement. And she wore a matching smirk.

Slowly, Rachel lifted the goblet she held, in a salute that Jasmine knew wasn't meant to be congratulatory in any way.

No, she didn't!

In that instant, Jasmine knew. Rachel wasn't playing—this witch was ready to rumble for real. Jasmine rolled her eyes, turned away from Rachel, and prayed that somehow, someway, somebody would find a room. She'd heard that hotels always kept extras for VIP situations. Who was a bigger VIP than her husband?

"I'm sorry."

Now there were three people on the other side of the desk, facing Hosea and Pastor Griffith, singing their apologies.

"We just don't have any other rooms." A tall, stately man with a British accent (which Jasmine doubted was real) was explaining now. "We can make a few calls and see if there's anything available in a nearby hotel."

Jasmine shook her head. She was not about to leave this place. There was too much networking that could be done in the halls, on the elevators, in the restaurants. No, they were not leaving; she was not giving any kind of advantage to the Adams family.

But the alternative didn't make her smile either—she and Hosea would just have to share a suite with Mae Frances, Mrs. Sloss, and the children.

Once again, Jasmine's glance turned to Rachel, and like before, she was staring, as if she'd been expecting Jasmine to look her way. Then, knowing that Jasmine was watching, Rachel threw her head back and laughed. To everyone else, it looked as if she was responding to something someone in her circle had just said. But Jasmine knew the truth—Rachel was laughing at her.

"Excuse me, Pastor Bush?"

The woman's voice made Jasmine whip around quick. Rachel didn't have a thing on her when it came to radar and keeping an eye on the women here—especially now that she knew there were religious groupies rolling through the convention.

But Jasmine recognized the woman immediately from the dossier that Mae Frances had given her on all the players. This was Cecelia King, the current first lady of the Coalition.

She introduced herself to Hosea, gave Pastor Griffith a hug as if she knew him well, and then turned her attention to Jasmine. "It's so nice to meet you, Mrs. Bush, but it seems that you're having a bit of a problem?" Her eyes moved between the husband and wife.

Jasmine was glad when Hosea took the reins, and he and Pastor Griffith explained the situation. It gave her time to step back and assess this woman.

One thing pleased Jasmine—at least she didn't have to go up against Cecelia. Word on the street was that she was ruthless, a barracuda really, who could never be trusted. Everyone believed that she was the true president—her husband was just *her* figurehead.

Seeing her in person for the first time, Jasmine could believe those rumors. Cecelia King was an imposing figure—standing model-tall, although she would have been on a plus-size runway. Her stance was elegant, her gestures were grand. She was in charge of the whole room, even though she was speaking to just Hosea and Pastor Griffith.

"Well, I think I can fix this for you," Jasmine heard her say. Cecelia turned toward the desk. "The executive suite that the bishop and I reserved. Please put that in the Bushes' name."

Jasmine watched, astonished, as the personnel moved swiftly. With just a few clicks on the computer, new keys were made.

Cecelia faced Jasmine. "There are two suites on the top floor," she explained. "The bishop and I took both because we wanted our privacy. But I'm more than happy to share the floor with you," she said, handing Jasmine one of the keys.

"Thank you so much, Lady Cecelia."

"Not a problem. We know that all things work together for good to them that love God."

Jasmine kept her smile, though inside she frowned. That was another thing she'd heard—that Cecelia was a walking Bible, quoting scripture constantly.

Cecelia said, "This will give us a chance to get to know one another better."

Jasmine nodded. "Definitely." It would be a good thing for the past first lady to spend time with the present one.

Hosea and Pastor Griffith thanked her again, and like royalty, she bowed her head slightly.

"So, darlin', you ready to go up?" Hosea asked Jasmine.

"Yes!" she breathed, relieved. "First, though, I want to check on the children."

She turned toward the elevator, but before she could take a single step, Rachel Adams was there, blocking her path. The victorious smile that had been painted on her face just minutes before had been washed away, replaced with a confused scowl.

As the men walked ahead of Jasmine, her first instinct was to just run over Rachel, push her down to the ground. But Jasmine knew that Rachel would get up and go ghetto. That wouldn't work for either one of them.

Brains, Jasmine, brains.

"Oh, Rachel, have you met First Lady Cecelia King?"

Cecelia extended her hand. "We haven't had the pleasure. Nice to meet you, Rachel . . ." She paused, as if she wanted Rachel to say her last name.

Inside, Jasmine laughed. Cecelia had no idea who Rachel was.

With nothing but benevolence in her tone, Jasmine said, "Oh, this is Reverend Adams's wife," she said, purposely not giving her name.

"My name is Rachel Adams," she said, her voice a mixture of attitude and confusion.

"Ah, yes," Cecelia said. "So nice to meet you. We must all get together—the three of us, during this week." Then, with just the slightest turn of her body, she dismissed Rachel. To Jasmine, she said, "I really want to show you and Hosea to your suite."

Jasmine nodded, but Rachel did not move. Once again, Jasmine thought about just knocking the trick down. But she wasn't going to resort to Rachel's level and her childish games. No, she was in control and was going to stay that way.

How you like me now? Jasmine thought as she sidestepped Rachel, leaving Pastor Adams's wife standing in the same spot, as still as a statue, and gaping as the Bush entourage passed her by.

It was nothing but willpower that kept Jasmine from turning back and gloating. But why was she wasting her time on such thoughts, such things?

She and Hosea had been in the hotel for less than twenty minutes and already she was mixing with the most important people of this convention.

The Adamses were irrelevant. Jasmine needed to keep her mind on greater things, on her one mission, and that was to be the first lady of the Coalition by the time this convention ended.

Chapter
EIGHT

Rachel was still reeling. It had been three hours since that fiasco in the lobby and Rachel still felt like an outcast in high school. It burned her insides to watch the one woman she couldn't stand walk away with the one woman that she admired the most. Just like they were old buddies. Rachel had done her homework on Cecelia King. She knew everything there was to know about the woman and the first lady all but dismissed her to walk off with Jasmine, of all people.

"I wonder if they already knew each other," Rachel mumbled.

"Why are you sitting in here talking to yourself and why aren't you dressed?" Lester asked as he appeared in the bathroom doorway. "The welcome reception has already started."

Rachel hadn't even realized that she'd gotten lost in thought. She leaned into the mirror, dabbed some lip gloss on, and puckered her lips to smooth it out.

"Gimme just a minute," she said.

"Honey, you look fine, really." He pointed to his watch. "We need to get going."

"I have to look better than fine," Rachel said, running her fingers through her curls once again. She loved her youthfulness, but at the same time, she wanted an air of maturity about her so that these people would take her seriously.

He leaned against the door frame, a small smile creeping up the side of his mouth. "I'm still trying to understand why all of a sudden you're so into this."

Rachel scooted past him as she walked into the bedroom and

picked up her suit, a cute peach Kasper number she'd gotten on sale at Macy's. "Well, good grief, I can't win for losing. You want me to be more of a first lady, then when I try, there's still a problem." She held the suit up. Suddenly, visions of Jasmine strutting in with some specially designed Vera Wang outfit turned her stomach. That's another thing that would change when she became first lady—discount shopping.

Lester waited until she slipped the skirt on, then reached out and pulled her to him. "Sweetheart, don't get me wrong. I love this side of you, when you're not causing mayhem." He wrapped his arms around her waist. "I love seeing you excited about something. I love our life and I just want you to know, regardless of the outcome, I'm excited. I'm happy no matter what," he gently said.

She patted his cheek. "Me, too, but I'll be happier when you win." She wiggled away and reached over to grab her suit jacket.

"Well, the kids are ready," he said, pointing toward the sitting area of the suite.

"I know they are. That's why I'm not." She stopped and turned to face her husband. "We need a nanny like the Bushes have," she said, thinking about the old woman traveling with Jasmine and Hosea. Although she didn't look like she was playing with a full deck in that long, gnawed-off-looking mink coat, at least they had help.

"How do you know they have a nanny?"

"Didn't you see Miss Jane Pittman, the old lady that got off the plane with them?"

"Rachel, that's mean."

"I can't help it that she's old as dirt. She probably was a secretary for Jesus." She picked up her clutch. "But the fact remains that she was probably in there getting the Bush kids ready while Jasmine had all evening to primp. We should've brought a nanny."

"We don't have one," he said matter-of-factly.

"Well, we should! We had to hire a freaking hotel babysitter to watch the babies tonight. Jasmine only has two kids. We have four.

So getting a nanny is something we're going to have to look into because as first lady of the ABC, I'm going to be pretty busy."

Lester shook his head as he motioned toward the door. "Okay, sweetie, we'll cross that bridge if we get to it."

"Well, I'm letting you know now, that's not open for discussion," she said as she walked out of the bedroom.

"Yes, darling," Lester said, following behind her. "Kids, let's go," he said as soon as they entered the sitting area.

Nia came barreling toward them. "You like my dress, Daddy?" she said, spinning around to show off her pink taffeta dress. Rachel loved how Lester treated Nia like a true daddy's girl, loving her like she was his own. He treated both of her children like that and it was one of the qualities she absolutely adored about him. At the same time, he didn't try to stop Jordan from having a relationship with his father, Bobby. They didn't have to worry about Nia's dad because that jerk had signed over his rights years ago and they hadn't heard from him since.

"Yes, that dress is adorable, as are you," Lester replied, lightly kissing Nia's hand.

"Brooklyn and Lewis are still sleep," she said, pointing to the toddlers who were napping in the playpen. The sitter was quietly perched next to them, engrossed in a book. "And Jordan won't stop playing that stupid game and entratain me like Mommy said," Nia continued.

"It's *entertain,*" Jordan snapped, not glancing up from his PS2. "Learn how to talk."

"I know how to talk!" she snapped. "But if I didn't, at least I can fix it. You ugly forever!"

"Kids, stop that fighting," Lester snapped. "Come on, Jordan."

"Why I gotta go?" He pouted as he stood up. "This thing hurts my neck," he said, pulling at the black-and-gray tie. "Why can't I just stay here with her?" he said, pointing at the sitter.

"You don't have to stay long," Lester said, sighing. "But our children have to be introduced as well. Please don't fight me on this."

Rachel didn't even pay attention to any of them. She'd gone back to the mirror and was surveying her reflection, debating whether she should change into the purple Donna Karan suit she was saving for tomorrow.

"You're fine," Lester said, as if he were reading her thoughts. "Can we please go?" He grabbed Nia's hand and walked to the door, not waiting to make sure Rachel and Jordan were following.

The room was already packed with people, mingling and networking. An assortment of women in fancy suits and pillbox hats dotted the room, and almost every man in the room wore a black or gray suit. Rachel tried to pause in the doorway to give her family a moment to be noticed, but leave it to Lester to just walk on into the room before anyone could see them.

Lester immediately made his way over to a group of ministers who were standing around deep in conversation.

Rachel scanned the room, her eyes stopping on an elegantly dressed Cecelia King. She was standing in the center of the room, commanding that the circle of women give its full attention to her. She exuded power. Rachel found herself wondering how Cecelia would take no longer being the head Mrs. In-Charge.

Rachel was just about to head over to the circle when Cecelia walked away, Jasmine right at her side. The whole way Jasmine was clinging to the woman was sickening. The two of them stopped at the side of the room as Cecelia leaned down to shake a little girl's hand. That must be Jasmine's child, the way Jasmine glided to her side.

"Mommy, I'm thirsty," Nia said, pulling on Rachel's skirt.

"Okay, wait, I'll get you something in just a minute." Rachel took Nia's hand and pulled her over to where Cecelia stood.

"Well, hello, ladies," Rachel said, acting like she'd just bumped into them.

"Hello . . . ummm, Rachel, isn't it?" Cecelia asked.

Rachel nodded, pleased that she'd remembered her name. "Yes, Mrs. King, and don't you look lovely this evening."

"Thank you," she said, running her hand down her knit royal blue skirt. "Jasmine here got the St. John memo as well." She laughed, motioning toward Jasmine's cream suit.

Rachel struggled to keep her smile. "Jasmine."

"Rachel," Jasmine replied.

"And who do we have here?" Cecelia asked, leaning down to look at Nia.

"I'm Nia," the little girl said.

"Well, Nia, it's a pleasure to meet you," Cecelia said, shaking her hand.

Rachel looked around for Jordan. She spotted him just a few feet away, plopped down in a seat. "That's my son Jordan."

Cecelia glanced his way, lost her smile, then struggled to get it back. "Is he playing a video game? Here?" she asked.

Rachel was horrified. "Excuse me for a second." She walked over and snatched the game out of Jordan's hand. "Boy, what are you doing? Put this thing up," she hissed.

"Awww, Ma," he whined.

She leaned in and whispered in his ear. "Don't 'aww, Ma,' me. We're supposed to be making a good impression, so get it together before you make me act a fool." Rachel stood, composed herself, then walked back over to Cecelia and Jasmine.

"Boys," Rachel said, laughing lightly. "They can be a handful, huh?"

Jasmine just looked disgusted, but at least Cecelia smiled. "They sure can."

Rachel glanced around, a flash of panic setting in. "Where's Nia?"

Jasmine reached over and gently touched Rachel's arm. "She's okay. She's right there, getting something to drink with my daughter." For a moment, Rachel saw something in Jasmine's eyes, a soothing maternal spirit. But just as quickly, it was gone.

"They both were thirsty," Jasmine said, dropping her hand and turning icy again.

Cecelia must've sensed the tension because she stepped in. "So, are you ladies ready for the voting?"

Rachel was just about to reply when a loud wail filled the air. All three women turned toward the sound, to see Jacqueline crying hysterically as she raced toward them. Horror filled Jasmine's face as she noticed the big red spot on the front of Jacqueline's dress.

"Jacquie, what in the world happened?" Jasmine asked.

Jacqueline held her arms out like she was Carrie from the *Carrie* movies. You would've thought she was drenched in blood, the way she was acting.

"M . . . m . . . my dress," Jacqueline sobbed. "She messed up my dress!"

"Is that punch?" Jasmine asked. "Oh, my God! This is a four-hundred-dollar Dior dress!"

Four hundred dollars! Rachel wanted to scream. *For a kid's dress?*

Jacqueline continued sobbing as her mother dropped the dress and held her tightly. Rachel would've thought Jasmine would be too concerned about messing up her designer duds to hug her daughter so tight. But it was obvious Jasmine's only focus was Jacqueline. The way she was trying to comfort the little girl almost made Jasmine seem, well, human. Almost anyway.

"Calm down, sweetie," Jasmine said, finally pulling away from her daughter, "and tell me what happened."

"Sh . . . she did it," Jacqueline wailed, pointing to Nia, who was standing off to the side, her head held low.

Everyone turned to Nia, who suddenly started crying herself as she raced into her mother's arms. "It was an accident, Mommy!" she cried. "I didn't mean to do it."

Rachel's eyes grew wide. *Nia did this?*

"I was tryna to pour me some more punch and she bumped into me." Nia buried her head in her mother's midsection.

"Shhhh, calm down," Rachel said soothingly as she stroked her daughter's hair. While Rachel didn't condone messing up the girl's dress, she couldn't help but feel that's what Jasmine's bourgie behind got. Really, who would spend four hundred dollars on a kid's dress for a reception that the child would only be at for thirty minutes?

Jasmine cut her eyes at Nia like she was trying to determine if it was indeed an accident.

"I told her I was sorry," Nia sniffed.

Rachel looked over at Jasmine. "I'm so sorry about this," Rachel said, sincerely.

Jasmine took a deep breath but didn't respond. Some of the punch from Jacqueline's dress had seeped onto her suit, from when she'd hugged the little girl. She glanced down at the spot on the front of her suit as well. "Let's go get cleaned up," Jasmine said, pulling her daughter toward the door.

Wow, this couldn't have worked out better, Rachel thought as she watched them walk off. She made a mental note to remind Nia about being more careful, then she'd take her out for ice cream to celebrate a job well done.

"Jordan," she called out to her son, who was still sitting against the wall, pouting. "Come get your sister and take her upstairs to the sitter."

"Can I stay in the room?" he asked, finally getting excited.

Rachel nodded.

"Yes!" Jordan exclaimed. "Come on, clumsy mumsy."

"I'm not clumsy, it was an accident." Nia pouted as she stomped off behind her brother.

Rachel took a deep breath and turned back around to Cecelia. The woman had stayed silent during the entire exchange. "I'm so sorry about that," Rachel said.

"I understand," Cecilia said, although she didn't sound believable. "I have two grandchildren myself and they can get rather rambunctious."

Rachel released a sigh of relief as she tried to change the conversation. "So do you mind if I ask, how do you enjoy being the first lady?"

"Well, it has its challenges, but it's a position I enjoy tremendously. I was actually quite disheartened the reverend has decided not to seek reelection." She was talking to Rachel but her eyes seemed to be scanning the room. "So are you worried at all?" she asked, her gaze settling back on Rachel.

"Not at all," Rachel lied, even though she was getting more worried by the minute, especially with her kids acting up. "I think Lester would make an excellent president and when I look at all that he's done for our church and our community, I can only imagine what he could do if allowed to branch out. I love our church, but I feel like he's been limited there. He'd be able to soar as president of the ABC. Personally, I think the membership wants a young, seasoned, *Southern* minister. I understand your entire family is from Alabama?"

"We are," Cecelia replied, turning her full attention back to Rachel.

"So you know all about those Southern roots?"

"And we're very proud of them."

"My point exactly. I have nothing against Rev. Bush, but I think that we don't want to lose the family-feel of the ABC. We don't want to become just another organization filled with members who do nothing."

She pursed her lips as she glared at Rachel. "So is that what you think we are now?"

"Oh, no, no," Rachel said, cleaning things up. "I think the organization is wonderful under Reverend King, and as a matter of fact, I just told Lester on the flight here that I wish Reverend King weren't retiring. But if he does have to be replaced, Lester should be the one replacing him."

Cecelia gave Rachel a fake smile, before saying, "Well, it's been nice chatting with you, but I see some other people I must go mingle with. Enjoy the rest of the reception."

Rachel watched as Cecelia walked off. This had not gone at all like she'd planned. She had to take a deep breath and get it together. Cecelia was going to be a hard nut to crack. And Rachel didn't know how she'd do it, but she knew she couldn't rest until she got Cecelia King on her side.

Chapter
NINE

The women filed in—two by two, three by three, a few came alone—and each time Jasmine greeted another first lady, she breathed a little easier.

It looked like she was actually going to pull this off. Not that she had any doubts that she would—well, not until last night, after the disaster created by Rachel's clumsy crumb-snatcher. Jasmine still couldn't believe how those hillbillies had ruined Jacqueline's dress. She had almost gone off on Rachel and her daughter. Did that Kmart blue-light-special chick have any idea what her daughter had done?

But then, why would she ask herself a question like that? Rachel didn't know a thing about quality. That was apparent not only from the way she dressed, but also by the way her children behaved. Video games, dumping punch on other children . . . though Jasmine couldn't really blame Rachel's offspring for having no home training. Low class begat no class.

But even though she'd had to take Jacqueline upstairs and calm her down, Jasmine's plan had moved forward.

This plan had begun to formulate in her mind right after Cecelia had escorted her and Hosea to the penthouse suite yesterday. Jasmine had called Mae Frances up to the room, and while Hosea napped, the two schemed.

"We need to make that Adams woman look totally inept," Mae Frances had said.

"That's not going to be too hard." Jasmine told Mae Frances about her suspicions that Rachel was behind the limousine and hotel fiasco. "But do you see how it backfired on her? She needs to recognize that she is nothing nothing more than a tire-slashing, key-a-car, turn-off-utilities kind of trick. She is not even ready for me, and besides that, she can't do anything to block the blessings that God has for me and Hosea."

Mae Frances grinned like a Cheshire cat. "I have a big plan for her . . . a big fall. But from the look on your face, I can tell that you have a plan, too. What are you thinking?"

"We don't have much time, but . . ." That's when Jasmine had revealed the first phase of the plan.

As Mae Frances's mouth opened wide, her eyes filled with pride. "I've taught you well, Jasmine Larson. This is brilliant. And I have a way to make it even better."

In the twenty hours that had passed since then, Jasmine and Mae Frances had plotted. While Jasmine worked the first ladies at the welcome reception, Mae Frances had done the behind-the-scenes planning.

Now Jasmine stood in the room next to the banquet hall where the first ladies' luncheon would be held in just two hours.

"Welcome," Jasmine said, holding her smile while sneaking a glance at her watch. She couldn't show her impatience with this last group of stragglers.

"Excuse me, Lady Jasmine?"

Jasmine turned to the voice and her smile went right away. "I just wanted to thank you for inviting me to this luncheon," Reverend Penn's wife said.

"I'm glad to have you here, Coco," Jasmine said stiffly, though she meant what she'd said. She fully subscribed to the keep-your-enemies-close theory. And when she wasn't with Hosea, she wanted to make sure that Coco Penn wasn't near him, either.

Following the last of the first ladies into the ballroom, Jasmine scanned the space and found Mae Frances barking orders to the waiters who'd been assigned to them at the last minute. And in the center of the room, Cecilia King held court, surrounded by several first ladies who were as stylish as she was—though none of them could hold a candle to the red Chanel suit that Jasmine wore.

"Showtime!" Jasmine whispered to herself.

She strutted toward the center, knowing that females were watching her—which was a totally different dynamic from the men. She had to stroll with confidence, but lose the sexiness. She had to balance it all with grace, with deference. It was a dance that didn't come easy to Jasmine.

For years, Jasmine had never cared what any woman thought about her. After all, how could she when she was so busy stealing their men?

But being Hosea's wife made her not only want to please him, but to be a proper first lady as well. She'd had to take a few lessons to make it happen, though. Her teacher? Mae Frances, of course.

"The key with women," her friend had told her, "is to be admired by them. You cannot be threatening. They cannot feel less than you in any way, because by nature women are a jealous bunch." Mae Frances had spoken as if she didn't share their gender. "So lesson number one—when you meet a man and a woman together, greet the man, but then turn all of your attention to the woman."

Dozens of lessons had followed; Jasmine had learned to make and keep eye contact and smile, even if a woman snarled. She still never trusted women, that was her life's mantra. But she'd learned how to get women to trust her.

"Pardon me." Jasmine stepped inside the small circle that surrounded Cecelia. "Mrs. King, I'm going to get started now, if that's all right with you."

The woman nodded her approval, as if she appreciated Jasmine's deferential approach. Both of them knew that this was Jasmine's event—she'd just come to Cecelia out of respect, another lesson she'd learned from Mae Frances.

"Excuse me, ladies." Cecelia bowed out. Then to Jasmine she said, "Okay, let's begin." For a second, she turned away from Jasmine and scanned the room. "Where is . . . what's her name again? The Adams lady?"

"Oh, yes, Rachel," Jasmine said, as if she had the greatest regard for her enemy. "I don't know; we invited her, of course, but . . ." She lowered her voice. "Well . . . you know."

Cecelia smiled. "Yes, I do." Then, "This is your program, but would you mind if I introduced you?"

This was a coup that wasn't expected. Just an introduction by Cecelia would feel like an endorsement.

"Oh, my goodness. Would you?"

Gently, Cecelia took her hand and guided Jasmine along the perimeter of the room, then up the portable steps that led to the temporary stage brought in for this reception.

For a moment, the two stood side by side, watching the first ladies in their Sunday-best suits meet and greet, chat and chuckle. The women sipped on sparkling cider that Mae Frances had ordered in every flavor, and they sampled the chef's special hors d'oeuvres. Jasmine smiled—she knew she could trust Mae Frances to create one of this week's finest events.

When Jasmine saw Mae Frances stick her thumb in the air, she knew that she and Cecelia made quite a picture.

"Ladies," Cecelia began. She didn't even use the microphone that was set up at the podium, yet all the chatter and laughter faded away.

This is power, Jasmine thought. And she shuddered with anticipation of being passed the torch of that power in just a few days.

"Thank you for coming," Cecelia continued, "to this . . . what shall I call it?" She turned to Jasmine. But she didn't wait for an answer. Cecelia said, "Thank you for coming to this reception before the luncheon. It's that simple, right?"

Jasmine frowned; she didn't like the word "simple" used in any sentence that had anything to do with her. And what Cecelia had said didn't sound funny at all. Still, the first ladies chuckled.

Cecelia said, "Isn't this just lovely? I think we should all thank our host, Mrs. Jasmine Bush."

Jasmine kept her gracious smile, bowed her head slightly, and held up her hands as if she felt like she didn't deserve this attention.

"Before we begin, I just want to say, that whenever we gather together, we must praise the Lord!"

The women applauded and shouted their praises into the air.

Cecelia said, "For we must bless the Lord at all times; His praise must be continually in our mouths!"

The clapping continued until Cecelia held up her hands. "Thank you for praising the Lord with me, and now, let's get to the second reason why we're here. Ladies, please help me welcome perhaps the next first lady of the American Baptist Coalition—Mrs. Jasmine Bush."

The ovation was polite, dainty, but filled with curiosity. The first ladies wanted to know what this was all about. Why had this reception been added to the program just last night?

"Thank you all so much for joining me here today," Jasmine began. "I know it was last-minute, so I appreciate you giving me an hour out of your morning."

Low murmurs told her that she was welcome.

"I'll get straight to the point since we don't have much time before the luncheon. I asked you to join me today because I wanted to introduce a program for the American Baptist Coalition that I think will not only benefit each of us, but will help every African American in this country."

Jasmine paused. She had to take a deep breath before she continued with this part. "As you may know, a few years ago, my daughter Jacqueline was kidnapped—"

Gasps rose throughout the room, which startled Jasmine just a bit. She knew that this would come as a surprise to some, since Hosea had been added to the ballot just last week. So not many had had time to research the Bushes. Still, hadn't any of them heard about the trial?

"Yes, kidnapped," she repeated. "And . . ." She stopped. Could she really do this? Could she say it aloud. "And . . ." She stopped again. When Cecelia stepped to her side and took her hand, Jasmine whispered, "And raped."

The sound of shock surged through the room.

"She was only four years old." Jasmine's voice trembled. "But you know what? God held her and kept her and finally brought her home!"

The women clapped, much louder now than they did before and praises rained down.

"Thank you, Jesus."

"Amen!"

"Hallelujah!"

"Yes, Jacqueline came home to me, with the help of our church, our community, and our friends." Jasmine paused as she glanced at Mae Frances. Once Jacqueline had been rescued two years ago, the two women had never spoken of those three weeks—until last night, when they were planning this. But they said few words about it, and Jasmine never asked Mae Frances if she was the reason why Jacqueline had been found. She didn't have to ask, not really. Mae Frances—and her connections—had come through for her like they always had, this time in the ultimate way.

Jasmine cleared her throat of the emotions that came with those sad memories and kept on. "There was something, however, that stood out to me during that time. As you know, my husband pastors one of the largest churches in this country, and let's be honest, because of that and because of his TV talk show, he is . . . a celebrity . . ."

"Yes," many said, and nodded in agreement.

"But do you know that after the first day, we were not able to get any media coverage?"

This time, the murmurs showed the women's surprise.

"Of course, everyone was with us that first day, but we were not able to keep our daughter in the news. Now, I don't believe in playing the race card. In fact, I abhor"—she'd chosen that word so carefully that she decided to repeat it—"I completely abhor people who throw race in our faces every chance they get."

"That's right."

"But I cannot think of another reason why the daughter of a New York pastor was not worthy of at least local media coverage."

The women stirred, now with discontent. Jasmine could feel their questions rising—what could be done?

"That's why if I become first lady of the Coalition, the first thing I will work on—with your help, of course—is a national Child Find Program."

Approval stirred through the crowd now.

"Our children cannot be invisible. Our children cannot go unnoticed. We must stand up for the little ones who have no voice."

"Yes!" The women applauded again.

"I want to set up centers like the one our church put together for my daughter in as many communities as possible. We need to have the centers in place, so that when something happens to one of ours, we are prepared. This way, we will be able to go into action, and not reaction."

"Yes!" the cheers came again.

"We need to be ready . . . to bring our children home!"

Applause.

"And, unlike many others who believe that abducted children only come in one color"—she paused so that the first ladies would catch her meaning—"we will take care of all children."

"Amen," and more cheers.

"And we will call these centers Jacqueline's Hope, because with all of us standing together, we can make sure that our missing children share the same fate as Jacquie—we can make sure that they will be returned to their homes and their loving families."

The shouts and the cheering were so loud that Jasmine had to wait for minutes to pass before she could speak again.

"But it's not going to be easy. I will need your help."

Every woman in the room nodded, seeming eager to hear how they could play a part in this fantastic program.

"I will work with planning committees in whichever communities and churches you decide. I will personally consult with you to set up these centers."

The women applauded again.

"And, we will need money." Jasmine paused because she wanted to make sure that every eye in the ballroom was on her for this announcement. "We will need money," she repeated. "And that's why, to get this program started, my husband Pastor Hosea Bush and I will personally donate one . . . million . . . dollars!"

Because Jasmine had purposely designed this reception with just tables and a few chairs, the women were already on their feet. But the way they applauded and cheered—it felt like a standing ovation.

"And let me be clear," Jasmine continued through the cheers of approval, "this is a personal donation. It has nothing to do with the money that my husband will speak about at the program tomorrow night. This is in addition to anything that has been raised by the Northern region."

On her left, Cecelia beamed. Jasmine's glance wandered to Mae Frances, who still stood at the back of the room, but now with eyes wide.

Well, yes, she'd just improvised that million dollars part. She and Hosea didn't have one million dollars to give to anybody's cause. But she'd been involved in a couple of major fund-raising projects for their church; she could do that again. She'd raise a million dollars easily. Plus, would anyone even really remember this million-dollar promise a week from now? This was all about this moment.

When the applause died down, Jasmine said, "The reason I wanted to announce this here, this morning, is that I didn't want to take away from the message that we will hear from our speaker at lunch today, the fabulous Lady Cecelia King."

Again applause, and Jasmine noted that the claps for Cecelia were not as loud as before. Had the torch already been passed? Were these women already looking to her as their new leader?

"So again, I thank you for coming out and for standing by me as we take care of our children. I hope I get the opportunity to work with each and every one of you very soon."

Cecelia hugged Jasmine as she stepped away from the

podium, holding her long enough so that Jasmine knew that Cecelia approved. The two held hands as they descended the stairs and then stepped into the crowd of waiting first ladies, who greeted them with approval and well-wishes.

"You have my support, Mrs. Bush."

"God bless you, Lady Jasmine."

"What an amazing testimony. You are an amazing woman."

And then through the tidal wave of accolades, Jasmine heard the shout, "Mama!"

The crowd parted as Jacqueline ran into her mother's arms. "Hi, baby," she said, hugging her.

It had been timed perfectly. As Jasmine was winding down her speech, Mae Frances called the suite and Mrs. Sloss brought the children to the reception.

"Oh!" many gasped. "Is this . . . your little girl?"

Jasmine nodded with pride. The women spoke words that Jasmine already knew. "She's beautiful." "She's blessed." "You must be so proud."

"Thank you," Jasmine said as she held Jacqueline's hand and led her through the mass. But it was hard to move with so many women crowded around, with the way so many wanted to shake her hand and give Jacqueline a hug.

This was one part of the plan that Jasmine had not been too sure of. She loved her children too much to use them, but Mae Frances had assured her that there was nothing wrong with the women seeing Jacqueline to help them understand the importance of Jacqueline's Hope.

"If they need to see Jacqueline in order to be moved to do the right thing and make Hosea the president, so that they can have these centers, then we need to let them see her. It's not like you'll be parading her up on the stage. It'll look like she just happened to show up."

But as Jasmine eased toward the doors, it felt a bit like Jacqueline *was* on the stage. Now she prayed that her seven-year-old wouldn't be hurt by all this.

She glanced down, and her daughter strutted by her side, her head high, her smile wide; she was beaming at the attention. She even had that little beauty-pageant-wave thing going on, and Jasmine couldn't have been more proud.

This was amazing on so many levels. It had taken a good year for Jacqueline to feel safe around anyone besides her immediate family. Her therapy sessions—which still continued—were obviously working.

But the truth was, Jacqueline Bush was *her* daughter. What else was to be expected?

"Thank you," Jasmine kept saying as she and Jacqueline glided toward the door.

The first ladies followed Jasmine as if she were leading them to the Promised Land, but when she stepped into the hall, Jasmine bumped into the only first lady who hadn't received a personal invitation to the reception.

Rachel glared at Jasmine, her eyes on fire with fury.

The two women stared each other down, locked in a silent showdown.

Which was why neither one of them noticed Cecelia King, off to the side, sipping grape apple cider, and watching. And, as the Jasmine-Rachel battle continued, Cecelia's lips spread into a slow smile.

Chapter TEN

Thank God she was somewhat saved. Because the evil thoughts racing through Rachel's mind right about now would definitely get her ticket to Heaven revoked.

This heifer thought she was slick. She almost pulled it off without Rachel even knowing about it, but then Rachel had heard two ladies in the elevator talking about it and inconspicuously followed them to the banquet room. *How long has this thing been planned?* Rachel thought as she peeked into the room. With a waitstaff, decorations, and everything, this had to be something Jasmine was plotting all along.

Rachel had stood by the door and listened for a little bit. She'd wanted to go in so badly, but she refused to give Jasmine the satisfaction. Plus, she didn't want to be embarrassed or called out, so she just stood outside listening to the whole dog and pony show. The applause was sickening. But when Jasmine played the my-daughter-was-kidnapped card for sympathy, Rachel was appalled. Even Rachel wouldn't sink that low.

Oh, and of course, there was that whole grandiose pledge. *A million dollars?* Yeah, Rachel's research revealed that the Bushes had money, but she didn't think they had it like *that*. Jasmine knew doggone well they didn't have a million dollars to just give away.

Rachel ducked out of sight when she saw a woman approaching with Jacqueline. When they passed, she peeked her head through the door again and saw the group of women parting like Moses and the Red Sea as Jacqueline ran into her mother's arms.

"Oh, good grief," Rachel mumbled. "And cue child running in, three, two, one . . ."

Rachel had had enough. She made her way around to the front entrance, where the obviously planned reunion was taking place. She'd just made it to the hall when she came face-to-face with Jasmine.

"Well, hello, Rachel," Jasmine said, a big grin across her face. "I was wondering why you weren't at the reception."

"I would have been there, had I known about it," Rachel said, trying to contain the anger building in the pit of her stomach. She was about to go off until she realized there was a small crowd of women growing behind Jasmine. Instead, she was blessed with an inspiration.

"Honestly, I wouldn't have been able to make it anyway. I was upstairs in a conference call with Regina West," Rachel said sweetly.

"The Academy Award–winning actress Regina West?" someone behind Jasmine said.

Rachel's smile widened. "The one and only."

The chatter heightened. "Oh, my God. We've been trying to get her to do something with us for years," someone said.

"I just love her."

"She's phenomenal but very elusive."

"You know Regina West?"

"Yes." Rachel nodded. She didn't even know who had asked the question. "Regina used to be a member"—she looked Jasmine in the eyes—"of our *little* church. Of course, that's before she went and took Hollywood by storm."

"So you really know Regina West?" Jasmine asked skeptically.

Rachel could understand her skepticism. Regina West was only the hottest actress in Hollywood—black or white. Last year, she'd surpassed Angelina Jolie as the highest-paid actress. She'd been the only black woman ever to win two Academy

Awards. "Yes, she's a dear family friend. She and I actually were talking about this fantastic program I'd like to start on women empowerment, empowering women mentally, physically, and financially—that is of course, if I were to become first lady."

Rachel wanted to jump for joy as the women left Jasmine's side and hurried over to bombard her with more questions about Regina.

"Ms. King," Rachel said, waving to Cecelia, who was standing off to the side, taking all of this in. "Regina would like to meet with you personally in the near future. She's a fan and said she'd love to do some work with you."

Cecelia looked pleasantly flattered. "Of course."

"I'll have her people get with your assistant to set something up after the conference." Rachel didn't want to remind them again that Lester had to win first, but she could tell by the looks on the women's faces that it was a fact many of them duly noted.

"I must get going," Rachel said, relishing Jasmine's silent fury. Steal Jasmine's shine. Checkmate. This couldn't have worked out better had she planned it. "I need to make another call before the luncheon."

"Another famous person?" someone asked.

"We'll just have to wait and see." Rachel winked as she waved and rounded the corner. She wanted to turn cartwheels down the hallway. But she couldn't get too excited just yet. She ducked into the stairwell, whipped out her cell phone, and punched in a number.

"Hey, Daddy," she said, when her father, Reverend Simon Jackson, answered.

"Hey, baby girl. How's the conference going for you?"

"It's great. You think you're going to feel up to coming?" she asked. Her father had been battling prostate cancer. It was in remission, but his doctor had severely limited his activity.

"I am. Jonathan and David wanted to come with me so they could support you and Lester, but Jonathan has to work and David, well, we have a little crisis here with David."

"Crisis? What kind of crisis?"

"Your brother's crazy ex has been showing up around here, acting a fool, talking about wanting to see D.J."

Rachel rolled her eyes. "When did Tawny get out jail?" There wasn't a motherly bone in that crackhead's body, so if she was coming around, she had to want something. Tawny had been the whole reason David had gotten hooked on drugs. Luckily, David eventually dropped her and tried to get his life together. Too bad he'd had a child with that nutcase. Everything worked out, though, because David got custody of D.J. after Tawny was arrested for trying to run down Rachel with her car.

Simon tsked. "I guess she just got out. I don't know. I just know David is doing so well and we finally got some stability in my grandson's life. I just don't want her coming around messing things up."

Rachel shuddered at the thought of Tawny causing any havoc in their lives. Jasmine would have some kind of field day with that. No, David and his drama needed to stay right there in Houston.

"Well, you tell David to stay there and handle that crazy girl, and you and Brenda can come on."

"We will. We actually leave in the morning after my doctor's appointment. We'll be there in time for the election."

"Okay, great," Rachel said hurriedly, ready to shift the conversation back to the real reason she called. "Well, look, I need a favor before you come."

"Anything, sweet pea."

"Whew, glad you said that." Rachel took a deep breath. "I need you to call Regina West."

"Who?"

"Regina, you know the actress."

"Call her for what? I haven't talked to her since I baptized her."

"Yeah, but you baptized her. That has to count for something."

Simon let out a long sigh, like he knew Rachel had gotten caught up in another drama. "Rachel, Regina and her family moved away when the girl was five. What do I look like calling her after all this time?"

"But you still talk to her father."

"Occasionally. They visit the church whenever they're home, but it's been almost a year since we spoke."

"Well, now's the perfect time. I mean, really, you're the reason the girl is going to Heaven."

"Rachel, that's ridiculous."

"No, it's not. You introduced her to God, so she owes you." Rachel exhaled in desperation. "Daddy, I really need you to do this for me."

He was quiet; then, "Rachel, what have you gotten yourself into?"

Rachel could hear her father's disapproval in his voice. She'd have to listen to him lecture later, but right now she needed him to act.

"Please, Daddy?" She hesitated. She hated to guilt him into anything, but she was desperate. "You know when I was growing up, you—"

"Okay, fine," he said, cutting her off. He knew she was about to remind him how he hadn't supported her or anything she wanted to do her entire life. He'd tried to get much better over the last few years and make up for all the time he neglected her for the church. "I'll call Allen today and see if he can have Regina call me."

"Thank you, Daddy. You're the best! You guys have a safe trip. Can't wait to see you so we can celebrate our win."

"Fine, Rachel. We'll see you tomorrow night. And can you just stay out of trouble?"

"Trouble? What's that?" She laughed. "Love you, Daddy."

"Love you, too, baby girl."

Rachel hung up the phone and leaned back against the wall. Things looked shaky for a minute, but now everything was falling into place. If that wasn't a sign that they were destined to win, she didn't know what was.

Chapter
ELEVEN

"Would you calm down, Jasmine Larson?" Mae Frances demanded.

But there was no way for Jasmine to do that. Not with what had transpired twenty minutes ago still so fresh in her mind. She couldn't believe the trick that trick had pulled.

"You know she doesn't know Regina West," Jasmine fumed as she paced the length of the master bathroom in Jasmine's hotel suite where she and Mae Frances were hiding out. They were alone—with little time before the luncheon, but Jasmine needed these moments, away from everyone else, to calm down.

Mrs. Sloss had taken the children back to their suite and Hosea was at a meeting with Pastor Griffith and the Northern delegation, preparing for tomorrow's budget presentation. Jasmine had no doubt that if points were being kept, Hosea would blow out Lester Adams tomorrow; the money that had been raised by the North was staggering. So her plan had been to take care of today . . . and all the women who would be influencing their husbands.

And she'd handled her business, until Rachel entered and stole her thunder with that gigantic lie.

Jasmine said, "I would bet any amount of money that she's only seen that woman on a movie screen."

"That's probably true." Mae Frances leaned against the marble counter and folded her arms, patiently waiting for Jasmine's rant to end.

"And now she has all those wives believing that she can give them something that will never happen." Jasmine's hands sliced through the air with each word. "That was nothing but a stunt."

"Kind of like your million-dollar stunt?"

Jasmine turned her fiery eyes on her friend. "Whose side are you on, Mae Frances? Because if you——"

"Stop being so dramatic," Mae Frances said, cutting off her friend before Jasmine got too indignant. "First of all, who cares about Regina West? You know I know everybody from Al Sharpton to Stevie Wonder, so if she wants to play the who-knows-who game, we'll stomp her with that."

Mae Frances was speaking nothing but the truth. But still, Rachel was the first one to pull a celebrity out of her hat. Anyone she and Mae Frances came up with now would make Jasmine look like the follower, not the leader.

Mae Frances added, "And you knew this was going to be a fight from the moment Preacher Man was offered this opportunity, or else you wouldn't have come to me."

That pissed her off. Did Mae Frances really think that she couldn't pull this off without her? Jasmine pressed her lips together and swallowed the words that she wanted to say—that Mae Frances shouldn't think too highly of herself. That she could've done all of this without Mae Frances's help. But since they both knew that wasn't true, Jasmine sucked in air and instead said, "Well, since I came to you, do you have any more bright ideas?"

Mae Frances raised one eyebrow, then shook her head slightly just to let Jasmine know that she was totally unaffected by her little tantrum. "Don't lose it now, Jasmine Larson. You know Pastor Griffith and I have something big that we're saving, but we're not even there yet. You're forgetting the major plan for today." She paused, then reminded her, "Today is about the luncheon."

I must be getting soft, Jasmine thought to herself.

It had been a long time since she'd schemed like this, and clearly she'd lost some of her edge, because Rachel had totally thrown her off her game. That was the only way she could explain how she'd forgotten about the rest of today's plan. She didn't need to be up in this suite ranting; she and Mae Frances needed to get downstairs to set the rest of this day in motion.

"I'd almost forgotten," Jasmine said, turning to the mirror. She finger-fluffed her curls, then reached for her makeup kit. "You think we can really pull this off?"

Mae Frances glanced at Jasmine in the mirror and smirked. "We're dealing with Rachel Adams, aren't we? She's young and dumb. She's so eager to impress these women that she's going to jump at the bait. Trust me."

That's just what Jasmine wanted to hear. She clicked off the light in the bathroom, turned to Mae Frances, and said, "Let's roll."

In the hallway, Mae Frances gave Jasmine the folder that she'd prepared last night; these would be the last moments Jasmine had to study. Once the elevator came, their talking ceased and they rode down in silence. The elevator stopped on almost every floor as the first ladies made their way to the biggest event of the week for the women. Along the way, Jasmine was greeted with pleasant smiles and a few congratulations, but the soft chatter was all about Rachel Adams and Regina West.

Jasmine sighed. After this morning's session, she'd expected the women to be groveling at her feet, ready to crown her queen.

But there was no need to sweat this. In just a couple of hours, she'd be the one back on top—where she deserved to be. And Rachel? Well, the women of the American Baptist Coalition would realize that Rachel was nothing more than a ghetto-not-so-fabulous street girl who couldn't stand next to her, or any of them, no matter how many lies she told.

As the women filed from the elevator into the hall leading to the Grand Ballroom, Jasmine and Mae Frances pressed through the crowd as politely as they could. At the door, they paused, and with eagle eyes they scanned the massive space. In moments, Jasmine zoomed in on Cecelia King. She was in the center, as always, her majesty surrounded by her royal court. But this time she wasn't alone. Rachel Adams stood at her side as if she were the princess preparing to take her rightful place.

Jasmine had to take a breath. Rachel was standing where she was supposed to be.

"This is better for the plan," Mae Frances whispered, as if she knew Jasmine's thoughts. "Just go on up in there, do it the way I told you, and I'll handle phase two." She patted the envelope she held in her hand, then gently pushed Jasmine forward.

Jasmine sauntered toward the group in the center, as if she wasn't in a hurry. But each passing second pulled them closer to the start of the program and Jasmine had to make this happen right now.

There was a crowd around Cecelia and Rachel, and if she hadn't had a plan, Jasmine would be fuming again. But she delighted in the fact that it wouldn't be long before Rachel was flat on her face.

How am I going to get Cecelia's attention? Jasmine thought. But there was no need for her concern. The moment Jasmine caught Cecelia's gaze, the older woman smiled. With a nod, Jasmine beckoned her, as if she had something important to share.

"Excuse me, ladies," Cecelia said before she stepped toward Jasmine.

But as Cecelia moved away from the group, Rachel did, too, as if she'd been invited to join Jasmine's discussion.

It was rude . . . it was immature . . . and it played right into Jasmine's hand.

Cecelia spoke first. "I didn't get a chance to tell you before, but I wanted to say what an awesome testimony you gave at the reception. What you want to do for the ladies of the American Baptist Coalition, and the whole country really, is simply amazing."

"Thank you." Jasmine lowered her eyes properly, as if the compliment was too much. "I just want to do what I can to make sure no mother has to go through what I did."

"Oh, yeah," Rachel said. "What you did up there was really special. A million dollars, huh?"

Both Jasmine and Cecelia stared at Rachel for a moment, letting her know her comment was inappropriate. "Rachel, honey," Cecelia began in a teacher's tone. "This has nothing to do with money. Her child was taken away and violated. Don't you know that?"

"Yeah, but . . ."

Cecelia sighed as if she was exasperated. "This offer came from Jasmine's heart, to protect other children and other parents." To Jasmine, Cecelia said, "You are to be commended for going through and coming through that. And to stand up there and share it with all of us . . ." She pressed her hand against her chest, shook her head, then pulled Jasmine into her arms.

Over Cecelia's shoulder, Jasmine saw Rachel roll her eyes. Oh, yeah. This was gonna be fun. It was time to take the wench down.

"Thank you so much," Jasmine said, pulling back. "And I wanted to thank you for introducing me at the reception." She paused, glanced at Rachel, who stood in place as if she had no intention of leaving Cecelia's side. "I'm hoping, Cecelia, that you'll let me return the favor. I'm sure there is someone already assigned to introduce you, but"—she hoped this was the part that would get Rachel—"since the women have already met me and are really getting to know me now, which is positive for my husband, I'm hoping you'll give me a chance to make a few more points . . . and introduce you."

"Oh . . . well . . . that's an idea." Cecelia lowered her head as if she was pondering the suggestion.

"It would mean a lot to me." Jasmine glanced at Rachel, who stood now, with her arms folded, with her eyes squinted, as if she was in deep thought. But Rachel hadn't jumped in yet, so it was time for Jasmine to go in for the kill. "It would mean a lot to Hosea . . . if you know what I mean." Jasmine shared a chuckle with Cecelia.

Rachel stepped in—literally. With her elbow, she nudged Jasmine aside. Any other time, Jasmine would've knocked the trollop upside her head. But she stepped back and allowed Rachel to fall into her trap. "Ummm . . . Cecelia, really, I would love to introduce you." Turning to Jasmine, she added, "I mean, you've already had a chance to speak to the women and many of them don't know who I am. So, I would love the opportunity and I think it's only fair . . ." She paused, then added, "And I'm sure you don't want it to look like you're favoring one of us over the other."

Fool! Jasmine thought as Cecelia's eyes narrowed at Rachel's words.

"I mean," Rachel began, as if she knew she had to clean this up, "I would never say that, but I heard some of the other ladies talkin'."

Jasmine was sure that Rachel was going to ruin her plan if she kept on, so she jumped in. "You know what? That's probably a good idea. Rachel, you should introduce Cecelia." Both looked at Jasmine as if they didn't believe her. Jasmine added, "I mean, you've been so gracious to me, Cecelia, and I don't want Rachel to feel bad . . ."

"I don't feel bad," Rachel said with too much attitude. "I'm just sayin'. . ."

Would you shut up? Jasmine wanted to scream. *You're going to ruin my plan!*

For a moment, Cecelia stared hard at Jasmine, as if she suspected that Jasmine didn't have a polite bone in her body— that this had to be part of some kind of trick or scheme. But finally, Cecelia relented. "Are you sure you're okay with this, Jasmine?"

"Absolutely!"

Cecelia motioned toward the tall, lanky woman who'd been following her around since they'd arrived. Though Cecelia never introduced her to anyone, Jasmine was sure she was her assistant.

Cecelia whispered something to her friend that neither Jasmine nor Rachel could hear. When they moved apart, the woman motioned for Rachel to follow her.

With a smirk and a "Hmph," Rachel sashayed away, putting way too much swing in her hips, as if she'd forgotten where she was.

Cecelia shook her head slightly, and frowned as she watched Rachel saunter away.

But Jasmine was all smiles. *Some people are just perfect victims, perfect idiots!*

This was one of those good news–bad news scenarios. The good news was that as the wife of one of the top contenders for the position of president, Jasmine was placed on the dais next to Cecelia King. The bad news—on the other side of Cecelia was Rachel, who did her best to keep Cecelia engaged and away from Jasmine throughout the entire program.

Even after lunch had been served, Rachel never stopped talking. It was only when a short break was announced before dessert and the women stood to mingle that she finally shut up.

When Cecelia stepped away and Jasmine and Rachel were alone, Rachel said, "You know, Jasmine, when Lester is voted in as president, I'm sure he can find a place for your husband to work for him." She pushed her chair back from the table and stood. "In fact, I may ask you to do a few little things for me, too." She laughed softly as she swung her fake Gucci purse that was a perfect match to the Kmart special dress she wore, and stepped down from the dais.

Jasmine's eyes followed Rachel as she sauntered through the crowd, stopping here and there, roaming to and fro . . . just like Satan. She kept her eyes on Rachel as she left the ballroom, obviously on her way to the restroom to freshen up for her grand introduction.

And then Jasmine's eyes wandered to the folder that Rachel had left beside her place setting. In the next instant, Mae Frances joined her on the stage, but neither woman said a word to the other. With the slightest movement, Mae Frances exchanged the manila folder at Rachel's seat with one that she held. Then she left the stage just as quickly as she came.

By the time Rachel returned, Jasmine was shivering with anticipation. When the mistress of ceremonies quieted the group, the women settled at their seats for coffee, tea, and dessert . . . and to hear from their leader, First Lady Cecelia King.

"It is my honor," the mistress of ceremonies began, "to present Mrs. Rachel Adams, who will introduce our keynote speaker."

The applause was polite as Rachel pushed back her chair, grabbed the folder with the bio, and then took her time strolling to the podium.

Rachel stood for a moment, her shoulders back, her head high—with much more poise than Jasmine expected. And for the briefest of moments, Jasmine wondered if Rachel was going to be able to pull this off. Would she scan the paper ahead of time, or would she just read, knowing that she'd already reviewed the bio?

But then Jasmine calmed herself. There was no way Rachel would be smart enough to glance over the sheet once again. The truth was, even she would just get up there and start reading if she were in Rachel's position.

Rachel opened her mouth and Jasmine took a breath. "Thank you all so much. It is such a pleasure to be here and to introduce a woman whom I've admired from afar for many years."

Jasmine raised an eyebrow. Afar? Impressive. She'd expected Rachel to just go up there, stutter a bit, and then start reading.

Rachel said, "As many of you may know, my father, Simon Jackson, has been the pastor of Zion Hill for many years. And if I've learned one thing from him, it's that our leaders are important because they are the ones who help us set the tone to bring others to Christ. So, Lady Cecelia, thank you for setting a wonderful tone for all of us to follow."

The applause was a little louder this time and Jasmine had to release a long breath. Where was this coming from? Rachel Adams sounded like she had a little bit of class. Was she ever going to open that folder? Was she ever going to read what Mae Frances had prepared?

Rachel cleared her throat, leaned closer to the microphone,

then did what Jasmine had been expecting—she began to read. "Cecelia King wasn't always a first lady. In fact, few know that she was a wildcat often found butt-naked . . . in college . . ." She paused as her eyes scanned the page.

Gasps and the clanking of dropped forks filled the air. Followed by whispers and glares.

"Oh, my God," Rachel said, though no one in the room heard her.

The chatter grew louder as the women stared and pointed, their disgust palpable.

The moments that passed had to feel like minutes to Rachel as she looked from side to side, not knowing what to do.

Jasmine jumped from her seat and rushed to Rachel's side. She put her arm around Rachel's shoulder and spoke into the microphone. "Obviously, there's been a mistake," Jasmine said. "But together, Rachel and I can tell you about the real Cecelia King. The woman who was raised in Smackover, Arkansas, who's been working since she was fourteen years old. The woman who helped her mother raise her six brothers and sisters while she put herself through the University of Arkansas at Fayetteville."

Jasmine continued the litany of Cecelia's accomplishments, never looking down at a single paper and never letting go of Rachel. This was the important part, Mae Frances had told her. The women had to see them side by side.

"The Bible tells us how important a helpmate is," Jasmine continued, "and it is because of Cecelia King that her husband, Reverend Andre King, has held the position of president of the American Baptist Coalition for eight years."

She paused as the women applauded.

Jasmine said, "But she leaves her own legacy with the National Head Start program that she initiated, along with the Reading Is Fundamental book drives that occur all over the country because of her vision."

More applause, and this time Jasmine paused long enough to take in the crowd. Rachel's blunder was not forgotten, but in their eyes Jasmine could see that the women were impressed with her. She was snapping off Cecelia's accomplishments as if she'd been by Cecelia's side for every one of them—and without reading from any notes whatsoever. And Rachel had to continue standing silently next to her, Jasmine's protective arm still around her shoulder—the princess and the pauper.

"And to quote one of Lady Cecelia's favorite scriptures . . ." Jasmine paused. She had no idea if this was Cecelia's favorite scripture or not, but Mae Frances had said with the way that woman went around quoting the Bible, they could pick out anything and it would work. Jasmine said, "For the Lord is great and greatly to be praised. Ladies, let us praise the Lord for our first lady! Without any further ado . . . or mix-ups"—she paused at the laughter and felt Rachel stiffen beneath her hold—"I bring to you the first lady of all first ladies, Mrs. Cecelia King."

This time, the women rose to their feet, but as Cecelia walked past Rachel and hugged Jasmine, Jasmine knew that the ovation was as much for her as it was for Cecelia.

When Cecelia finally leaned back and caught her eye, Jasmine took a quick breath. It was the smirk that Cecelia wore that made Jasmine wonder—it was a smirk that said she knew Jasmine was behind this whole setup.

Well, so what? Of course, she probably knew. But even if Cecelia suspected that, it didn't matter. Jasmine's goal was to please many more than Cecelia King. There were many other first ladies who had to be impressed with her, and the reaction from the other women just moments before told her that she'd accomplished her goals.

Rachel moved like a zombie as Jasmine led her back to her seat. She actually had to help the girl sit down—but that was wonderful because Jasmine knew the women were watching and she demonstrated her compassion for the poor, stupid child.

Then Jasmine took her place, folded her hands in her lap, and turned to Cecelia King as if the woman was about to give the most important speech in the world.

Chapter
TWELVE

Uggghhhhh!!!!" Rachel screamed as she threw the hotel's lamp against the wall.

"Have you lost your mind?" Lester screamed.

Rachel stopped mid-rant. She didn't know how long she'd been in the hotel suite, but judging by the broken lamp, the overturned coffee table, and the way Nia was cowering in the corner, it had been long enough to terrify her children.

Her son was standing behind Lester in the doorway, looking scared out of his mind. He must've run outside and called Lester when she came stomping into the suite like a stark raving lunatic.

Lester's admonishment and the silent tears trickling down Nia's face brought her back to reality. She hadn't had an angry explosion like that in years. Rachel closed her eyes and inhaled. *How in the world had she let that woman push her to this point?*

"I . . . I'm sorry, kids," Rachel said, her eyes watering. "Mommy didn't mean to scare you. I was just really mad."

"But when I got mad and broke Jordan's airplane, you said no matter how mad you get, you shouldn't break other people's things," Nia softly replied.

"And you shouldn't," Rachel responded, walking over and pulling her daughter out of the corner. "Mommy did a very bad thing, but she's going to use her own money to pay for the lamp."

"Like you made me use my allowance to pay for Jordan's plane?" Nia asked.

Rachel nodded. "I'm sorry I scared you." She looked up at Jordan. "You, too, Jordan."

He looked relieved that she wasn't mad about him going to get Lester.

"Why don't you take your sister down to the gift shop and buy her some ice cream." She pulled a twenty out of her purse and handed it to her son. "Keep the change."

"For real?" Jordan exclaimed. If anything could make Jordan forget about problems, it was money.

"For real."

"What about me?" Nia said.

Rachel reached in her purse and pulled out two five-dollar bills.

"Yay!" Nia said. She waved the money in her brother's face. "I got more than you. I got more than you."

"No, you don't."

"Unh-huh. You only have one bill. I got two," she sang.

"You are such a dumb dork," he said as he walked toward the door.

"Jordan, don't talk to your sister like that," Lester said, before moving to let them pass.

Lester let the sounds of their arguing fade before he stepped inside and closed the door.

"Do you want to tell me what's going on?"

"It's that bi—that witch, Jasmine," Rachel said, her anger returning. "You will not believe what she did at the luncheon."

Rachel paced back and forth as she relayed the whole sordid story. After Jasmine swooped in with her fake Wonder Woman cape, the whole atmosphere had shifted. Cecelia had barely said two words to her the rest of the luncheon. Some of the women even spent the whole time throwing her dirty looks. Rachel had tried to apologize afterward, even telling Cecelia that someone had switched out her bio. Cecelia had barely listened to her apology, and quickly made her exit. Rachel didn't know how, but she knew exactly *who* that someone had been.

"Rachel, I'm sure it wasn't as bad as you're making it out to be." Lester motioned around the room. "It surely didn't warrant this."

"Are you freakin' kidding me? It was worse than bad, it was horrendous. And what if it costs you the election?"

"Then it wasn't God's will for me to win," Lester said, walking over to begin picking up the broken pieces of the lamp. "I just thank God the babies weren't in here. Jordan said they were with your dad and Brenda."

"Do you hear yourself?" Rachel screamed. "This is not something to be taken lightly. This tramp is trying to sabotage everything we worked for."

Lester released a frustrated sigh. "First of all, I doubt it's that serious." He turned and looked Rachel in the eye. "And if this election is going to turn you into this crazed woman, I will just withdraw from the race."

"You'll do no such thing." She knew there was no way Lester was going to play dirty. But *she* wasn't above it at all. In fact, she had just the dirt she needed. Her trump card. She hadn't planned to stoop this low, but the game had changed. That old freak had proven she could *and would* play dirty. But Jasmine didn't know dirty and Rachel was definitely about to show it to her.

"I'm going to tell the front desk that we have a lamp to pay for," Lester said, dumping the last of the shattered ceramic into the trash. "Then, I'm going back to the budget meeting. The public praise and worship session starts in four hours and I'd like to get some rest."

Rachel didn't reply as her husband walked out. She didn't have time to be concerned with him. Four hours was just enough time to put her plan into action.

Rachel couldn't help but notice how Jasmine kept staring at her throughout the worship service. She was probably wondering why Rachel was smiling, seemingly carefree as she got caught up in the praise and worship. But Rachel was focused, her eye was on the prize, and she was ready for her plan to be unveiled—right in front of this packed ballroom.

When she had found out this little tidbit, she'd filed it away because it was a little too much, even for her. She knew what she was about to do would really make Lester mad. But he'd just have to get over it because there was no way Rachel was about to let that tramp get away with what she did at the luncheon.

"Can I get an amen?" Reverend King said as the music took on a softer tone.

Amens reverberated throughout the ballroom.

"After that powerful message from this evening's guest preacher, Rev. Payne, I know there's some soul that feels the need to come to Jesus."

Yes! Rachel silently proclaimed.

"I know there are a lot of saints in the house, but if there are any sinners among us who long to know God, come, come now and share your testimony," Reverend King said.

A couple of people made their way up front. Rachel's smile spread as the third person stood. She looked exactly like Rachel expected her to. The long, platinum blond wig. The leopard-print spandex pants. The black crop tank that was cut too high at the bottom and too low at the top. And the makeup. Whew. The bright blue glitter eye shadow was overpowering and it looked like she'd used ruby red lipstick on her lips *and* her cheeks. She had to be pushing forty, but years of hard living made her look a lot older. Rachel couldn't have picked a better representative if she had created her herself.

Rachel waited anxiously as the first two people gave their testimony. She wasn't even sure what they had said. All of her attention was focused—like most people in the room—on the harlot standing at the end, smacking on a wad of gum like it was the last piece on earth.

Rachel sneaked a look over at Jasmine, who was sitting across the aisle with her husband. Jasmine looked like she'd seen a ghost and Rachel knew instantly that her source had been right on the money. She actually was grateful Jacqueline wasn't here. It would be a shame for the little girl to witness what was about to go down.

"Hey, e'rebody," the woman said after Reverend King handed

her the mic. "First of all, givin' honor to God and all that stuff. My name is Alize. Well, my real name is LaQuanta, but e'rebody call me Alize. Thank you for lettin' me say my piece. I just happened to be here in the hotel meeting a . . . a . . . umm, a customer." She paused and released a giggle. "But don't worry, it wasn't nobody from y'all's convention," she said to a few nervous chuckles. "Anyway, I was waiting on him, when I spotted somebody I knew from back in the day." How she continued to chew her gum and talk was beyond Rachel, but it just added to the outrageousness of it all.

"Anyway," she continued, "I couldn't get close enough to her to say hi, so I followed her in here to try and talk to her because I used to really look up to her back in the day when we was stripping together."

Gasps filled the room. It took everything in her power for Rachel not to look over at Jasmine and burst out laughing.

"Anyway, she was always one of the classy strippers down at Foxtails. And even when we used to, um, give private lessons, she was still one of them high-class h—"

"Yeah, okay," Reverend King said, snatching the mic away.

The woman snatched the mic right back. "I ain't done. You said you wanted to hear from people that had a testimony. Well, ain't nobody been tested like me!" She scanned the crowd until her eyes settled on Jasmine. "And if Pepper Pulaski, oh, my bad, I guess you don't go by that anymore. If Jasmine Cox can pull herself up and be all up in here with all you sidity folks, then maybe I can, too. Thank you, Jazzy, for showing me that I don't have to keep turning tricks and showing my body. I'm gettin' too old anyway. I need a new come-up, so I wanna be like you and do this church thang. You my she-ro, girl. Call me. I'm still at Foxtails, although I just mostly do private stuff and bartending now cuz I can't shake it like I used to." She did a little wiggle. "So drop by before you leave LA. We moved, though. We on Crenshaw now. Most of the girls are gone, but Buck is still there. He'd love to see you, so come by tonight. And bring the bishop," she said, blowing Hosea a kiss.

Every eye in the room turned to Jasmine, including a horrified Cecelia King. Rachel tried her best to look surprised as well, but this was so absolutely perfect that she couldn't contain her joy. Lester eyed Rachel suspiciously, but she'd already planned to lie, deny, and lie some more. This actually hadn't even been something Rachel had discovered. This was divine intervention. Some hoochie-looking lady had walked up to her in the lobby yesterday and handed her an envelope with all the info on Jasmine's stripper past. When Rachel had eyed her with skepticism, the woman had used Rachel's phone (she said she didn't want to be linked to anything) and called this Alize.

At first, Alize had been hesitant because she said it had been so long ago that she barely remembered Jasmine. But the three hundred bucks Rachel offered helped to refresh her memory. Suddenly, she recalled how "uppity Jasmine Cox was" and how she always "thought she was better than everybody else," and she said it would be her pleasure to "help put Jasmine on blast."

Rachel hadn't planned to use the information, as juicy as it was, but then Jasmine had pulled that stunt this morning and the game changed. So Rachel called Alize back, offered her another five hundred to come over to the hotel tonight, and Alize had been all too willing.

"Okay, so am I saved now?" Alize asked, turning her attention back to Reverend King.

"Umm, I'm sorry, little lady. It, um, it isn't that easy," he stammered.

"Awww, hell. Guess it's gonna have to wait until another time. I gotta private party with some rappers in an hour and until the Good Lord put some Benjamins in my pocket, I'm gon' have to keep doin' what I do. But y'all pray for me. I feel an anointin' coming on. Hallelujah!" she sang as she strutted down the center aisle and out the door.

Shame" and "sorry" were two words that were foreign to Jasmine; they'd never had any place in any part of her psyche. She'd never been ashamed—not of the millions of lies that she'd told, not of the humiliation she'd bestowed upon her first husband, not even of all the heartache she'd caused for the women whose husbands she'd bedded over the years.

No, there'd never been room for shame because she'd always had a reason. And her days as a stripper? Please! That was when she had the greatest reason of all. Without that pole, she would've never graduated from college.

So never any shame, never any reason to be sorry.

But now, as she held Hosea's hand and stepped down the aisle of the convention center, her head was high, though she moved humbly . . . with shame. Not that she was sorry for what she'd done; it was just that she'd been caught . . . and so publicly . . . and at the worst possible time.

She'd prayed last night that this revelation wouldn't cost Hosea this election. But already, she was sure that God hadn't been listening to her. The arena was packed. There were more people here this morning than at the worship service last night. All to see her, no doubt. All to hear what Hosea was going to say.

As she approached the front, Jasmine caught sight of Lester and Rachel holding court at the edge of the platform that had been set up as an altar.

That skank Rachel.

There was not a single doubt in Jasmine's mind—Rachel Adams was behind this. Jasmine's eyes stayed on the woman, glaring, willing Rachel to turn and face her.

As if she felt Jasmine's glare, Rachel turned around.

At first, Rachel wore a smile, a grin really, her face shining with the delight of triumph. But as her eyes remained locked with Jasmine's, her smile faded slightly, became just a smirk, then vanished. Right there, Rachel seemed to shrink before Jasmine's eyes. Oh, yeah, Rachel still held her head up and stuck her chin out. But Jasmine could almost see the woman's heart beating through the cheap fake silk blouse that looked like it had been purchased at a swap meet several years ago.

Good! Jasmine thought, feeling just a bit of satisfaction at Rachel's fear. It was clear that the Adams girl had done her homework, but she hadn't delved deep enough. Because if she had, she would've known that Jasmine Cox Larson Bush was not the one to be messed with.

Rachel was going to pay; Jasmine had decided it was time to finally implement the big plan that Mae Frances had been talking to her about.

But first, she had to get through this session.

At the front, Lester shook Hosea's hands and the two men exchanged a greeting that Jasmine didn't hear. But she didn't say a word. Just kept her glare on Rachel, instilling more fear until the trick lowered her eyes.

At least Rachel wasn't totally dumb. At least she was smart enough to be afraid.

Jasmine took her seat, the same one she'd been sitting in last night when the stripper had called her out. She didn't have to turn around to see the stares; she could feel them. If she wasn't trying to get her husband elected, she would've stood up at the altar and told every single last one of them to go to hell.

But that was not how a proper first lady behaved.

She would just have to endure it. If this went down the way they had planned, in an hour she would be back in all of their good graces. The men had decided how to handle this situation.

It was not the way she would've handled it; but since she was the problem, she didn't have a big voice in what was to be the solution.

At least they had a plan, one that she prayed was going to work. One that they'd come up with last night after they left the arena . . .

Never had hundreds of black people been in one place, sitting together in such absolute silence. But that was what filled the convention center as Alize handed the microphone back to Reverend King and then sauntered up the aisle, swaying her hips as if she was naked on a stage right now. The hundreds had been stunned, never taking their eyes away from Alize, not until she sashayed right out of the door.

Jasmine had been the most shocked of all. Had Alize been a stripper with her twenty years ago? Really? And she was *still* at Foxtails? Really?

If that was true, that woman needed to be arrested—not because she was too young, but because she was way too old. There had to be a law against anyone who was closer to fifty than to forty taking off their clothes and scaring people like that.

She had wanted to run after that heffa, call her out, call her a liar, and demand that Alize restore her good name in front of these women and their husbands, whom she'd worked so hard to get on her side.

But as the silence broke and the arena filled with shocked chatter, Hosea had pulled her to follow Pastor Griffith as he led Hosea, Jasmine, and the rest of their entourage through the side door.

"There was no reason for us to leave," Hosea protested, though he quickly followed behind his father and Pastor Griffith. "That's not how I operate. I stand up and face the enemy."

"I appreciate that, but we need to regroup," Pastor Griffith said, taking a quick look at Jasmine. "This election is too important to make the next move without thinking it all the way through."

Back at the hotel, Pastor Griffith had given instructions to

Reverend Penn and the other assistants who'd followed them while he pushed Hosea, Jasmine, and Reverend Bush into the elevator.

"Mae Frances," Jasmine yelled.

"I have something I need to take care of, Jasmine Larson," the woman growled. "I'll be right up." Then she marched away as if she were going off to war.

The elevator doors shut before Jasmine could beg Mae Frances to stay with her. There had never been a time in her life when she needed her friend more. Didn't Mae Frances know that? Jasmine lowered her eyes, shook her head. She truly regretted never having told Hosea about her life as a stripper. It was horrible that he had to find out on this day, in this way.

What was she supposed to do now? What was she supposed to say? All kinds of lies flashed through her mind. But she didn't have enough time to figure it all out. When they stepped into their suite, she still had no idea what she was going to say, since lying wasn't an option. She couldn't lie—her father-in-law knew the truth.

The moment they closed the doors behind them, though, Pastor Griffith was on it. "Is what that stripper said true?"

Without a word, Hosea walked toward the massive windows and looked down as if he was studying the traffic below. Reverend Bush stayed just as silent as his son as he moseyed toward the bar, dropped two ice cubes into a glass, and then added ginger ale.

Jasmine watched both of them—the two men whom she loved the most—turn their backs, and keep their eyes away from her. And she trembled. Was she going to lose Hosea finally? Over this?

That was when she felt it for the first time in her life . . . shame. And sorrow. And then another emotion—rage. Because if she lost Hosea over what Rachel Adams had just done, Rachel was going to die.

It was clear that the men didn't plan to say a word, so Pastor Griffith turned to her. "Jasmine?" His eyes roamed over her in a way that she didn't appreciate, as if she were swinging from a stripper pole right now.

She squirmed beneath the heat of his glare. "I need to talk to my husband first."

Hosea turned slowly, and said, "Yes. It's true."

His voice was flat, without emotion, and the tears in her eyes were instant. Jasmine didn't know what to think.

Hosea continued, "She worked as a stripper while she was in college. To pay her tuition."

Jasmine blinked, fighting more tears.

"Her mother had just died," Hosea continued, "and her father didn't have any money to help her."

"You knew?" she asked. "All of that? You knew?"

He nodded.

"But you never said a word to me."

He shrugged and gave her a little smile. "What was there to say? Pops told me that you did what you had to do."

She turned to her father-in-law with eyes full of gratitude, and in return he gave her a smile of unconditional love.

Hosea said, "And that's why I wanted to stay downstairs." He faced Pastor Griffith. "Because I don't see how what my wife did twenty years ago affects this election."

Pastor Griffith shook his head. "You're naive if you believe that this won't make folks jump off the Bush train."

"He's right, son," Reverend Bush chimed in.

Pastor Griffith paced through the room. "We've got to come up with something," he said, as if he was the one who was running for president and about to lose it all. "Something!"

Three loud bangs on the door startled them all and Jasmine held her breath as Reverend Bush moved to answer it. There was no telling who was on the other side, no telling what Rachel Adams was going to do next.

Reverend Bush swung the door open and Alizé stumbled inside.

"Would you stop pushing me?" she growled as she looked over her shoulder at Mae Frances.

Mae Frances shoved the girl again. And she looked like she would have done a whole lot more if Reverend Bush hadn't grabbed her arm.

"Mae Frances!" Reverend Bush shouted. "What's going on?"

"I found this ho trolling the lobby looking for her next trick."

"Troll? Who you calling a troll, old lady?"

"I didn't call you a troll. I called you a ho."

"Oh," Alize said.

Mae Frances said, "Go on. Tell them what you told me."

"What?" Alize paused, glancing around the room. Making a 360-degree turn, she scoped the room, nodded her head as if she was impressed. Her smile was wide, until her eyes met Jasmine's. "Look," she began. "I just told them what I knew," she said, as if she owed Jasmine an explanation.

Mae Frances said, "Yeah, after they paid you for it."

"Who paid you?" Jasmine and Pastor Griffith asked at the same time.

"Cynthia," Alize said.

All kinds of thoughts and suspicions swirled through Jasmine's mind. "You mean Cecelia?" Jasmine asked, shocked that Rachel wasn't the one behind this. But why would Cecelia do this? Was she turning against her? It didn't make any sense.

"I said," Alize began, as if she had an attitude, "Cynthia. I speak English. Don't you?"

"So, wait," Pastor Griffith jumped in. "Someone named Cynthia paid you to do what?"

She shrugged a little. "Got a call from this lady who hooked me up with Cynthia, who offered me some cash to just get up there and tell my story. She said it was testimony night and they were looking for people to testify."

"Where did you meet Cynthia?" Reverend Bush asked.

"I didn't." Alize swung her waist-length platinum blond wig over her shoulders as if it were a weapon. "I got a call from this country-talkin' chick saying what she wanted me to do and how she would leave me some money at the desk if I did a good job."

Jasmine inhaled deeply. Country-talkin' chick. It *was* Rachel.

"Okay." Pastor Griffith began pacing again. "This is good! This is good!" he said, excitedly. "We can use this."

"To do what?" Hosea asked.

"We can get her"——he pointed to the stripper, in her leopard-print spandex pants——"to get back up there and tell everyone how someone paid her to make this whole thing up. It will look like someone is out to fix this election—probably someone on Adams's team." Pastor Griffith laughed. "This is perfect. You'll be a shoo-in for sure. All she has to do is get up there and tell everyone that she was lying."

"No," Hosea, Reverend Bush, and Alize chorused together.

"I ain't no liar," Alize said. "I told the truth, the whole truth, and nothin' but the truth." She grinned. "I watch *Law and Order*."

Hosea crossed the room and opened the door to the suite. "Alize, we're sorry that we troubled you. I'm sure there's someplace you have to be."

She looked around as if she'd hoped to stay a little bit longer. "That's all you want from me?"

"That's it." Hosea nodded.

She moved hesitantly, then looked back at Jasmine. "You know, maybe I could say a few things about lying . . . you know, if the price was right . . ."

Gently, Hosea placed his hand underneath Alize's elbow. Jasmine said a quick prayer, begging God to make sure Hosea didn't catch anything. "I think you've been paid enough." He escorted her to the door, then as politely as he could closed it, even though she was still standing there, facing them.

Hosea turned back to the others. His eyes wandered from Jasmine to his father, Pastor Griffith, and Mae Frances, before he glanced back at his wife.

"I want to handle this with the truth."

Pastor Griffith shook his head. "Truth is not going to play well with this crowd."

"Really?" Hosea said. "With what some of those pastors have been through? Accusations of adultery, homosexuality, and a couple of years ago, didn't one of the pastors get arrested right here at the convention for burning down his mistress's house because she'd gone public with their affair?"

"Yup. And that's exactly why. Because let's be honest . . . a lot of these folks ain't nothing but saints with sinners' hearts. They need this gossip to keep the spotlight away from them."

"Well, if this is gonna cost me the election, then so be it. But I'm not going to lie and no one is going to lie for me."

Jasmine glanced at Mae Frances, and she knew that her friend was thinking the same thing that she was—sometimes the only way to win was to lie.

But this was Hosea Bush. No one in the world would be able to convince him of that.

Hosea put his arm around Jasmine's shoulders. "Pastor Griffith, I just need you to get me a little time to speak before the budget meeting tomorrow." And then he went on to share his thoughts with everyone in the suite . . .

Now here they sat, ready to give their budget presentations. This meeting was just a formality for the general population. The voting board had already seen how much the North and the South had raised and the North, behind Pastor Griffith, had broken the fund-raising record, raising four times as much money as the South. So, the budgets were not the news. But what Hosea was about to say was.

As the meeting was called to order and the announcements were made, Jasmine sat stiffly, her eyes not wandering a bit from the pastor who stood at the podium. All she wanted to do was to get this over with.

At least, this meeting was the first order of the day. After what went down last night, Jasmine was actually grateful that they'd convened this morning; she wouldn't have to go through the entire day without knowing which way this was going to play out.

From the corner of her eye, she saw Cecelia King, followed by her husband, ease into seats next to Rachel and Lester. Jasmine steamed, but only on the inside. On the outside, she kept her cool.

Just a few more minutes.

Jasmine was surprised when Reverend Penn leapt from his seat and galloped to the stage to introduce Hosea. The reverend wouldn't have been her first choice to present her husband, but since they'd all arrived, the good reverend and his porn-star wife had been nothing but totally supportive of Hosea. Now that she thought about it, Reverend Penn was actually the perfect choice for this task—everyone knew that he had wanted to be the North's nominee, and if he could stand up for Hosea at this time, then the entire Coalition could.

It felt as if everyone in the arena was holding their breath. But that didn't seem to faze Hosea. He was as calm and collected as always. It was his nature to leave everything up to God. For a moment, Jasmine wanted to have some of his understanding, some of his peace. What would her life be like if she trusted God the way Hosea did? Maybe she would try it . . . really try it this time. She would . . . right after this election.

"I present to you," Reverend Penn said, "Pastor Hosea Bush."

With a squeeze of her hand, Hosea stood, then trotted up the three steps that led to the podium.

He gave Reverend Penn one of those brotherman hugs, before he started. "Giving glory and honor to God who is the head of my life," Hosea began, "I just want to thank Him and you for being here today. It is an honor and a privilege to stand before you as one of your candidates for president." He paused for a moment, placed his Bible on the podium, and bowed his head before he said, "I know that the purpose of today is to discuss money . . . the amounts that have been raised and the plans as we see them." He stopped. "But what I'd like to do is take just a moment. Would you mind turning with me in your Bibles to the Book of Hosea?"

Low mumbles rippled through the congregation. Clearly, this was not what they expected. No one was interested in opening Bibles and reading scriptures. They were waiting for the drama. Either the man onstage needed to let go of some tears as he begged for forgiveness for his wife, or he needed to be defiant in his denial and protection of his wife. Either way would lead to some good gossip.

But Hosea was never about the drama, and as Jasmine flipped through her Bible she knew that these people were about to see what a true man of God was all about.

Hosea said, "Before we read, I want to tell you a little about this book. The facts, you already know: God told this prophet, Hosea, to find a wife. He told Hosea, ahead of time, that his wife wouldn't always be faithful to him."

What? Jasmine screamed so loud in her head that she wondered if anyone else had heard her. Maybe she should have asked Hosea exactly what he'd planned to say this morning. Because she would have told him to leave out this part.

"And even before they married," Hosea continued, "the prophet Hosea knew that his wife would have children—some who would not be fathered by him."

Dang! Did he really have to go there? Did he really have to tell it like that?

"But here's the thing"—Hosea's voice came through her thoughts—"the Book of Hosea is a story of love, not a perfect love, but it's a story that's real and tragic and true. It's about love—God's love for His people."

"Amen!"

"Preach!"

"Now, because of time, I'm not going to actually read scripture to you," Hosea said, "but I asked you to open your Bibles so that you would make a note to go back and read the entire book yourselves, especially the last chapter. And once you read, I know that God will talk to your heart and you'll have a different opinion today about what you heard here last night."

Hosea closed his Bible and came down one step to get closer to the congregation.

"See, here's what I know. God made me, He loved me before I was even born, and He put on my parents' heart that I should be named after that prophet who was just a man, but a man who heard God's voice. The Lord knew that I would be such a man—a man who would have a wife who wasn't perfect, but because of Jasmine's imperfections, many would watch our walk together. And learn from it. And, many would come to Christ because of it."

The applause that started shocked Jasmine at first, and then she put her hands together like everyone else, though across the aisle, only Lester clapped.

Hosea said, "My wife and I don't owe you any explanations about what she did twenty years ago. We don't have to tell you that she did whatever she had to do because she was a young girl who desperately needed money for college."

"All right, now!"

"We don't have to tell you that this happened months after she lost her mother and years before she really found God. We don't have to tell you that to the young girl my wife used to be, working in a gentleman's club was the only way. We don't have to tell you any of that because truly, it's not really your business." He paused. "So here is the part that is your business. If you elect me, you will get a man who loves God and who has God's favor. You will get a man who listens to the Lord and who, despite the imperfections of his wife and others in his family and especially himself, can stand up proudly at all times because it's not about tricks." He paused and looked toward Lester Adams.

"Tell it!" several shouted.

This was the only part of Hosea's speech that Pastor Griffith had insisted upon. It wasn't in Hosea's character to go after someone like this, but even last night Jasmine could tell that Hosea was upset by the stripper's sudden appearance; that's why he'd agreed with Pastor Griffith.

He said, "You will never find me in the middle of any kind of scandal, paying people to interrupt a celebration that should be all about the Lord."

It took every shred of self-discipline that Jasmine had not to lean forward. She wanted to see the look, not only on Rachel's face, but on Lester's as well. Hosea's words accused them both.

"But whatever happened last night is in the past. The American Baptist Coalition is all about the future."

This time, Hosea received a standing ovation.

But he stopped them. "Please sit down, because I'm not looking for any kind of applause. All I wanted to do was to bring you what you deserved—and that was the truth. You didn't get the truth last night. You heard lies and innuendos by someone who'd been paid off by one of us . . ."

Shocked gasps filled the air.

"If we are truly going to move this Coalition forward, we are going to have to do it with honesty and decency and in the ways of the Lord."

He couldn't stop the ovation this time, and when they finished, Hosea said, "But you know what? I'm not the only one who believes this. I know our brother Lester Adams stands with me."

Hosea tipped the microphone away from his mouth, and motioned toward Lester. "Do you have anything that you wish to share?"

Jasmine frowned and she could feel Pastor Griffith stir in the seat next to her.

"What is he doing?" Pastor Griffith mumbled.

This wasn't part of the plan. The idea was that Hosea would get a few extra minutes more than Lester. They knew that Hosea could preach and move people and make up whatever points had been lost last night. But if Lester spoke, Hosea could lose the edge that he had clearly gained this morning.

Quiet seconds passed, then Lester stood up. He walked up to the podium, took the microphone from Hosea, hugged him, then stood shoulder-to-shoulder next to his opponent.

"Saints, I just have to say that I am honored to be standing in the presence of a man such as Pastor Hosea Bush."

He waited for the applause to subside before he continued.

"You are so right; we all live in glass houses. And before we cast a stone, we need to clean our windows because there is not a one of us who could stand up here blameless. Not one of us who doesn't have something that could shame us if someone resorted to the deceitful action that we all witnessed last night." He paused and looked at Rachel. "Even my wife and I have things that have happened. An affair that I'm not proud of."

Jasmine heard Rachel's groan all the way across the aisle.

Lester kept on, "But while I'm not proud of it, I don't have to walk in shame because I've been forgiven by the Almighty!"

"Yes!"

"Preach!"

"I've been washed in the blood and God did what He always does—He turned something bad around for the good!"

"Say it!"

"Just like God did this morning," Lester preached. "Today, because of my affair . . ."

Rachel groaned again.

"My marriage is stronger," Lester continued. "And just like Brother Bush and his wife, Rachel and I are better for the trials we've been through. Amen!"

"Amen!" the arena roared.

Lester said, "And the Bible says that if we confess our sins one to another, and that if we pray for one another, then we shall be healed."

"Amen!"

"Hallelujah!"

"So, I ask all of you right now, to bow your heads and pray for me and Brother Bush. Whichever way this election turns out at the end of this week, one thing's for certain. Pastor Bush and I are brothers, men who love God with all of our hearts. And in the end, when we stand before Him, isn't that all that will matter? It's all about God and the American Baptist Coalition!"

Lester Adams had pulled the crowd to their feet and Jasmine was sure that very few remembered how this morning had started.

"Let's bow our heads," Lester said, "as Pastor Bush and I pray for all of us."

Jasmine bowed her head, but didn't close her eyes. Instead,

she glanced over at Rachel. Her nemesis's head was bowed, but with her arms folded across her chest, her shoulders hunched, and her lips poked out, it was clear that Rachel was seething. She'd probably believed that last night was her knockout punch. And she probably never would've believed that her husband would've provided the help that the Bushes needed.

Jasmine's eyes were still on Rachel when suddenly Rachel looked across the aisle at her. The two held their stares, locked as if they were in the middle of a battle.

It was Jasmine who smiled; it was Rachel who looked away.

Oh, yeah, Jasmine thought. Of course, there would still be people whispering and wondering and wishing for more trouble. But they were going to have to get it from someplace else. Clearly, Hosea had handled this.

And now that her husband had done his part, it was time for Jasmine to do hers.

She was going to handle Rachel Adams. Once and for all. That witch was about to pay . . . and Jasmine couldn't wait.

Really, Lester? I mean, you had to confess to an affair in front of all those people? Really?" Rachel paced back and forth across the conference room, trying desperately to compose herself. They'd taken a ten-minute break so that the North and South could get their PowerPoint budget presentations together. Lester really should've gone over to meet with his team to get the presentation together, but Rachel guessed he knew what was best for him because he'd followed her into the conference room.

"It's humiliating enough that all of Houston knows about your affair," she continued. "Now the whole freakin' world knows my husband was unfaithful."

Lester sighed heavily. "Rachel, trust me, we are not the only ones that have endured infidelity. If anything, I think it makes us more palpable to people. It shows them that we're flawed humans and we're not without sin."

Every word out of Lester's mouth was making her madder. She was supposed to be celebrating the Bushes' slinking away in shame. Instead, they were back to square one, with everyone acting like the bourgie couple walked on water.

She raised a finger and pointed it at him. "And if you had to confess like you were in front of a priest, why didn't you tell them I adopted the child of the woman that you slept with? Even though it turned out not even to be your kid. Your mistress is rotting in jail and I took her child. How many women would do that, Lester, huh? Why couldn't you run and tell that?"

"Rachel, I hadn't intended to say anything at all but the Spirit just moved over me to speak my heart."

"Whatever," Rachel said, waving him off. "Right now, the Spirit is telling me I need to go upside your head."

"Besides," Lester continued, his voice getting stern as he ignored her threat, "we had to divert attention because I'm sure the Bushes weren't the only ones who thought we were behind that stripper showing up."

Rachel shifted uneasily as she tried to remain expressionless.

"I mean, that's absurd, isn't it, that anyone would think we would stoop to something so low?" Lester asked, narrowing his eyes.

Rachel nodded innocently. "It most definitely is."

Lester stared at her apprehensively before saying, "Rachel, tell me the truth. You don't know anything about someone hiring that woman to come and make up lies?"

Rachel huffed as she threw up her hands. "Why does everyone assume she's lying? Did you hear the Bushes deny it? No, so that means it's probably true that Jasmine used to make her cheeks clap on the pole, probably while they were sliding a dollar bill down the crack of her a—"

"Don't be disgusting, Rachel," Lester said, cutting her off. "And you still didn't answer the question."

Rachel released another exasperated breath, walked over to her husband, looked him in the eye, and calmly said, "I didn't have anything to do with that drama at praise and worship yesterday. I don't know anything about some stripper being paid off." Yes, she felt bad about lying to her husband, but she was the type of player who came to win, by any means necessary. So, God would understand her little white lie.

"Okay," Lester said, like he desperately wanted to believe her.

"You know, I'm getting sick of you always thinking the worst of me." She stuck her lips out as she folded her arms across her chest.

Lester sighed, then pulled her close to him. "I'm sorry, sweetheart. I just know how bad you want to win this, and well, I know you know a trick or two."

"You said you wanted to win fair and square, so, fine." She wiggled out of his grasp. "But if you ask me, you act like you don't want to win this at all."

"Of course I want to win, but I think God has already ordained who He wants to have that spot."

Rachel wanted to strangle him. "Faith without works, Lester. Faith without works!"

"I am very well aware of the verse," he replied. "But I'm tired of this discussion. Let's just let this unfold how it's supposed to unfold. Now, come on, we have to get back inside. You know tongues are already wagging."

Rachel didn't protest as she followed her husband back into the room. She hated the way she was now the one being watched. People were staring at her like they were trying to figure out if she was capable of hiring a stripper to come in and lie on the Bushes. Everything in her gut told her that Alize wasn't lying, and Rachel couldn't understand why everyone wanted to give Jasmine the benefit of the doubt.

Rachel tried her best to ignore their glares. She plastered on a smile and walked over to the table where their team was putting the finishing touches on the presentation.

Rachel saw the Bushes making their way back to the front. Jasmine's smug and confident attitude got under Rachel's skin. Earlier, the Kings had sat with them. Now they were back with the Bushes. This whole politicking thing was working Rachel's last nerve. She was tired of kissing Cecelia's behind, going back and forth with that trick Jasmine, and she was tired of fighting this battle on her own because her husband, Dudley Do-Right, wanted to win "fair and square."

But Rachel had never been a quitter and she wasn't about to start now.

"All right, everyone," the conference chairwoman said, taking the podium. "If we can get everyone to go ahead and take their seats, we'll pick up with our budget presentations, before dismissing you so you can go grab lunch."

Lester and Rachel made their way back up to the front as

Cecelia and her husband laughed with the Bushes like they were old friends. Rachel wasn't the only one watching. Several people in the audience were taking note of the comfortable relationship as well, and Rachel didn't want the members of the ABC to feel like Hosea Bush was a natural choice to succeed Reverend King just because they were so buddy-buddy.

She wished Lester were more aggressive. At the start of the meeting this morning, he should've been the one to stand up and profess his love of God first. And if he had to confess their affair, he should've done it before Hosea talked about his and Jasmine's personal issues. The way it had gone down made Lester seem like he was following the leader.

The chairwoman called the meeting back to order and Rachel's mind churned constantly as the North made its budget presentation. It was ridiculous, the amount of money they'd raised. She had to give them props on their fund-raising. Well, at least mentally. She wasn't about to say anything out loud. Suddenly, it dawned on her what she *hadn't* heard during the North's budget presentation. But it was too late to tell Lester. He was already making his way to the podium because it was their turn to speak.

"Wow, I almost hate to follow that presentation, that's such phenomenal fund-raising," Lester said jokingly as chuckles reverberated throughout the room. Rachel tried her best not to roll her eyes.

Lester continued, "Even so, I am proud to present the budget from the Southern division of the American Baptist Coalition." Lester went through the fifteen-minute presentation, listing the money they'd raised and how. Even though the presentation was more detailed, packaged much better, and presented in layman's language, the bottom line remained: they'd raised just a portion of what the North had raised.

But the bigger problem was that Lester wasn't even bothering to address the elephant in the room that Rachel saw clearly. *Oh, good grief,* Rachel thought as she discreetly grabbed her purse, pulled out her checkbook, and scribbled out a check. Then she stood and walked over to the podium.

Lester eyed her with confusion. He probably was worried that she was about to say something out of order.

"Honey, may I say a word?" she asked sweetly. The way Lester gripped the mic, Rachel could tell that was the last thing he wanted, but he slowly stepped aside.

"Good morning, everyone. My husband is a little modest, so I just wanted to add that we hope this is just the beginning of the funds we raise for the American Baptist Coalition." She turned toward Jasmine and Hosea, who were seated in the front row on the other side of the podium. "Rev. Bush, I think it's wonderful that you and Jasmine have decided to donate so generously." Rachel placed a hand over her heart and smiled appreciatively. "And if we could, everyone, please give Rev. and Mrs. Bush another round of applause." She led the clapping. "God has truly blessed them with an abundance of wealth. So much so that not only were they able to raise so much money, but in the women's luncheon yesterday, Jasmine pledged one million dollars of their personal money to the American Baptist Coalition." She paused as gasps filled the room—mostly from men who hadn't heard the news.

"Rev. Bush, I think it's phenomenal that you all are willing to share your blessings," Rachel continued as the applause died down. "Now, as you know, Zion Hill isn't as prosperous as City of Lights Church." She smiled at Hosea, who sat with his eyes wide, obviously stunned. Bingo! He didn't have a clue that his wife had pledged a million dollars. Jasmine was visibly upset, but she kept her fake smile plastered on.

"We can only hope that God will continue to bless our small church, well . . . if you call three thousand small," she added with a smile as she glanced back out at the congregation. "We hope we can one day give so generously. I'm sure many of you can relate to our situation, since most of you have medium-size and small churches. So, I hope you understand why we can't raise as much money, and personally, you'll understand that there is no way in the world we can match the Bushes' one-million-dollar donation. I know we all get so busy when we get back to our respective cities—that's why I think we should leave our checks now." She paused for dramatic effect. "Therefore, Lester and I would like to present a check for ten thousand dollars from our personal funds." She hadn't discussed making a personal donation with Lester, but it wasn't like the ten grand would leave them homeless. Lester had a nice little trust fund from his parents and grandmother and he'd invested it wisely, so the donation wouldn't break them. They were nowhere near millionaire status, but they could comfortably invest ten thousand in his race to be president. At least that's what she would convince Lester of later.

Rachel leaned down and handed the check to Reverend King, then turned her attention back to Jasmine. "Rev. and Mrs. Bush, I'm sure you'd like to present your million-dollar check as well?"

"Ah-umm," Hosea stumbled.

Rachel narrowed her eyes. "I'm sorry, Rev. Bush, is something wrong? I mean, surely your wife wouldn't say you guys were giving a million dollars if you weren't?"

Jasmine suddenly stood. "Of course, we plan to give it. I wouldn't have pledged it otherwise."

"Well, great! The treasurer can come get both of our checks." All eyes turned to Jasmine, who was still standing next to her husband, looking like she wanted to disappear.

Rachel wanted to break out in a cheer. Maybe things were turning around after all. Sure, the Bushes could probably come up with a million dollars, but from the astonished look that still blanketed Hosea's face, it was definitely not something on their to-do list. Oh well, Rachel thought. Since Jasmine and her "megachurch mentality" wanted to fight dirty, then they were definitely going to have to pay to play.

The treasurer stood, a gigantic smile across his face as he made his way to the front. "Wow, this is unprecedented," he mumbled to the sound of "Amen" and "God is good." He took the check from Reverend King, then walked over and stood anxiously in front of the Bushes. Every eye in the room was on them. Hosea almost looked like he wanted to stand up and say something, but before he could, Jasmine snatched her purse off the pew, pulled out the checkbook, and wrote a check.

Rachel was the first to clap as Jasmine handed the treasurer a check. She gave Jasmine a thumbs-up, and had to fight back a laugh at the look of pure anger on the woman's face.

Chapter
FIFTEEN

The arena was still humming with the news.

Eyes were wide as pastors and their wives rushed to greet and congratulate Hosea and Jasmine, the golden couple who'd just contributed one million dollars to the Coalition out of their own account.

Who did that sort of thing? so many of them asked one another. For sure, it was a done deal now. Hosea Bush would certainly become the president of the American Baptist Coalition.

"That was just amazing." Cecelia King beamed as she hugged Jasmine. "I know that's what you pledged, but to write out a check, from your own account . . . and to do it today . . . in front of everyone." She shook her head. "And ye shall serve the Lord your God and He shall bless your bread." Cecelia paused. "Well, the Lord has most certainly blessed the Bushes."

Jasmine stepped back; the ache that was in her heart had made its way to her face and it was a pained, pasted-on smile that she wore. She nodded at the women who encircled her with their own words of amazement and congratulations. For a moment, her eyes focused on Rachel, standing on the edge of the circle, her arms crossed and a look of pure amusement shining on her face.

Jasmine was going to kill that monkey-midget.

But first, she had to survive her own murder—the one that was sure to come at the hands of her husband.

Her eyes found Hosea, in the center of his own congratulatory circle. His face was stiff and hard, almost frozen with shock at what had just happened. Then he turned toward her and sent her a laser-sharp glare.

"Excuse me," she heard him say as he pushed his way through the crowd of men.

Jasmine wanted to cut and run. But the only way she'd be able to outpace Hosea was if she ditched her brand-new Louboutins. And since that was never going to happen, she just stood firm and poised in those five-hundred-dollar red-bottom stilettos.

Hosea grabbed her wrist and almost dragged her from the center of all of the attention. As the two scampered up the aisle, the crowd broke into spontaneous applause, which made Hosea's steps quicken. He held her as if she were his child, and they pushed their way toward the elevator.

Hosea jabbed the button with his fist and Jasmine flinched. When the elevator doors parted, it took a moment for Jasmine to step inside—did she really want to get in there with her husband alone?

But then a glance over her shoulder told her that she was safe. Her father-in-law and Pastor Griffith were right behind them. They all stepped inside and there was silence among the four until the doors closed.

Pastor Griffith spoke first. "I don't like surprises," he said. "I need to know everything so that we can time every move. I had no idea you two were making this kind of contribution."

"We're not," Hosea said before Jasmine could speak.

The pastor's eyes narrowed in confusion.

Hosea said, "Can we talk about this later? I need to talk to . . . my wife first."

Pastor Griffith glanced at Jasmine. For the second day in a row, his eyes asked if she was trying to sabotage her husband on purpose?

Pastor Griffith said, "Call me as soon as you can."

When the doors parted on the ninth floor, Reverend Bush asked, "Do you need me, son?"

Hosea shook his head and Jasmine wished her father-in-law had asked her. But he hadn't even looked her way before he stepped out and the elevator doors closed.

Where is Mae Frances when I need her the most? Jasmine asked herself, though she knew her friend was in the hotel's spa—taking advantage of a half-day massage and more that Jasmine had given to her as a surprise that morning. Now she wished that she could take that back and have Mae Frances standing at her side as her protector.

But then she realized that she'd known her husband long enough, loved him deeply enough, to know exactly what he was going to say. His first words were going to be "What were you thinking?" and she would tell him everything. That this wasn't her fault. That all blame could be laid with that wench Rachel.

Jasmine stepped into their suite first, tossed her bag onto the sofa, then turned with a smile that was supposed to disarm Hosea. "Babe—"

But he spoke before she could say anything more. "You've been a liar ever since I've known you, but now you're a cheat?"

What? His words were like a stun gun, paralyzing her. "What are you talking about, Hosea? I haven't cheated anyone out of anything."

"How much money do you have in your account, Jasmine?" He cocked his head a bit. "You know, the account from which you just wrote a check for one million dollars?"

Okay . . . she saw where this was going. "I know, I don't have a million dollars in my account, but—"

"But what?" His voice was low, but the volume didn't hide his anger. "You just wrote a check, and by tomorrow morning the Coalition will know the check is not worth anything. You *knowingly* wrote a bad check."

"Okay, let me explain."

"Please do, and make it quick because I need to get down to the treasurer and let him know that he shouldn't cash that check. I need to let everyone know."

"No! Don't do that."

"Jasmine, you don't have a million dollars! I don't have a million dollars! *We* don't have a million dollars, yet you pledged that to the Coalition. A personal pledge."

"I told you that I was going to speak to the first ladies about Jacqueline's Hope."

He frowned. "You said you were going to start a foundation, that if I was elected, that would be your platform. Nowhere in the conversation did you mention it would cost us a million dollars."

"And it didn't. And it's not."

Hosea sat down on the couch. Folded his arms like arrows on his chest. "Explain this to me."

She sidled up to the couch, but decided to keep standing instead of easing down next to him. "It all happened so fast. I was telling the ladies about Jacqueline's Hope and everyone was so excited and we started talking about funding or something . . . and I'm sure I said something about a million dollars, but not out of our money. I was going to raise it."

"Oh, really."

"Yes. You know how good I am at fund-raising. I must've said something about a million dollars being my goal."

"So, when Rachel Adams stood up, she had it wrong."

"Yes."

He waited for Jasmine to say something more, but when she didn't, he asked, "Well, why didn't you correct her?"

"Because . . . because everybody was looking at us. And I didn't want to make you look bad, because that's all Rachel was trying to do."

He shook his head. "So, you don't think we're going to look bad now, when we tell them that check is going to bounce."

Now Jasmine eased down onto the couch. "First of all, I don't think we have to say a thing." When Hosea's eyes widened, Jasmine said, "Let's figure this out. They won't be able to cash the check until sometime next week, and by then, I was thinking that we might be able to cover the check."

"Oh, this I've gotta hear."

She ignored his sarcasm and continued, "We have a million dollars, Hosea. Between our retirement accounts and the kids' college funds . . ."

He chuckled, though there was no humor in the sound. "You're telling me that you want to spend your children's college money to cover up your lie."

"First of all, Hosea, I didn't lie, because I had a plan. We won't be spending their money. We'd just be using it—for now. And then we'll have a fund-raiser and put the money from that back into our accounts."

Hosea lowered his eyes, shook his head.

Jasmine released a long breath. Clearly, he wasn't understanding what she was saying. "We'll transfer the money on Monday, when we get back to New York, and in a month or two, we'll replace it. All one million dollars. In fact, it will probably be more, because the last time I did that fund-raiser for the hospital annex, we raised one-point-seven million. That would be a seven-hundred-thousand-dollar profit for us. We're going to come out ahead of this, Hosea."

She'd provided him with a solution, but Hosea glared at her as if there was still a problem.

Hosea pushed himself off the sofa, then ambled toward the door.

Jasmine jumped up behind him. "Where are you going?"

He stopped and faced her. "I'm going to tell the treasurer to destroy that check. Then I'm going to stand up in praise and worship tonight and tell everyone that there's been a mistake."

"You can't do that, Hosea," she said, on the verge of whining. "It could cost you the election."

He shook his head. "I don't know if I even want this anymore."

She frowned, confused. "You're so close . . . why would you want to walk away now?"

"Because this election really *has* turned you into a cheat."

"Why do you keep saying that?"

"Because now you're talking about doing a fund-raiser and

then putting the money into our bank accounts. *That's illegal,* Jasmine!"

"I'm only talking about replacing the money that we're putting out."

"I don't care what you're talking about . . . it's illegal. And you're so caught up in this election that you're not even thinking. You have a degree in finance, for God's sake. You ran your godbrother's nightclub for years. I know you know a little something about this."

"I didn't think it was illegal," she said, her voice softer now.

"Well, it is. So, before my wife is thrown into jail, I'm just going to end this."

"Hosea, don't," she said.

But he stepped out into the hallway and closed the door behind him.

"Hosea!" she called again. Her heart thumped. This was bad—really bad. Because even if Hosea didn't quit the race, it would be over when he stood in front of the congregation tonight and told everyone that they didn't have a million dollars.

She couldn't let this happen.

She grabbed her cell and punched in Mae Frances's number, but the call went straight to voice mail—just as she expected. Of course, Mae Frances was still at the spa. Mae Frances had always been her savior, the one who could solve anything and everything.

Who could help her now?

In a second, she had the answer to her question. Shoving her purse onto her shoulder, she dashed through the door and turned to the stairwell rather than to the elevator. She didn't have waiting-for-the-elevator kind of time.

On the ninth floor, she scanned the numbers on the doors until she found 9302. She knocked—three raps, hard—as if she were the FBI, and Pastor Griffith answered accordingly.

"Where's the fire?" he asked when he swung open the door.

"It's Hosea," she said, stomping into the room. "You have to stop him." Then she noticed the pastor, still in his suit pants, but his jacket was gone and his shirt was gone and all he wore was his wifebeater. She sighed and took her eyes away from his chest and focused instead on his face, especially his lips.

That wasn't any better. She had to find a way to concentrate on the task in front of her, so she focused on his nose. "Hosea said he's going to quit. He's going to tell the treasurer not to cash that check."

"I take it he didn't know anything about the million dollars," Pastor Griffith said calmly.

"No, I pledged that. But I was going to raise the money, not take it out of our account. Rachel Adams set me up," Jasmine said, her words coming quickly, knowing she was talking against time. "And now Hosea is down there," she said, pointing toward the door, "giving up everything that we've worked for."

Pastor Griffith raised an eyebrow. "We?"

"Yes, we. Pastor Griffith, I know you've done a lot of work on this campaign, but I haven't been just sitting back."

"And that"—he pointed toward her—"may be our problem."

He motioned to Jasmine to have a seat, but she stayed standing, her arms crossed. The pastor reached for his cell phone, then paced back and forth as he barked orders to whoever was on the other end.

Less than ten minutes passed before Pastor Griffith said, "Okay, great. Tell Pastor Bush to meet me in his suite in five minutes."

He clicked off his cell, then said, "It's taken care of. The check is good. Hosea is still in the race; he's being informed right now how this is gonna go down." The pastor sat down in the chair adjacent to his bed and crossed his legs as if everything was going to be all right. "He'll be fine with it."

Jasmine exhaled a long breath. "Thank you."

He nodded. "But now I need to ask you for something." He stood and walked toward Jasmine.

Everything inside of her made her want to back away, but she stayed where she was, showing him that she wasn't intimidated, she was not afraid. Didn't he know that she was Jasmine Cox Larson Bush?

Sure, he was fine, but she'd taken down men even finer than him. Still, her heart pounded as he came closer; he only stopped when there was nothing more than an inch of air between them.

"Now that I've helped you out"—he licked lips that seemed plumper when he was this close to her—"are you willing to do something for me?"

From the moment she'd first seen the gorgeous pastor, Jasmine knew that he'd been attracted to her.

She stood strong, though, and told him the truth. "I love my husband."

He frowned. "What does that have to do with anything?"

"I love Hosea," she repeated, "and I'm not going to ever do anything to jeopardize our marriage."

He chuckled. "Well then, you'll have no problem doing what I was going to ask you." He paused and stepped back, giving her room to breathe. "Can you please stay out of this, Jasmine?" he asked. "Please let me do what I know how to do, and that's get your husband elected."

It took her a moment to digest his words. This wasn't the come-on she'd expected.

He said, "Isn't that what we both want?"

She nodded.

"Well, if you want it as much as I do, you'll stay out of this from now on."

All she could do was nod, then scurry from the room.

Oh, my God! Jasmine thought once she was outside. Pastor Griffith must've thought she was a fool! How could she have been so wrong? She'd been sure that he was making a pass at her. It couldn't have been just her imagination.

Well, whatever Pastor Griffith was doing or not doing, it didn't matter. He'd made that million-dollar check good, and though she wondered what he'd done, she pushed it out of her mind. It wasn't like she needed to know. She just needed to concentrate on this election—and Rachel Adams.

It was funny. Rachel had probably thought she was destroying Hosea's chances today, but instead, she'd almost certainly just secured Hosea's election. Still, Jasmine wasn't about to let Rachel get away with this. She needed to pay for what she'd done. It was finally time to execute Mae Frances's big plan.

Yeah, Pastor Griffith had asked her to stay out of this . . . and she would . . . the day after tomorrow.

Jasmine moved down the hall as she pressed the keys on her BlackBerry.

"First Lady," she exclaimed the moment Cecelia answered. "I hope I'm not disturbing you."

"Not at all," Cecelia said. "I will always take calls from the first lady and the pastor who were willing to put so much of themselves into the Coalition even before the election. The bishop and I were just talking about you two."

"Well, thank you," Jasmine said, relieved because this conversation could have been going in a whole 'nother direction—if Pastor Griffith hadn't stepped in. "But actually, I was calling to ask if you would join me in doing something tomorrow."

"What do you have in mind?"

"Well, since it's Men's Day and a free day for us, I was thinking about leaving the hotel. I was born and raised in Los Angeles, you know."

"Yes, I read that about you."

"Well, none of us have had the chance to get out and I was thinking that it might be good for you and me . . . and Rachel Adams to go out . . . to the Beverly Center maybe. That's an amazing mall and they have great restaurants, too."

"That's a wonderful idea. And Lady Jasmine . . ." She paused. "I'm glad you want Rachel to go with us. I can tell there's a bit of a strain between the two of you."

"Yes, but I want to fix that," Jasmine said as she rolled her eyes. "Because whether her husband or mine is elected, this has to be all about the Coalition. So I want Rachel and me to get to know one another better because in the end, we'll probably be working together."

"This is true."

Jasmine inhaled—she'd come to the most important part of the call. "I would like your help, though. I'm not sure Rachel will accept an invitation from me and—"

"Consider it done," Cecelia said before Jasmine could even ask the question. "I'll talk to her this evening."

"Great. Thank you so much, Cecelia."

She hung up the phone, so pleased. Either way, she'd won. If Rachel refused to go, Jasmine would have Cecelia to herself. And if Rachel decided to go with them . . . well.

Jasmine sighed, suddenly feeling exhausted. This day had taken so much out of her. All she wanted to do now was to spend some time with her children. And then maybe even get in a nap.

Because it was going to be a long, late night—for her and Mae Frances.

Chapter SIXTEEN

"Y ou're a piece of work, you know that?"

Rachel smiled as she sashayed in front of her husband in their hotel suite. He'd followed her up after the meeting and she knew it was only to lecture her about what had just happened. But Rachel wasn't about to let her husband spoil her good mood. She softly patted his cheek. "And that would be why you love me, my dear."

"Did you really have to do all that grandstanding?" Lester asked, shaking his head. Although his tone was chastising, he smiled. "And what's really going on? Because I know you wouldn't have called all that attention to the Bushes' donation if you didn't have an ulterior motive."

"The only motive I had is letting everyone know that Jasmine Bush is a liar," Rachel replied matter-of-factly. Game recognized game and Jasmine could act all sanctified, but Rachel saw her for what she truly was. "I just wanted that fact to be exposed, which it will be the minute that check starts bouncing like it's in the NBA."

"The Bushes are rich. What makes you think their check will bounce?"

Rachel eased down onto the sofa and slipped out of her heels. "Yeah, they may be rich, but they're not *wealthy*. Wealthy people are the only ones who can just up and donate a million dollars of their own money."

"Rachel . . ."

"Lester, let's stop talking about that horrid woman. I'm

worn-out and I would love to relax before the kids come back from the children's day excursion."

"I just——" Rachel's cell phone rang, cutting Lester off. Her eyes lit up when she glanced at the caller ID. "Ooh, be quiet. This is the call I've been waiting on." She took a deep breath and answered. "Hello."

"Hey, Rachel, it's Jetola." Rachel held her breath as she waited for the news she'd been anticipating all day.

"Hey, Jetola. Thanks so much for getting back with me. Were you able to get in touch with your sister?"

"I was. And she was all too happy to do anything for you."

Rachel breathed a sigh of relief. She'd been working on this plan since she'd arrived, and it looked like it was going to finally come to fruition. "That is wonderful."

"How's ten o'clock in the morning?"

Rachel enthusiastically pumped her fist. "Ten in the morning is fine. I'll make sure Cecelia is there. You just don't know how grateful I am. I owe you sincerely."

Jetola laughed. "Girl, please. We're the ones that owe you. But it all worked out. My sister really played it up so she was able to get her boss to approve the story."

"Wonderful. And it'll air nationally?"

"Yes, there in LA and nationally. My sister also does freelance reports for TV One, and since the ABC is so huge, she said they'll probably be interested in the story as well."

Rachel wanted to jump from her seat and do a jig around the room. First, Regina West, now this? Oh, she was about to be in like Flynn.

"Well, her name is Melinda," Jetola continued, "and she'll meet you in the hotel lobby at ten. Take down her number in case there are any problems."

"Oh, there won't be," Rachel said, jotting down the number anyway. Rachel said her good-byes and let out a yelp as she hung up the phone. She ignored Lester, who had been standing there looking at her throughout the entire conversation.

"What was that about?" Lester finally asked.

Rachel tossed the cell phone on the coffee table, then stood with her arms outstretched like she was modeling a new outfit. "Yours truly has negotiated some media coverage."

"How'd you manage that?"

"That was Jetola Jones, from home, the mother of one of my Good Girlz. Her sister works at a TV station here in LA and they're going to come out and interview me and Cecelia."

Lester frowned. "You? Why would they interview you?"

"Because I'm the one hooking this thing up."

"But it seems like they'd want to talk to Rev. King, or even me or Rev. Bush, since one of us will be the next president."

"Oh, I knew you were busy, so we pitched the whole women's empowerment thing," Rachel said as she pushed by him and walked into their room. She had to go find something to wear. She'd go with a vibrant color so that she would really stand out on camera.

"How do you know Cecelia will even want to do the interview?" Lester asked, following her.

"Please. Cecelia King never met a camera she didn't like." Rachel paused. "I'd better call her, though, and make sure she can do that time. Don't you have a meeting to get to?" She ushered her husband out the door, covering his mouth as he started to protest.

After Rachel got rid of Lester, she picked up the hotel phone and called the front desk. "Yes, can you connect me to Cecelia King's room, please?"

She waited with giddy anticipation while the call was patched through.

"Mrs. King," Rachel said when Cecelia picked up.

"Rachel, I was just about to call you."

Rachel's heart skipped a beat. Cecelia actually sounded pleasantly surprised to hear from her. "You were?"

"Yes, but go ahead and first tell me why you're calling."

Normally, Rachel would've let Cecelia talk first, but she was so excited, she was about to burst. "Well, I was just seeing if you were free in the morning to do an interview with KNBC."

"KNBC? As in the TV station?"

Rachel was glad Cecelia couldn't see how hard she was grinning. "Yes, they want to talk with you about the convention." She left off the part that she would be interviewed, too. Right now, she wanted Cecelia to think it was all about her.

"How in the world did you manage that? Our publicity people have been trying to get them for weeks and can't even get a return call."

"I have a friend who works at the station, so I called in some favors. They're going to do a piece for the news and a separate piece that will air on TV One."

Cecelia gasped. "Rachel, that's fantastic! I'd love to do it. Do I need to get the reverend as well?"

"Actually, their focus for this story is on the women of the American Baptist Coalition."

"Spectacular!" Rachel could hear her beaming through the phone.

"Wonderful, they'll meet us in the hotel lobby around ten fifteen." Rachel wanted to allow fifteen minutes for her and Melinda to talk, so there would be no questions about the interview.

"That is so great, Rachel. I'm looking forward to it," Cecelia said.

"I am, too." Rachel was just about to hang up when she remembered that Cecelia was about to call her for something. "Oh, yeah, you mentioned that you were just about to call me?"

"Yes, since tomorrow is a free day, I was going to go over to the Beverly Center for lunch and a little light shopping, and I was wondering if you wanted to join me?"

Rachel paused, her heart skipping a beat. Cecelia wanted to go shopping with *her*? "Of course I'd love to go. We can head out right after the interview."

"That sounds like a plan." She paused, then added, "And, um, I feel I must tell you, Jasmine will be with us as well."

Rachel's bubble burst and silence filled the phone.

"I think it's important that you two spend some time together, because regardless of the outcome of the election, you two could forge a powerful coalition," she added hastily.

Hell would freeze over before Rachel ever worked with that scallawag, but she kept her thoughts to herself. Rachel wished she could take back her enthusiastic response, because spending an afternoon with Jasmine ranked right below getting a root canal. Then, suddenly, an idea hit her.

"You know, that's great. As a matter of fact, why don't you make sure that Jasmine is there for the interview as well, so we can just head out after that?"

"What a splendid idea, and thank you for extending the olive branch. You continue to amaze me."

Rachel rolled her eyes as she hung up the phone. She picked up her cell phone and the piece of paper with Melinda's number on it. She quickly typed a text message to her, then went to get her beauty rest so she'd be alert and ready for her television debut.

The next morning, Rachel was dressed in a fuchsia Tahari suit—the nicest suit she'd brought with her—and a pair of black Nine West pumps as she made her way down to the lobby. At ten on the dot, a tall, slender woman wearing a designer pantsuit walked in, followed by a portly, gray-haired, shabbily dressed man carrying camera equipment.

Rachel would've recognized her even without her photographer. She was the spitting image of her sister. "Melinda?"

"Rachel, it is such a pleasure to meet you," Melinda said, hugging her. "I've heard so many wonderful things about you. My niece raves about the Good Girlz program and I am eternally grateful to you, because I tell you, we were worried about that girl." She shook her head.

Rachel waved her off. "Your niece is a doll. She just needed someone to help her channel all of that anger into a positive direction."

"Well, you did just that. She's at college now, doing well, and we have you to thank for that."

"It was my pleasure. I miss the girls so much."

The photographer motioned to the people milling around in the lobby. "Hey, I'm gonna go ahead and start getting video."

Melinda nodded, then turned back to Rachel. "So, I got your text and that's no problem."

Rachel breathed a sigh of relief. She'd been nervous about sending it, but Melinda didn't seem fazed. "So you understand?"

Melinda smiled wickedly. "All too well. And I told you, my family owes you, so we're good."

Rachel glanced over Melinda's shoulder to see Cecelia coming off the elevator. "That's awesome. And here's Cecelia King." She smiled as Cecelia approached as if she were British royalty. She was dressed in a royal blue St. John suit and just the right amount of accessories to make her look sophisticated and smart. Jasmine was close on her heels. She, too, was camera ready in a black St. John suit.

"Hi. Melinda Jones, KNBC," Melinda said, extending her hand to Cecelia.

Cecelia graciously shook it. "Cecelia King. Thank you so much for coming by to do a story."

"Anything for Rachel," Melinda said, smiling at Rachel.

Jasmine stood behind Cecelia, waiting to be introduced. Rachel gave her a terse nod, but didn't bother with an introduction. "Well, I know Melinda is on a tight schedule, so let's get started."

Melinda summoned the photographer over and a small group of people stopped to watch as she began interviewing Cecelia. That woman was made for the camera, Rachel thought as Cecelia effortlessly recited facts about the ABC, goals of the organization, and how women were working to empower the community. The crowd grew as many admired the ease with which Cecelia handled the interview.

After about ten minutes, Melinda turned to Rachel, who had been standing to the side, watching in awe. "Rachel, why don't you join Cecelia? I'd like to ask you a few questions."

"Oh, I'm not an official," Rachel said innocently.

Melinda pulled her arm. "Yes, but you are a woman and we're

talking about women of the ABC. And you'll probably be the next first lady. So, we can talk about your visions for the future and what the organization means to you."

Jasmine's brow furrowed as Rachel stepped into the camera shot.

"So, Rachel, tell us how you feel to be taking part in this event," Melinda said.

Rachel flashed a winning smile, then said, "I am thrilled to be a part of the American Baptist Coalition. My husband, Reverend Lester Adams, is in the running to take over for the honorable Reverend King. Regardless of the outcome, he and I are committed to making sure the ABC is a viable force in the community. The Kings have done such awesome work with the food ministries, the women's shelter, and the literacy programs, and it is our goal to continue their good work."

Melinda asked several other questions, and with each answer, Cecelia smiled her approval, as did several of the onlookers. After a few minutes, Jasmine loudly cleared her throat.

"I have something I'd like to add," she said, raising her hand like she was in class.

"Oh, I think I have enough." Melinda turned and flashed a tight smile, then focused her attention back on Cecelia and Rachel. "So, ladies, your interviews were phenomenal," she continued.

Jasmine looked stunned, but quickly recovered.

"I think that it's only fair that I be interviewed also," she said sharply, but then immediately softened her tone. "I mean, I'm sure your station has some type of equal-time rule or something."

Melinda turned up her nose. "Yeah, we do. For politicians running for elected office. This is a story profiling the good one religious organization is doing. Do you have a problem with that?" Melinda loudly asked.

"Oh, no . . . I, I mean, I didn't mean it like that," Jasmine stammered.

Rachel couldn't even look at Jasmine, because she didn't want to burst out laughing at the look of humiliation she was sure was on Jasmine's face. Half the people in the lobby were staring at the exchange between Jasmine and Melinda, including Cecelia, who looked horrified that Jasmine was embarrassing her. Rachel decided to step in. "No, Melinda, it's okay. Interview her, too. What the ABC is doing is bigger than any one person, and besides, we wouldn't want anyone to feel slighted."

Melinda shrugged. "Fine," she said, motioning for the photographer to turn the camera toward Jasmine. Cecelia definitely didn't like having the camera taken off her for Jasmine.

Melinda didn't have the same enthusiasm as she put the mic in front of Jasmine. "Could you please state your name?"

Jasmine took a deep breath, tossed her hair, and said with a smile, "Jasmine Bush, first lady of—"

"Oh, dang!" Melinda said, cutting her off as she looked down at her BlackBerry. She turned to her photographer. "Scott, I just got a text from the station. They found a house full of starving dogs over on West Twenty-ninth. They want us to get over there ASAP. Shut it down."

"But it'll only take a moment for my interview," Jasmine said desperately.

Melinda held up her BlackBerry. "Sorry, when the boss says move, we move. Maybe next time," she said with a smile as she patted Jasmine's hand. The photographer was already breaking down his camera equipment.

"Mrs. King, it was a pleasure talking with you," Melinda said quickly. "The story will air tomorrow, and then on TV One Saturday morning."

Rachel wanted to turn a backflip. That was right before the vote. This couldn't have worked out better in her dreams.

Melinda turned to Rachel, hugged her quickly, and said, "Good luck on the election, and if Rev. Adams wins, you know I'll be right there to cover the celebration! Ta-ta," she said as she and her photographer raced toward the door.

Jasmine was seething. Soon, Cecelia and Rachel were surrounded by people showering them with praise and trying to get more details on the interview.

Jasmine stood off to the side, eyes blazing. "Are you okay?" Rachel asked Jasmine, loud enough for several people to hear. Jasmine didn't reply and Cecelia must've sensed the tension, because she stepped in.

"Well, ladies, the car service is here. Are you ready to head to the Beverly Center? After that fantastic interview, I'm looking forward to lunch and some great shopping."

"I definitely second that," Rachel said with a smile.

"Well, let's go!" Cecelia said, walking ahead of them.

Jasmine still hadn't moved. It was almost as if she was trying to process what just happened. Rachel strutted past Jasmine, then gently leaned into her ear and slowly whispered, "It's amazing what us country bumpkins can do."

She popped her shades on, released a hearty laugh, then followed Cecelia out to the car.

Chapter
SEVENTEEN

Jasmine sat in the front of the Town Car, seething that Cecelia had assigned her to sit next to the thin-lipped driver. Behind her, Rachel and Cecelia lounged in the back, chatting like a pair of girlfriends.

"I still cannot believe you got us that interview," Cecelia said, her voice saccharinely sweet. "Do you know how long we've been trying to get coverage like that?"

"It was nothing." Rachel waved her hand.

Jasmine's blood pressure inched higher.

"Oh, no, give yourself credit, Rachel. That was a big deal," Cecelia complimented her. "I know everyone in the Coalition will be so grateful for the positive press."

"That's all I wanted to do—just help out the Coalition."

Jasmine wanted to throw up—on both of them.

"Anytime I can bring attention to the Coalition," Rachel began, "I'll be happy to do it."

Oh, you're about to bring attention to the Coalition, all right, Jasmine screamed inside.

That was the only thing that kept Jasmine going—knowing that in a few hours, Rachel would be going down in the biggest way possible. Now Jasmine was sorry that she hadn't gone along with Mae Frances's plan before—then she wouldn't have had to put up with everything that Rachel had thrown her way over the past few days. But there was no reason for her to look back; it was finally going to happen.

"Do you know anyone else in the press?" Cecelia asked Rachel.

That's when Jasmine began to hum, under her breath, of course. Inside, she sang the Black Eyed Peas anthem: *I got a feelin' that tonight's gonna be a good, good night!*

As she hummed each verse and as each mile passed, Jasmine calmed. Good things were about to happen for sure. The humiliation that Rachel tried to bring onto her—first with the stripper, then with the million-dollar check, and finally this morning with the TV interview—was all going to drop right back on her.

By the time the car stopped in front of the Beverly Center, Jasmine was beginning to think that the interview had been a very good thing—and the fact that it was going to air the morning before the election . . . *wow!* It had been hard to see all the possibilities as she'd stood there in the lobby, stunned and embarrassed by another one of Rachel's tricks. But the thing was, the way this was about to play out . . . she couldn't have planned it better herself. She hadn't thought of media coverage, but if they aired that interview, they'd have to report on what was about to happen, too.

This was brilliant.

And Rachel had done this all to herself.

She shouldn't have messed with Jasmine.

Because Jasmine had Mae Frances.

And Mae Frances had connections.

"Well, here we are," Cecelia said, all giddy, as if she was still on a high from the interview. "Ladies, after working the convention all of these days, I am ready to do some serious shopping." She leaned over to give instructions to the driver and Jasmine eyed Rachel.

Rachel said, "You sure are quiet. What? You don't have anything you want to say?"

Jasmine curled her fingers into the palms of her hands. Just one punch, that's all she wanted. One chance to punch Rachel right in the nose! "Oh, I'll have plenty to say real soon."

Rachel's smirk was full of confidence. She leaned closer and whispered, "Why don't you just admit that you lost? After the way you acted during *our* interview, trying to take the attention away from Cecelia . . . she's not happy with you. And that means that my husband is all but in."

"We'll see about that," Jasmine said.

Rachel looked down at her nails as if she was examining her gold-frost-colored manicure. "It's such a shame. Jasmine Cox Larson Bush is going home . . ." She looked up, poked out her lips, and twisted her neck as she said, "A loser."

Just as Jasmine raised her hand to slap the little bit of sense this woman had out of her, Cecelia turned around. "Okay, I'm ready, ladies. Let's go."

Cecelia had saved this little girl, but actually, that was a good thing. There was no need to go violent . . . no need to mess this up when she was so close to Rachel's end.

Cecelia asked, "Should we start with lunch or shopping?"

Jasmine and Rachel spoke together.

"Lunch," Rachel said.

"Shopping," Jasmine said, just a bit louder. "It's a little early for lunch. Let's browse through a few shops, then break for lunch, and go back to shopping, since we have all day."

"That sounds like a plan," Cecelia said, though she turned her attention back to Rachel. "So, do you think Melinda would mind doing another interview once the new board is in place this weekend?"

Rachel glanced at Jasmine before she said, "Oh, I can definitely get her to do that."

Cecelia said, "Great, because I'd really like to stay in touch with Melinda. I have so many big things planned for the Coalition."

"You do?" Rachel asked with a frown. "Really? Like what?"

Cecelia waved her hand as if she had misspoken. "I didn't mean that I, specifically, had plans. I mean the Coalition in general."

"Oh!" Rachel said. "Well, I know that Lester is committed to not only helping the Coalition become more active in our communities, but helping the Coalition grow in membership as well."

Jasmine rolled her eyes. Rachel sounded like she was repeating Lester's nomination speech.

"That is exactly the kind of thing I'm talking about," Cecelia gushed. "I'm so pleased, Rachel. You and your husband understand what's important to our organization."

Jasmine had to break up this lovefest now or she was going to throw up for real. "This way," she said, leading Cecelia and Rachel toward the escalators. As the two strolled behind her, Jasmine pulled her cell from her purse and texted Mae Frances. Then she prayed that her friend would get this right.

This whole idea had belonged to Mae Frances, but this was going to be the hardest part for her—the cell phone. Mae Frances had had a cell for a few years now, but she never could seem to master any part of it. Jasmine had practiced with her last night, and this morning Mae Frances had assured her that all was well.

Still, Jasmine held her breath as they ascended the glass-enclosed escalators that gave a clear view of the expensive homes in the Hollywood Hills.

By the time the three women reached the top, the text came in: *he's ready. :-)*.

Jasmine had to hold back her laugh. Yesterday, Mae Frances didn't even know how to send a text. Today, she had the nerve to add a smiley face.

"Well," Jasmine said, "where shall we go first?"

It must've been the singsong tone in her voice that made Rachel frown. And if Jasmine could have, she would've broken out into a happy dance right then.

Little girl, you are never going to play with me again.

"Well, let's see," Cecelia said, glancing into Bloomingdale's.

"I know," Jasmine said, eyeing Cecelia's purse. "Let's go to Louis Vuitton."

"Great!"

Jasmine led the way, though this time there was little talk coming from Rachel. Inside the designer store, Jasmine and Cecelia perused the purses, oohing and aahing over the new designs.

"I saw this on the runway at Fashion Week," Cecelia said, pointing to one of the black bags.

"You're kidding," Jasmine said. "You were at the show? So was I."

"Really?"

"Yes, I go every year, but the highlight of the week, to me, was Kimora's show."

"Oh, I wanted to get into that one so bad," Cecelia said. "But you know, those shows are all about who you know."

"Well, let me know if you want to go next year. Hosea and I have known Kimora . . . and Russell for several years."

"Really?" Cecelia's eyes widened.

Cecelia seemed so excited that Jasmine half-expected her to break out a scripture. "Oh, yeah," Jasmine said nonchalantly. "I can get you into just about anywhere you want to go. You know all those celebrities are always calling, wanting to be on Hosea's show."

"That's right," Cecelia said, pausing for a moment. "Hosea's show. Just by him being the president . . . that would get the Coalition a lot of publicity."

"Definitely," Jasmine said. "But neither he . . . nor I want to push our connections on anyone. You know, we want this race to be all about merit." She paused and looked at Rachel. "It should be about who brings the most to the Coalition." She smirked. "Speaking of connections, Rachel, when are you going to connect Regina West with Cecelia?"

Cecelia put down the bag she'd been looking at. "I'd forgotten about that. I'd love to meet her."

Jasmine could almost see the color draining from Rachel's face.

"Well . . . um . . . Regina . . . she's busy right now. You know . . . actors are always working and . . ."

Inside, Jasmine laughed. Just as she thought—Rachel didn't know Regina West. As if Rachel hadn't spoken at all, Jasmine turned back to Cecelia and changed the subject. "About Fashion Week, let me know if there are any particular designers you want to see this fall."

"I will!" Cecelia beamed.

Jasmine glanced at Rachel, who was sulking as she leaned against the counter. "What about you? I know you're a fan of Kimora with all of the Baby Phat that you wear," she said, meaning for her words to be a jab. "Have you been to her show or any of the others?"

Jasmine was just waiting, waiting, waiting for Rachel to mention some little country fashion show that her church had put together as some kind of scholarship fund-raiser or building drive.

"Uh . . . Lester and I . . . haven't traveled . . . you know, to Europe for the shows . . . because . . . you know, we have the kids."

"Europe?" Jasmine said in a tone that made Rachel sound stupid. "I said Fashion Week; I wasn't talking about any of the individual European shows."

"Fashion Week is in New York, dear," Cecelia explained. "Every September."

Rachel gulped. "Well, I was talking about the bigger shows," she said with just a little too much attitude. "The ones in Europe."

Cecelia and Jasmine exchanged a glance, before Cecelia motioned to one of the saleswomen.

"I definitely want to take a look at this one." Cecelia pointed to the vintage-inspired iconic doctor bag. "I've been eyeing it for a while now."

"And I like this one." Jasmine had chosen a monogrammed tote. Again, she turned to Rachel. "Aren't you going to get anything?"

"I don't really like Louis," she said, as if she was on a first-name basis with the designer. She folded her arms and turned up her nose. "You know, it's not real leather."

The saleswoman frowned, Jasmine laughed, and Cecelia said, "Who told you that?"

"Well, uh . . . isn't it just like canvas?"

As Cecelia schooled Rachel on the Louis Vuitton line,

Jasmine handed her credit card to the clerk. Being in this store wasn't even part of the plan. This was just Jasmine's idea of a little payback, just a little reminder to this pickup-truck chick that she wasn't anywhere near her league.

As Jasmine paid for her fourteen-hundred-dollar purse and Cecelia passed her platinum American Express to cover the three-thousand-dollar bag she'd chosen, Rachel stood to the side, arms crossed, lips pressed together in the thinnest of lines.

Jasmine almost skipped out of the store. "Let's go to Gucci," she said with glee.

Again, this store wasn't part of the plan. But by the time Jasmine and Cecelia had bought their three-hundred-dollar sunglasses, Jasmine knew that Rachel had been securely put in her place.

Actually, the girl had much more willpower than Jasmine had imagined. She was sure that Rachel would have found something to purchase—a keychain or something—just to keep up with her and Cecelia. But she didn't spend a dime. Jasmine was sure that the ten-thousand-dollar check Rachel had written had depleted any spending money that she'd had. Once again, Jasmine had to thank God for Pastor Griffith. She didn't know where that million dollars was coming from, but Hosea had told her last night—although he wasn't happy about it—that her check was already covered.

When the three stepped outside of Gucci, Cecelia said, "Where to now, Jasmine?"

That made Jasmine's heart beat just a bit faster.

It was time.

"Oh, there's a fabulous store in here called Bling. They compete with Swarovski crystal, only they're much more upscale. And they have the best pieces—"

"Say no more," Cecelia said, holding up her shopping bag. "Lead the way."

Jasmine wanted to sprint right into the store. But she took slow, casual steps, as if she wasn't in any kind of a hurry. As they strolled toward the escalator that would take them to the third floor, she thought about Mae Frances, and how once again, her friend—and her connections—were coming through.

Even though she'd only known this woman for a bit over seven years, it felt like Mae Frances had always been in her life. Mae Frances and her connections had saved Jasmine in her most devastating moments. Mae Frances and her connections had helped her to pass off her daughter as Hosea's child. Mae Frances and her connections had helped her track down the blackmailer who had wanted the world to know that she'd been a stripper. And though they'd never discussed this, Jasmine was absolutely convinced that it was Mae Frances, and her connections, who had found Jacqueline and saved her from her kidnapper.

Mae Frances knew influential people who were now dead and plenty who were very much alive. And now she had a connection who had a connection with a little security guard, in a little store in Beverly Hills.

They stepped into Bling and the unsmiling, white-haired guard eyed the three of them as if he was trying to determine if they were worthy of entering the store. Finally, he glanced at Jasmine for just a second and gave her a short nod.

She nodded back and followed Rachel and Cecelia deeper into the store. Her eyes moved toward the three cameras that Mae Frances told her hung from the corners.

"Make sure you stay out of the camera's vision," she'd warned. *"Buster's security company gets all the tapes, but he said it would be better if he didn't have to fix anything. Though he would, it'll work better if this whole thing is clean."*

"Oh, my goodness," Cecelia said. She was already standing at one of the glass counters. "These pieces are beautiful."

The salesclerk smiled. "You've never seen our pieces before?"

"No, I haven't. Can you believe it?"

"Well, let me show you." The tall, lean woman unlocked a case and lifted a bracelet from the display. "We mix diamonds and crystals," she explained. She wrapped the bracelet around Cecelia's wrist.

"Isn't this divine?" Cecelia asked.

"I want to try one," Jasmine said.

The clerk took out another bracelet, hooked it around Jasmine's wrist, then Jasmine and Cecelia held their wrists together and compared their pieces.

"That is so classy," Cecelia said, admiring the black and white crystals that Jasmine wore.

"What about you, Rachel?" Jasmine asked. "What do you think?" She held up her wrist for Rachel to take a closer look.

"They're all right." Rachel pouted.

Jasmine pointed to a charm bracelet with a cross hanging from the center. "Oh, let her try this one," she told the clerk.

"No, that's okay."

"Oh, come on, Rachel," Cecelia said, helping Jasmine's plan without even knowing it. "It's not as much fun if we're not all shopping."

Rachel sighed as the clerk hooked the bracelet onto her arm, but then she smiled.

"And that's only nine hundred dollars," Jasmine said.

"Oh, I'm not worried about the price," Rachel said. "It's just that I'm not much of a jewelry person."

"Don't you like it?" Jasmine asked, pushing. "It definitely looks good on you."

With Cecelia, Jasmine, and the clerk watching her, Rachel hesitated for a moment, as if she was considering the piece. Then she shook her head. "Naw." She began to unhook the bracelet.

Right then Jasmine diverted Cecelia's attention. "Did you see the necklaces?" She pointed to the counter in the back.

"Where?"

The clerk said, "Oh, you have to see the necklaces. I have a piece that would be perfect for you."

When Rachel followed Cecelia and the clerk, Jasmine glanced at the cameras, then at the guard. He nodded, and she slipped the bracelet that Rachel had left on the counter into the palm of her hand. Her heart pounded as she edged toward Rachel. She glanced up once again at the camera, took a deep breath, then leaned forward, bumped Rachel, and dropped the bracelet into her purse.

"Dang," Rachel said as she stepped away from Jasmine. "Why you gotta get all up in my personal space?"

"I'm sorry," Jasmine said, backing away. "I just wanted to get a look at this necklace." But she turned around, glanced toward the guard, and they nodded at each other.

Her heart still hammered—the deed was done. All she had to do was wait.

"You know what?" Cecelia said. "I'm going to think about this. I want to check out a few more stores."

The clerk nodded and began returning the pieces that had been taken out.

"Why don't we go to lunch now?" Rachel said, as if she'd had enough of shopping. "I really just want to sit down for a while." She walked in front of them, and Jasmine slowed her own pace a bit so that it would look like Rachel was rushing.

To Cecelia, Jasmine whispered, "I think Rachel's upset. She's in such a hurry to get out of here."

Cecelia nodded and frowned. "I wonder what's wrong."

Then . . . Rachel crossed the threshold and the guard scooted to his left, blocking her path.

"Excuse me, miss," he said, his voice low and steady. "You need to come back in here."

Rachel whipped around. "What?"

The guard said, "In fact, all three of you ladies need to follow me."

"Why?" Jasmine and Cecelia said together.

"Please," he said, motioning with his hands toward the back of the store.

The three stood frozen for a moment before Cecelia said, "I'm not going anywhere until you tell us what this is about."

"It's about shoplifting, ma'am——"

"Shoplifting," the three women said together.

The guard continued, "And I'm trying to straighten this out before I call the police."

"I ain't going nowhere," Rachel said belligerently. "I didn't shoplift a damn thing." She turned back toward the door and the man blocked her path once again. This time, he unlatched his walkie-talkie from his waist and spoke into it.

"Ah, Rachel, Cecelia," Jasmine said as people in front of the store slowed down to see what was going on. "Maybe we should just go with him and get this cleared up." She turned to Cecelia. "We know it's some kind of mistake, so after he figures that out and we get an apology, then we can get out of here."

Cecelia nodded. "Rachel, come on," she demanded. Then, to the guard, she said, "When you finish with us, you're not only going to give us an apology, but I want your supervisor's name."

"I'll be happy to give it to you, ma'am." He motioned toward the back of the store.

It was the middle of the day, a Wednesday, and so there wasn't the crowd that Jasmine would have liked. But just being marched to some back office had to be too much for Cecelia King.

As Cecelia, Rachel, and Jasmine passed the salesclerk, she eyed Rachel as if she was sure she was the culprit.

In the back, which was much more of a storage room than an office, the guard said to Rachel, "May I look into your purse?"

"Naw! You can't look in my purse; I didn't do anything."

"Look, if it will help us to get this over with," Jasmine said, "you can look in mine." She opened her bag and shoved it under his nose.

"I don't need to look in your bag," he said. "I didn't see you take anything. I saw her."

Jasmine made sure her eyes were as wide as Cecelia's.

"What?" Rachel yelled. "You didn't see me do anything because I didn't even like this funky stuff. You better step back and stop lyin'."

"Miss . . . just let me look in your bag," the guard said, still maintaining his calm professionalism.

"No." Rachel pressed her bag against her chest. "You not gonna treat me like some common criminal."

"Well, then," he said, "we can wait for the police."

"Rachel!" Just the way Cecelia said her name was a demand.

"I don't want us to get caught up with the police . . . even if it is a mistake."

Rachel pushed out a breath. "Here," she said. She crossed her arms. "That's why I can't stand coming into stores like this because y'all always thinking it's the black people stealing something. This ain't nothing but racism and——" She stopped as he slowly lifted the bracelet with the dangling cross from her purse.

"Oh, my God," Jasmine whispered.

"Rachel!" Cecelia exclaimed.

"I . . . I . . . that's not mine."

"You're right," the guard said. "It's not yours."

"I mean, I mean, I didn't take it!"

Three pairs of eyes stared her down.

"I don't know how that got in there," Rachel said, her voice raised now.

Cecelia stepped forward. "How much does that cost? I'll pay for it."

Jasmine said, "It's nine hundred dollars. Remember, that's the bracelet that Rachel was looking at." To the guard, she said, "Yes, we'll pay for it. I'll pay for it. I'll pay double just to make this go away. She's sorry, I'm sure."

"I'm not sorry about nothin'," Rachel said indignantly. "'Cause I didn't do anything."

The security guard shook his head. "Well, *I'm* sorry, but in this store, we prosecute shoplifters."

"Oh, my God!" Rachel's tears were instant. "I didn't put that in my bag." She turned toward Cecelia. "I wouldn't do that!" And then she glared at Jasmine. She was crying a river when she screamed, "You did this!"

"What? No!" Jasmine shrieked. "I would never. And I could afford to buy it."

Behind them, there was a quick knock and two uniformed officers entered the room.

"Oh, my God!" Rachel repeated as the guard told the LAPD what he'd seen and what he'd found.

Cecelia went into damage-control mode again. "Officers, this is a huge mistake. We were all trying on bracelets and there was so much going on. I can vouch for this woman." She paused and glared at Rachel as if she wished she could let her rot in hell, but for the sake of the Coalition, she wouldn't. "The bracelet probably just slipped into her bag."

Both of the officers smirked at Cecelia's explanation.

"Slipped?" one of them asked, almost laughing.

The other said, "We have to take her down to the station. That's the store's policy. If it just . . . slipped, we'll straighten it out down there."

"Oh, my God," Rachel cried again as the other officer cuffed her hands behind her back.

Jasmine stepped closer to the officer and Rachel. "Is that really necessary? Handcuffs?" she asked, as if she wasn't delighted.

He didn't even acknowledge Jasmine as he began, "You have the right to remain silent . . ."

"I didn't steal that bracelet," Rachel screamed.

"We'll figure this out, Rachel," Jasmine said. "Officer, what station are you taking her to?"

"The one over on Rexford."

"Call Lester, please!" Rachel cried as the officers flanked her and escorted her from the store.

Jasmine and Cecelia walked quickly behind her as the light afternoon crowd slowed their steps to stare at all three of them. At the elevators, the officers stopped.

One turned to Jasmine and Cecelia. "You won't be able to come with us. You can meet her at the station."

When the officers gently nudged Rachel into the elevator, Jasmine and Cecelia stood in the middle of gawking shoppers with their mouths as wide open as everyone else.

"I don't believe this," Cecelia said.

"Neither do I. But she was really looking at that bracelet." Jasmine sighed as if everything that had just happened was completely unbelievable. "Should we go to the police station?"

Cecelia shook her head. "I've never set foot in one and I'm not going to do it today. We'll go back to the hotel and get her husband to take care of this."

Jasmine nodded and led Cecelia back the same way they'd come into the mall. There was so much that she had planned to say—like telling Cecelia that she didn't know Rachel had wanted the bracelet so badly, or even telling her that Rachel had been arrested before.

But Jasmine said none of that. The thrill that she'd expected to feel when she watched Rachel being carted away just wasn't there.

She didn't know what had stolen her joy. Maybe it was the look of total shock and fear on Rachel's face. Or maybe it was the thought of Rachel's children being without their mother, even if it was just for one night.

Whatever it was, as Jasmine and Cecelia descended in silence on the escalator, Jasmine almost wished that she could take it all back.

Almost.

What Mae Frances had concocted, and what she'd just implemented, had to be done. Because Hosea had to win this election—by any means necessary. And Hosea would have won . . . if Rachel had just left it alone. But she hadn't, and now Rachel had to pay.

She and Cecelia were still silent when they jumped into the car waiting at the curb exactly where the driver had left them. They were still silent when he edged away and sped down La Cienega, in the opposite direction of the police station where Rachel had been taken. And they were still silent when the car hit the freeway that would take them back to the safety of the hotel and the convention.

All Jasmine could think about was that the deed was done. And that was a good thing.

So why did she feel so bad?

Chapter
EIGHTEEN

As God was her witness, Rachel was going to strangle Jasmine Cox Larson Bush until she took her last breath. Right now, Rachel was thinking of a thousand and one ways for Jasmine to die. And if it took the rest of her life, Rachel wouldn't rest until she made that Botox bimbo pay.

"Hey! No one has come for me?" Rachel screamed from the holding cell. She was so angry she couldn't stop shaking.

"For the five-thousandth time, no!" the female deputy shot back. "I will let you know when someone gets here, so quit asking, you're getting on my nerves!"

"I've been here fifteen hours and my husband should've gotten me out by now." Rachel had been so hysterical when she'd arrived that they'd let her call Lester as soon as she got through booking. Cecelia had already filled him in and he was horrified at the news, but promised that he'd get her out as soon as possible.

The deputy appeared in front of Rachel, her hands plastered on her hips. She looked like she was about to explode out of her too-tight uniform. "You've been here less than two hours," the deputy said, exasperated. "Now shut up and have a seat before I put you in the real cell."

Two hours? That's all? Rachel slinked away from the bars and then began pacing back and forth across the cell. She was no stranger to jail. She'd been put behind bars once when she was a teenager for stalking Bobby and pulling a knife on his new girlfriend. But that was a lifetime ago. She might lead a drama-filled life, but nothing about that life was criminal and she dang sure had never stolen anything. She couldn't believe she was being accused of it now. Rachel knew beyond a shadow of a doubt that Jasmine was behind this whole mess. If she had to stay in this place overnight, they might as well give her a permanent spot because she was going to be right back for murder anyway.

Rachel glanced around the dingy cell. There were four other women there, two that looked like they'd just walked in off the street corner, another that looked like she used to be a man in a former life, and a mousy-looking woman who sat in the corner, terrified. Rachel had heard horror stories about women in jail, but luckily everyone seemed caught up in their own problems and no one seemed to be worried about her.

"Adams, I guess you can calm down now."

Rachel jumped at the sound of the deputy's voice. She didn't even realize how long she'd been lost in thought. "Thank God, I'm getting out," she said, scurrying over to the bars.

The deputy held her hand up. "Whoa, not so fast. You're not going anywhere just yet. But you do have a visitor."

"I'm not getting out?" Rachel asked.

"You are, but just for a minute."

"This is so not fair."

The deputy unlocked the door and stepped aside for Rachel to walk out. "You should've thought about that before you stole that jewelry."

"I didn't steal anything!" Rachel protested.

"Yeah, that's what all you crooks say," she said, slamming the door shut.

Rachel had never been so happy to see her husband. She raced to him and had just thrown her arms around his neck when the deputy shouted, "No contact!"

Rachel stepped back and fought back tears. "Do you see how they're treating me? Like I'm some criminal."

"It's okay, baby," Lester replied soothingly.

"*Okay?* Lester, do you see where I am? How is this okay?"

He motioned for her to take a seat at the small table next to them. She did and he slid in across from her. "Please tell me what in the world happened. Why do they think you stole a nine-hundred-dollar bracelet?"

Rachel was so relieved to see that his face bore no judgment. In fact, he looked just as dumbfounded as she did.

"You know I don't steal. And I don't even like overpriced jewelry like that piece of crap they say I took," she said.

"Of course I know that," he replied. "I just don't understand how the bracelet got in your bag."

"It was that lying old trick Jasmine. I was thinking about this in the cell, and there was a moment in the store when she bumped into me. I know that she planted that bracelet, trying to set me up! She is the one——"

"Rachel——"

"Don't 'Rachel' me. I know she was behind this."

"But the security guard said he saw you."

"Well, he's lying. I don't know how or why. Maybe Jasmine paid him. I don't know. But ain't nobody saw nothing because I didn't do anything." Rachel was getting worked up all over again.

He tried to pat her arm. "Okay, baby, just calm down."

She pulled away and pounded the table. "No, this has gone too far! I've been set up and I don't deserve to be here." She took a deep breath to calm herself down when she saw the deputy staring icily at her. "Look, I've been thinking. I need you to call Melinda for me."

"Who is Melinda?"

"The reporter at KNBC just came out to interview me."

"Are you crazy? You want this on the news?" Lester asked incredulously.

Rachel had thought about this option while she'd been in the cell. She didn't personally know Melinda, but she knew her family, so she felt some level of trust. Besides, Rachel didn't have much choice. "No, I don't want this on the news. But I need her help. She can call that store and put that security guard on the spot or something. They'll react faster if a media person calls versus you calling. He's lying, and if she tells him she's gonna put that hoity-toity store on blast, or even prove he's lying and put it all on the eleven o'clock news, he'll tell the truth."

"I doubt that very seriously."

"Well, Melinda can get him to show the videotape or something. I know a store like that has surveillance tape. It'll show I didn't steal anything!"

"How can she make them show the tape?"

"Those reporters have power."

Lester shook his head doubtfully. "No, why don't we just let an attorney work all of this out. I already called one and——"

"No, Lester! I'm not about to sit in this jail cell while they try to prove my innocence."

"We're already working on getting you bailed out."

"*Bail?* I don't need bail because I didn't do anything!" she screamed.

"Hey, keep your voice down," the deputy called out.

Lester gently patted her hands, then pulled back when the deputy shot him a warning look. "Sweetheart, I'm doing my best to get you out of here ASAP."

Rachel gritted her teeth. She was not about to debate this with her husband. He wasn't the one stuck here. "Lester, call Melinda. Just call information and get the number to KNBC's news department. Tell Melinda what's going on and tell her I desperately need her help. Please, Lester. I'm going crazy in here."

Lester released a defeated sigh. "Okay, fine. I'll call her right away. But I'm still going to have the attorney work on bail."

"Whatever." She rubbed her temples. "We'll probably need the bail money anyway, because I swear, I'm going to kill Jasmine."

Lester's eyes widened. "Babe, even if Jasmine did do this, you can't prove it, so let's cool it with the threats."

Rachel glared at her husband. She thought about what she'd endured today. She thought about the humiliation she felt as they slapped handcuffs on her and carted her through the Beverly Center like a common thief. And she thought about the complete and utter disgust on Cecelia King's face. No. Rachel didn't care what Lester said. Jasmine was behind this. Rachel knew it and this was the last straw. There was no way in hell she'd rest until Jasmine had paid—and paid dearly—for this latest act.

Chapter
NINETEEN

This was the day before the nominating session and she'd just put Rachel Adams right where she belonged—in jail. This was her crowning moment, just about guaranteed a win for Hosea . . . so why wasn't Jasmine kicking up her heels?

"Will anyone be joining you?" the restaurant hostess asked.

"No, just a table for one." Jasmine's eyes scanned the huge space. The din was at a fever pitch, the room filled primarily with women finding a way to pass the time as the men remained in all-day, closed-door sessions. With the restaurant packed with first ladies, this would have been the perfect time for Jasmine to work the room, to circulate among the pastors' wives and remind them, once again, of all the wonderful programs she had planned for the Coalition—once she became the first lady. And they would all believe her—after all, hadn't she and Hosea donated one million dollars out of their own pocket before a vote had even been cast?

This would have also been the time to drop a little piece of gossip: By the way, did you know that Rachel Adams was arrested a few hours ago in Beverly Hills? You didn't know? Oh, yes, the police dragged her away . . . for shoplifting!

In her mind's eye, Jasmine could see their shocked expressions, she could hear their gasps, as they all reacted to that juicy piece of scandalous news.

But instead of sashaying her way through the maze of tables, Jasmine pointed toward the empty booth in the back corner and then followed the hostess with her head down, raising her eyes just a bit every few steps, just enough to return the greeting of anyone who called out to her.

She slid into the booth, and breathed a long sigh of relief.

"Please ask the waiter to bring me a cup of tea," she told the hostess. "Any kind."

The woman nodded and left Jasmine alone to retrace the events of the last hours. It was only three o'clock, but the day had seemed so long it could have easily been three in the morning.

With her elbows on the table, she closed her eyes and rested her face in her hands, thinking about how Cecelia had jumped out of the car as soon as the driver had rolled to a stop in front of the hotel. Cecelia didn't even wait for one of the valets to open the door; she just slipped out, muttered something about seeing her later, and then rushed into the hotel as if Jasmine was tainted, too.

That was the only part of the plan that hadn't gone as she'd expected. She was supposed to get in the car and drive the stake deeper into Rachel's heart by bonding with Cecelia even more as she shared sordid details of all the trash Rachel had done in the past.

But Jasmine had said nothing; she'd hadn't told Cecelia anything. The two women had sat quietly, as if they'd both been shocked into silence.

Now Cecelia was gone; she and Jasmine hadn't bonded any more. The only good thing out of this was that Rachel was still behind bars in Beverly Hills.

"Jasmine Larson, why didn't you call me?"

For a moment, Jasmine was surprised that Mae Frances had found her. Then she remembered—this was Mae Frances. Her friend could find anything, do everything.

Slowly, Jasmine opened her eyes and Mae Frances slipped into the booth, right as the waiter placed the teakettle and china set in front of her.

"Are you ready to order?" he asked.

Mae Frances swatted at him as if he was a fly. "Go away. We'll let you know when we want something," she huffed.

When the waiter scooted away, Mae Frances leaned forward. "So?"

Jasmine kept her voice low, a reminder to Mae Frances that they were in a public place with ears all around. "She was arrested."

Mae Frances's lips slipped into a sly grin. "Did you just get back?"

Jasmine nodded. "A little while ago. Cecelia and I left the mall and came straight here."

Mae Frances took her eyes off Jasmine and glanced around the room. "So why aren't you up and working these ladies?" She spread her arms wide. "Every first lady in here needs to hear the story of Rachel's humiliating arrest."

Jasmine took a sip and nodded. "I know," she said. "And I'm gonna get around to telling them." She sighed. "It's just that . . ."

Mae Frances frowned. "What?"

"I don't know. It didn't feel as good as I expected. I mean, this child has been taking me through it this week and I just thought this would be the happiest moment of the convention. But then I started thinking. Suppose for some reason Rachel doesn't get out tonight."

"That would be even better," Mae Frances said with glee.

Jasmine shook her head. "Not if it means being away from her children." She shuddered as memories of that time, not long ago enough, replayed in her mind. All of those hours, all of those days, those three weeks that she'd spent without Jacqueline, not knowing where her four-year-old was or if her daughter would ever be found and returned to them.

"This is not the same thing," Mae Frances said, as if she read Jasmine's thoughts. "Not at all. Rachel's children are safe."

"I know. It's just that after what I went through, I don't think any mother should have to spend an hour without her children against her will."

Mae Frances waved her hand as if Jasmine's words didn't make any sense. "Those bebe kids will be with their father. And as bad as they are, Rachel should be thanking us for giving her a night or two or three away from them." When Jasmine said nothing and only took another sip of her tea, her friend added, "Don't go getting soft now, Jasmine Larson. You want Preacher Man to win this election, don't you?"

Yes, of course she wanted Hosea to have this position . . . she needed him to have it.

"That's all that counts," Mae Frances said before Jasmine answered. "Rachel being arrested for shoplifting was our knockout punch. Now we have to make sure that everyone at this convention knows about it." Mae Frances picked up her cell, punched in some letters, and then put the phone back on the table. "Earl will know what to do."

Ah, Pastor Griffith. Didn't they owe him enough?

"He told me to stay out of this, you know. He might not be happy with what I did today."

"Are you kidding me? Earl knew all about it. We'd come up with this plan before we left New York, when we got that first dossier and found out that Rachel had been arrested before. Earl is going to play that fact up—once a jailbird, always a jailbird."

Jasmine shook her head. Mae Frances may have been a couple of decades older than her, and she may have been behind on all this new technology, but when it came to scheming and strategizing, there was no one in the country who did it better.

"Ladies."

Jasmine looked up and into the green eyes of Pastor Griffith. No one did it better than Mae Frances—except for, perhaps, Pastor Griffith.

"Is the men's session out already?" Jasmine asked as she leaned to the side, hoping to see her husband not far behind. That's what she needed right now—to see her husband and then go hug her children.

"No," Pastor Griffith said as he slid into the booth next to Mae Frances. "We're still in session. I just got the text, though I figured it had gone down already when I saw Lester and his treasurer rush out of the hall like they were being chased. But I stayed in there and waited to get Mae Frances's text." His eyes moved between the two women. "We have to capitalize on this all the way. Did you discuss everything that Mae Frances told you to say with Cecelia?"

Jasmine looked at Mae Frances before she said to the pastor, "You knew that much about this setup?"

He smirked. "Mrs. Bush, you underestimate me. This shoplifting idea was mine. I told Mae Frances about it in New York."

She nodded; her friend had just told her that.

He said, "Maybe you're not getting it yet. Maybe you don't know how much work . . . and money I've put into your husband's campaign."

His words made Jasmine pause. For the first time, she asked herself why. Why was Pastor Griffith all up in this as if he was the one being elected? What was he going to get out of doing all of this for Hosea?

Up to this point, Jasmine thought Pastor Griffith's enthusiasm was a North and South thing—after six decades, finally the Coalition would have someone from the North as president. But now that she thought about all that Pastor Griffith had done, especially working out the million dollars. Now, this . . . there had to be more to his obsession.

"So, what about Cecelia?" he asked again.

Jasmine shook her head slightly. "We . . . we didn't talk in the car . . . she didn't want to." When Pastor Griffith frowned, Jasmine added, "But she was right there for the whole thing. She was standing next to Rachel when the guard pulled the bracelet from her bag and when she was handcuffed. She saw everything."

Her words made the pastor smile. "Good," Pastor Griffith said, sitting back as if he was beyond satisfied. "But we need more now. We need to make sure that everyone knows what happened."

The three sat in the booth, silent now, the two across from Jasmine pondering ways to make sure that everyone in the convention knew about the arrest. And Jasmine sat, reflecting, too, but her thoughts were different. Her eyes and her mind were on Pastor Griffith.

"I got it," Pastor Griffith said. "I'll rush back in the session, pretending that the emergency call I just got was about Rachel. I'll stand up, tell them that that's why Lester Adams had to leave in such a hurry and I'll make a plea for us to have a special offering to raise money for Rachel's bond so that we can get her out of jail."

"That's perfect!" Mae Frances said.

"I'll paint a picture," he said. "A whole story about how they found the bracelet, and the police coming and Cecelia being right there when they handcuffed Rachel and dragged her away."

Mae Frances beamed at him as if she was proud. Jasmine just continued staring and thinking.

"The only thing," Pastor Griffith said to Jasmine, "is I don't want you here; I don't want you in the hotel. I don't want anyone to be able to call your room or to see you anywhere in the hotel—at least not for the next few hours."

"Why not?"

"Because I want Cecelia hounded by these people. I want people calling her, I want people knocking on their door, I want people texting her. I want the Kings so overwhelmed that they will never again have anything to do with the Adams family! So, I don't want you anywhere to be found to answer questions."

"That's not going to work. Hosea is going to call me as soon as he hears about this. He knows I was with Cecelia and Rachel."

"I'll tell Hosea that since your children are hanging out at all the kids' events today, you knew they were safe and you wanted to get Mae Frances away from this craziness. Don't worry, Hosea will probably call you, but I'll take care of your husband. I've got him under control."

Jasmine and Mae Frances spoke at the same time. "What does that mean?"

He looked at Jasmine, then turned to face Mae Frances. "Don't get testy, ladies. I simply mean that I have the situation—the whole situation—under control."

"That's not what you said," Jasmine stated.

"Well, that's what I meant." The pastor stared at Jasmine as if he dared her to challenge him any more.

The women glanced at each other, but when Pastor Griffith picked his wallet from his pocket and tossed five one-hundred-dollar bills to Mae Frances, she seemed to forget his ominous words.

But the money didn't distract Jasmine. "What's that for?" she asked.

"You two go out."

"Where?" The questions all came from Jasmine; Mae Frances no longer had any concerns. She'd already scooped that money up as if it was a million dollars. "And for how long?" Jasmine kept the questions coming.

"Just a couple of hours. Go back to the mall, finish up your shopping. Go out to eat; all this work has got to have made you hungry." He had tucked his wallet away, but he opened it up again and passed five bills to Jasmine.

She stared at the money, then shook her head. "I'm fine." Looking him straight in the eyes, she said, "I don't need your money."

He chuckled. "Sweetheart, this is not about needs, it's all about wants. And because you and I want the same thing—for your husband to be the president of the Coalition—you *need* to take this money, and let me do my thing."

She stared at the five hundred dollars for a little while longer; and again, she wanted to ask him, what was in it for him? But after a few moments, her fingers slowly curled around the money.

He smiled.

Mae Frances laughed and said, "Let's go, Jasmine Larson."

It took her a moment to gather herself, but with a final glance at Pastor Griffith, Jasmine lifted her bags and followed Mae Frances out of the restaurant.

Chapter
TWENTY

The eight hours had felt like an eternity. But Rachel was just grateful to be out of that hellhole. Her idea to call Melinda had been right on the money. Melinda had marched over to the Beverly Center, flashed her ID, and asked that security guard to retell his story on camera. Naturally, he'd spouted some mess about the company's privacy policy, but when Melinda had demanded to see the surveillance tape, and it showed Rachel just standing around looking irritated and not blatantly stealing as he'd claimed, he'd stuttered, backtracked, and said maybe he'd been mistaken. Rachel had hoped the tape would've shown Jasmine setting her up, but Melinda said it only showed Jasmine's back to the camera and there was no way to prove she'd done anything.

That had been frustrating, but at least the flustered guard had decided he didn't want to go on camera lying about her. He never admitted to anything, but the manager had told Melinda they didn't want the "negative press," so they wouldn't be pressing charges.

Rachel had decided she, however, would be filing charges. Or a lawsuit. Or something for false arrest, false imprisonment, lying on a customer, anything she could make stick.

But right now, she had a bigger fish to fry. While she'd sat in that jail cell, she'd been consumed with thoughts of how to make Jasmine pay. But nothing she could think of was punishment enough.

"Are you okay? You're so quiet," Lester said, snapping Rachel out of her vengeful thoughts.

"I'm just happy to be out of that place." She leaned back in the car seat. Lester had been waiting with a driver when she'd walked out and she'd been so happy that he'd had the good sense to get a luxury Town Car. She sank down in the plush leather seats. "Where are the kids? Do they know what's going on?" she asked.

"No. Brooklyn and Lewis are with Brenda and your dad. Nia and Jordan are at the kids' coalition slumber party tonight. The only person that knows anything to my knowledge is Deacon Tisdale. I had to tell him so he could work on getting me the money for the bail."

Rachel sighed. At least Deacon Tisdale, the treasurer of their church, was discreet. "What about everyone else? I'm sure Jasmine couldn't wait to get back and blab to everyone at the hotel what happened."

"Actually, no one has said a word about it other than Mrs. King. When I was leaving to come pick you up, she asked me for an update."

"I hope you explained to her that they'd dropped the charges."

"I did and I told her how you'd never stolen anything in your life. She looked a little skeptical but relieved."

Rachel glanced out the window of the moving car. She'd made such progress with Cecelia this week. Even though the charges had been dropped, Rachel was sure the whole experience had left a sour taste in Cecelia's mouth.

Yet another reason for her to hate Jasmine.

The driver pulled up to the hotel. Rachel was grateful that the lobby was fairly empty. Lester said no one really knew but she didn't trust that for a minute. She was positive Jasmine had told anyone who passed about what happened. So Rachel just needed tonight to regroup, get her head together, and prepare for tomorrow's formal nominating meeting. She probably would need to address this whole matter. It was an issue she decided to bring up with Lester later.

Rachel had just made it to the elevator when one of the men who had been with the Bush entourage came rushing toward her.

"Rachel! Are you okay?"

Rachel raised an eyebrow at this old man and his fake concern.

"Excuse me?" she said, cutting her eyes at Lester.

"How are you, Pastor Griffith?" Lester said, stepping in.

The man took Rachel's hand. "Oh, don't worry about me. We need to be concerned about Rachel. I imagine it was horrific having to spend the afternoon in jail!" His voice was loud and carried across the corridor, causing a few people to stop and stare their way.

Rachel had to take small, deep breaths to keep from losing it. She didn't know this Pastor Griffith, but she did know he was on the Bushes' side, so his concern about her was a big act and she was about to tell him about himself.

She snatched her hand away. "You know——"

"Pastor Griffith"——Lester must have known Rachel was about to go off, because he stepped in, cutting her off——"thank you for your concern, but Rachel is fine. It was all a big misunderstanding."

Pastor Griffith shook his head. "I heard they found a nine-hundred-dollar diamond bracelet in her bag."

"Again, it was all a misunderstanding," Lester said.

"I just hate that for you. I am sure that was so traumatic for you," Pastor Griffith said, his voice still raised, "to be carted out of a mall in handcuffs, then just thrown into jail!" *Were his eyes actually watering up?*

"You don't need to be concerned about me," Rachel said as calmly as she could. She glanced over to the people who were blatantly staring her way. "Someone tried to set me up. The police figured that out, which is why they let me go."

"Well, that is fantastic news because I would hate for you to have spent the night in jail." He was a great actor, because he looked like he was really worried about Rachel. Luckily, she could smell a con artist a mile away and Pastor Griffith definitely bore the stench of someone who was up to no good.

"Again, thank you, Pastor Griffith, but as you can imagine,

my wife wants to go get some rest," Lester said, stepping to Rachel's side.

"Well, you just let me know if there's anything I can do," Pastor Griffith said.

"Like that would ever happen," Rachel muttered.

"Pardon me?" Pastor Griffith said.

"Nothing," Lester quickly interjected. "Come on, sweetheart. I know you just want to go upstairs and lie down." He led her on to the elevator.

"Can you believe the nerve of that man," Rachel said as she watched Pastor Griffith wave from across the lobby. "He knows doggone well he could care less about me being arrested. Everybody knows he's pushing for Rev. Bush, so why he's trying to fake the funk is beyond me." Rachel was pissed, but after the day she'd had, she couldn't waste any more energy on this Pastor Griffith.

"So, are you going to get some rest?" Lester asked as the elevator door closed.

"Actually, I want to see my kids."

Lester pushed the button for their floor. "Well, Brooklyn and Lewis are asleep, and you know if you wake them up, it's going to be brutal trying to get them back down."

She nodded. He was right about that. "Well, at least let me see Nia and Jordan."

"They're at the slumber party," Lester said.

"Okay, but I still want to stop in and see them, say good night at least."

Lester punched the button to the twelfth floor as the elevator rose. "Okay. They're in 1202. It's the suite at the end of the hall. Do you need me to go with you?"

"No, I'm fine. You go on up."

"Actually, I need to run by Deacon Tisdale's room and update him on everything." He handed her the room key. "Here's the extra key. I'll just see you back in the room."

"That's fine," Rachel said as the elevator doors opened on the twelfth floor. She stepped out and looked down the hall to room

1202. The sounds of squealing children reverberated through the door. She knocked several times but the kids were so loud they couldn't hear, so no one answered.

Rachel was just about to turn and leave when the door swung open. Her son Jordan and another little boy stood in the doorway.

"Ma?" Jordan said. "What are you doing here?"

"Hey, honey. I just came to check on you."

"Awww, Ma, why you checking on me?"

"I just wanted to come hug you good night."

Jordan looked mortified as the little boy next to him started snickering. Rachel shook her head, not about to get into it with her son. "Is Nia in there?"

"Yeah, all the girls are in one room. She's been whining for you since we got here."

That warmed Rachel's heart. "Can you go get her?"

Jordan seemed all too happy to dart off. The other boy was quickly on his heels. Rachel stood with her foot propping the door open. She would've gone in, but all that noise was making her head hurt.

A few minutes later, the door swung back open and Nia bounced into her mother's arms. "Mommy!" she said.

"Hey, baby," Rachel said, hugging her daughter tightly. She was just about to say something else when she looked up to see who had just stepped out the door and was standing behind Nia. "Hi, Jacqueline," Rachel said slowly.

"Jacquie's my friend now," Nia said excitedly as she took Jacqueline's hand. "She's not mad at me anymore for messing up her dress."

"Well, that's wonderful. Are you girls having a good time?"

"The boys are being mean," Nia said. "They put them in another room, but they're still picking on us. Can I come with you?"

Rachel smiled. She was tired and really had wanted to just hug her daughter and keep moving. But how could she turn down such a sweet request?

"Okay, honey. We can pop some popcorn and watch a movie."

"Oooohhh." Nia stopped and looked over at Jacqueline. "Can Jacqueline come, too?"

Rachel's heart stopped as an idea for the perfect payback sprouted in her mind. But this was a low blow. Considering the horror Jasmine had gone through the last time Jacqueline came up missing, Rachel couldn't do that to her again.

"Ummm, well . . ." Rachel began.

"Please? I wanna come," Jacqueline said. "The boys are being mean to me, too. Can I come? Pretty please?"

She couldn't inflict that type of pain on another mother. But then Rachel thought back over the last ten hours. She thought back over the humiliation of being arrested, of sitting in that jail cell, of Cecelia's disgust. When she processed all of that, she found herself saying, "That sounds like a great idea. You can spend the night with us. We'll cut off the phone so nobody can disturb us and just have our own private slumber party. You can go back to your room in the morning." A sick feeling rose in her gut, but Rachel shook it off as she took both girls' hands and led them to the elevator. "I'll call the chaperones when we get to the room and tell them that you're spending the night with me."

Chapter
TWENTY-ONE

From the moment that Jasmine had married a man of such means, shopping had been her third love—behind Hosea and her children. But she found no love in her favorite habit today.

In fact, she felt like she'd been exiled to some kind of shopping prison and Mae Frances was her prison guard.

She and Mae Frances hadn't returned to the Beverly Center. Instead, Mae Frances had dragged her to Rodeo Drive, where Jasmine told her that the five hundred dollars that Pastor Griffith had given her would do nothing more than buy a good meal and some wine. But Mae Frances had insisted, and as the April breeze swept through Beverly Hills, they sauntered up and down the famed streets known for the designer stores and haute couture fashion. Mae Frances squealed like a tourist when she walked past Harry Winston and Chanel and Hermès and David Yurman, although Jasmine didn't know why. Mae Frances lived on the Upper East Side of Manhattan—she'd definitely seen these stores before.

Maybe it was just the California air. Or maybe she was still excited that they had pulled off such a scheme, and Rachel Adams now sat in jail not too many blocks away from where they shopped. Whatever it was that had Mae Frances smiling and figuring out how she was going to spend her money, it had Jasmine brooding.

"You need to get it together, Jasmine Larson," Mae Frances had said to her once. But after that warning, Mae Frances had ignored her friend, and focused just on the stores.

Even when Jasmine decided that they should go to Crustacean for dinner, and Mae Frances had marveled at that famous walk-on-water entrance, Jasmine's mood had not changed.

"What has your panties in a bunch?" Mae Frances asked right after they'd both ordered the charbroiled colossal tiger shrimp from the Special Kitchen. "Don't tell me that you're still thinking about Rachel? There's no need to worry about her."

"No, it's not her," Jasmine said, though she wasn't sure if her words were totally true. She didn't really know if it was Rachel or what that had her stomach churning—like something bad was brewing.

"How well do you know Pastor Griffith?"

Mae Frances frowned as if she didn't understand the question. "I can't even count the years," she said. Jasmine wondered if she was purposely being evasive.

But she didn't ask any more questions. When an hour had passed, and Mae Frances texted Pastor Griffith, Jasmine held her breath.

"Great!" Mae Frances said as she looked down at her phone. "He said it's safe to come back." Then she laughed. "He added that the Kings have had enough. We need to celebrate, Jasmine Larson. With another glass of wine."

"We need to get back to the hotel," Jasmine said, signaling the waiter for the bill. "I want to see my children."

When they jumped in the cab to head back downtown, Jasmine offered the driver twenty dollars over the meter to get them to the hotel in fifteen minutes. It took him twenty-two minutes and she'd tipped him a twenty (from Pastor Griffith's money) anyway, just because she was so glad to be back.

And she was even happier when Hosea met her at the hotel's entrance.

"Babe!" she said, dropping her bags and wrapping her arms around him.

"Whoa!" Hosea chuckled. "I should send you out shopping more often."

She said, "It's just been a long day . . . and I missed you."

"Well, I don't know how you had time to miss me when you were in the middle of all the excitement today."

Jasmine glanced at Mae Frances before she said, "I know. Rachel arrested for shoplifting. Isn't that something?"

"It was, but thank God it was all cleared up."

The women spoke together. "What are you talking about?"

"Turns out the security guard at the store you guys were in retracted. Said he didn't see what he thought he saw, and the tapes in the store didn't show anything." He leaned over and whispered to Jasmine, "I have to admit, darlin', for a moment I thought you had something to do with it. But the tapes didn't show anything except for three ladies out doing their thing."

"So, how did the bracelet get in her bag?" Mae Frances asked.

Hosea shrugged as he took the shopping bags from his wife and Mae Frances. "No idea. I'm just glad that it's all cleared up now, though for a while this afternoon, Reverend King and his wife were quite upset. People were almost attacking Lady Cecelia with all of their questions."

Jasmine glanced at Mae Frances and she was sure that her friend's thoughts were the same as hers—at least that part of the plan had worked.

"Well, all I want to do is go to the children's suite, hug them, then go up to ours and crawl right into bed."

"Mind if I join you?"

"You better! Are you finished for the night?"

He nodded. "I think they know they kept the men away from their wives long enough. Plus, they want us well rested for the nominating session tomorrow."

Hours had passed since the last time Jasmine smiled. At least this whole process, this whole week, was coming to an end. Tomorrow, Hosea would officially be nominated, and then two days after that . . . it would be over. No more tricks from that trick. And, she wouldn't have to deal with Pastor Griffith anymore either. Jasmine didn't like mistrusting him, especially when he'd done nothing except help them. But there were too many things that made her uneasy and she just wanted to get away from all of these people.

Inside the elevator, Hosea said, "Oh, I forgot to tell you, darlin', Jacqueline is at the Coalition slumber party."

"What?"

"The slumber party, remember? She's been asking to go to that all week."

As the doors parted on the fifth floor, Jasmine asked, "So, Mrs. Sloss is with her, right?"

"No, she stayed behind in the suite with Zaya."

The three had been moving together, but Jasmine stopped in the middle of the hallway. "So . . . who's with Jacquie?"

Hosea put his hand on her shoulder, and said, "She's at the party with five chaperones. I dropped her off and checked out things myself. She'll be fine." He paused. "She's safe."

Jasmine turned around, marched back to the elevator.

"Where are you going?" Hosea asked.

"To get Jacquie."

"No, Jasmine." Hosea gently tugged her hand, pulling her in the direction of the suite. "She wanted to go to the party and we have to start letting her be a little more independent. She's begging for that and she needs it. And here in this hotel, at this convention, is a wonderful and safe place for us to start."

She took a deep breath, then followed Hosea back down the hall toward the suite where Mrs. Sloss and Mae Frances were staying with Zaya. "I just want you to know that I'm going to hug Zaya and then we're going to get Jacquie." The look on Hosea's face made her say, "Okay, we won't get her, but I want to at least give her a hug."

Mrs. Sloss greeted them with the news that Zaya was already asleep. Jasmine tiptoed into the bedroom, with Hosea behind her, and together they stood above the bed, watching their three-year-old sleep.

Hosea put his arms around Jasmine and held her close. "Our

children are fine," he whispered. "Our children are safe. You know that no matter what, I will always see to that."

Jasmine knew that was the truth—there was a castrated man in prison in New York who had dared to mess with their daughter. In her heart, Jasmine knew that her children were safe, especially here. But still, it was hard to let go of Jacquie, when she had such trouble letting go of the memories of that horrible time.

She kissed Zaya's cheek, and without looking away, she said, "That's all I want to do with Jacquie. Just kiss her good night."

"I already did that for the both of us," Hosea said. "If we go to the room now, we'll disrupt the fun and she'll probably want to leave with us. She has our numbers if anything happens. If she wants to call . . . if she wants to leave."

Jasmine shook her head, so unsure.

"We have to begin to trust again," he whispered. "Trust ourselves, trust Jacquie, trust God."

Jasmine leaned over and kissed their son again, then with everything that was inside of her, she let Hosea lead her to their hotel suite without stopping for Jacqueline.

They stepped inside their room, but never made it to the bedroom. Before the door was closed, Hosea had Jasmine in his arms. His kisses were as gentle as his touch and she remembered why she loved this man, in every way . . . this gentle man.

He slipped off her jacket; then the camisole that she wore underneath. His lips followed his fingers, his cool tongue setting every inch of her body—even the parts that he hadn't gotten to yet—on fire. When she reached for him, he held her hands away, letting her know that he was in control tonight.

On the living room couch, they made love for the first time since they'd arrived in Los Angeles; their kisses, and touches, and moans let the other know how much they'd been missed.

And then they took their love salsa into the bedroom, where they united again and again for more hours, until there was no more room for their pleasure.

Exhausted, they lay in each other's arms. In just minutes, Jasmine heard the rhythm of Hosea's sleep breathing. But though she was satisfied and wanted nothing more than to rest inside her husband's arms, she could not.

What was this disconcerting feeling that boiled inside her? Was it all because of what she'd done to Rachel? It couldn't be that. Rachel was out, and wasn't even going to be charged. So why was she so concerned about her?

Jasmine closed her eyes, but still she couldn't sleep. So she just lay in Hosea's arms and waited. Waited for morning to come.

Chapter TWENTY-TWO

Morning came, though it hadn't come fast enough. Jasmine was out of the shower before the alarm rang at six.

Hosea rolled over and slapped the clock. His eyes were still filled with sleep when he peered at Jasmine pinning up her hair in front of the mirror.

"Where are you going? Running?" he asked, eyeing her jogging suit.

"I'm going to get Jacquie."

He glanced at the clock as if he'd forgotten that he just turned the alarm off. "Darlin', they are not even awake yet."

"That's okay. I was thinking about bringing the children up here for breakfast. We haven't spent enough time with them."

Hosea plopped back down onto the bed. "Can't we do that in an hour or two? We don't have to be in the hall until noon."

Pushing the last hairpin in place, Jasmine turned to her husband. "Of course. I'll just hang out with the kids in their suite, and then we'll come up here about seven thirty or eight."

When she leaned over to kiss him, he grabbed her. "The point of waiting a couple of hours for the kids is so that I can have more time with my beautiful wife. What do I have to do to talk you into coming back into bed with me?"

She pressed her lips against his as her fingers tickled his naked torso. "Tonight. We'll celebrate after the nomination." Another kiss, and then she was gone.

It had felt like a week had passed since she'd last seen Jacqueline. Jasmine knew it was way too early for her not-a-morning-child daughter, but it didn't matter. She needed to lay her eyes on Jacqueline, and then after that, they'd spend some quality time as a family.

She didn't even bother to wait for the elevator; it was just a few flights down. It took several rounds of knocking before she even heard the first sounds of someone stirring on the other side of the door.

"Who is it?" a woman mumbled through the closed door.

"Jasmine Bush."

Jasmine heard the lock click, then the door opened slowly to reveal a short, thick, young woman wearing an oversize American Baptist Convention T-shirt and leggings. "I'm here to pick up Jacqueline Bush."

With her fist, the girl wiped her eye. "None of the kids are up yet." She yawned.

Jasmine folded her arms; her expression and her stance asked her question—what does that have to do with anything? Aloud, she said, "That's okay, I'll wake up my daughter."

When the girl sighed as if Jasmine was intruding, Jasmine wanted to ask where *her* mother was, but she stepped inside, and saw bodies everywhere . . . on the couch, on the floor, in the chairs.

"These are all the boys." The girl yawned again as she led Jasmine through the maze of kids. "Some of the chaperones are in there." She pointed to one side of the suite. "And the girls are in this room."

She opened the door and Jasmine was once again faced with bodies. Tall ones, short ones, under covers, in sleeping bags—about twenty altogether.

It was Jasmine's turn to sigh. Wasn't a mother supposed to know her children anywhere, anytime? It would have been easier to just call out her name, but it really was early, and these kids had probably been up until just a few hours ago.

So, she stepped over the bodies, stopping at each one, absolutely sure that the next one would be her darling daughter.

And then Jasmine got to the end of the room.

She felt her heart begin to race, but she took a deep breath and calmed herself. She turned to the girl. "Where's Jacquie?"

The girl shrugged. "I didn't really get to know all their names."

"What do you mean?" Jasmine asked, her voice rising as she stepped through the sleeping bags once again.

"We just let the kids play and hang out. We didn't ask their names."

The panic attacked like a lion. "Jacquie!" Jasmine yelled out. Now she ripped the sleeping bags from the girls, waking each one up in the process. "Oh, my God! Jacquie! Jacquie!"

It was exactly the way it was before. Searching, calling for her daughter . . . and no answer.

"Jacquie," she screamed, waking up everyone in the suite.

The chaperones dashed into the room.

"What's going on?" a gray-haired woman asked.

"Where's my daughter?" Jasmine cried. "My husband, Pastor Bush, brought her here last night and now she's gone." She tore through the girls again; most were standing up now. Then she raced into the bathroom before she rushed into the living room, waking all the boys.

"Jacquie!" she screamed. "Jacquie!" she cried.

"Mrs. Bush, Mrs. Bush, calm down," the older woman said to her.

Jasmine whipped around and had to fight hard to keep her hands from closing around the woman's neck. "Calm down? Someone has taken my daughter!"

Two of the chaperones were on cell phones, and as Jasmine rushed to the other side of the suite, she yelled out to no one in particular, "Call my husband!"

Not many minutes passed before Hosea burst into the room, and Jasmine was still searching—under the beds, behind the sofas, in the closets.

"Jasmine!"

She wanted to rush to him for comfort, but it was his fault that they were back in this place. "She's gone!" Jasmine cried.

"You left her here and now she's gone!" Her intent was to beat his chest until he hurt as much as she already did. But when he pulled her close, she fell into his arms.

"We'll find her," he said. "I'll find her."

"My baby's gone again." She trembled in his arms. "My baby's gone again."

Three men from hotel security entered the room and Hosea told them how he'd dropped off their daughter last night for the slumber party.

"Would anyone else have picked her up?"

"No!" Jasmine cried. "Her nanny is in their suite with her grandmother, and her grandfather is probably still asleep." She crumbled in Hosea's arms. "Oh, my God. It can't happen again. Please, God! It can't be happening again."

Hosea helped Jasmine to her feet, then settled her onto the couch. But though he wanted to rush through the suite himself, he couldn't leave Jasmine—she would never survive without him by her side.

As he held Jasmine, he asked one of the security guards to call his father and Mae Frances. And while the other guards questioned the children, before they were escorted back to their parents, Hosea held Jasmine in his arms and fought his own tears.

This could not possibly be happening again.

Within minutes, they were joined by more security and hotel personnel. Then Reverend Bush, Pastor Griffith, and Reverend Penn and his wife rushed in.

"Lady Jasmine," Coco Penn called. "Is there anything I can do?"

Jasmine didn't respond. She didn't move at all; she couldn't.

And then Mae Frances came in. Without saying a word, she took Hosea's place, and now Jasmine rested in her arms.

"The police have been called," the visibly shaken hotel manager told them. "They'll be here in a few minutes."

"And I've informed Reverend King," Pastor Griffith said. "Mrs. King said that she'll be right down."

Jasmine closed her eyes, now wanting the sleep that had

eluded her last night. She would only survive through unconsciousness . . . because she was never going to live a day without her daughter. If Jacqueline was missing again, she would go, too. She'd much prefer to die than to live with the pain of another day without her child.

As the hotel suite came alive around her, Jasmine wondered what the end of this day would bring. Would Jacquie be back or would Hosea have to shoot someone else?

"Jasmine!"

Not even the voice of the woman whose attention she'd craved yesterday could make her open her eyes. She had no intention of coming back. She would stay in that dark place behind her eyes, because there she could pretend that Jacqueline was coming home soon.

She felt Cecelia sit beside her, though Jasmine kept her head on Mae Frances's chest, still not moving, only thinking.

Her thoughts were random and peculiar. Was there a *Guinness Book of World Records* entry for kidnapping? Would Buster, the security guard from Bling, be the one to find Jacqueline this time?

Her head was spinning with questions and with the clipped, efficient commands of the security officers taking charge, making calls, doing all that they could to find the missing child.

And then.

"Mommy!"

Jasmine's eyes popped open as Jacqueline ran into the room past the security guards, past Reverend King, past her grandfather and father, and into her mother's arms.

"Jacquie! Oh, my God. Jacquie!"

Everyone in the room exhaled together as Jasmine held her daughter so tight she squirmed.

"Mom," the seven-year-old coughed. "I can't breathe."

That didn't matter to Jasmine. Her plan was to find a way to live her life without ever letting Jacqueline go.

Around them, there were cheers and pats on backs as Hosea knelt next to his wife and daughter.

Cecelia stood and shouted, "And all things, whatsoever ye shall ask in prayer, believing, ye shall receive!"

Jasmine didn't hear Cecelia. All she could do was say, "You're all right," over and over again.

"Mommy, why are you crying?"

It was only then that she relaxed her arms and sat back a bit. Her eyes took in her daughter—her beautiful daughter, who was wearing the same jeans and sweater that she'd had on yesterday.

"Where . . . where were you?" Jasmine asked.

Jacqueline grinned. "With Auntie Rachel. We had our own slumber party . . . me, Nia, and Auntie Rachel." She pointed toward the door.

For the first time, Jasmine noticed her. Rachel. She was standing at the door, wearing a sleeveless summer dress and a sweet smile on her face.

Rachel said, "My son just came back to the room and said they were all let go early, without breakfast, because a little girl was missing. I came down here because I thought we could help in the search. I had no idea the missing girl was Jacquie." Rachel placed her hand across her chest as if she was shocked.

"Jacquie's been with you?" Hosea asked.

"Yes, we told one of the chaperones," Rachel lied. "Jacquie begged to come with me and Nia and I thought since she was spending the night out anyway, it wouldn't be a problem."

Every eye in the room was on Rachel, though she didn't seem to mind.

"I'm so sorry, Jasmine, Pastor Bush."

Jasmine pushed herself from the couch. Slowly, she stepped unsteadily toward the door where Rachel stood and everyone anticipated this beautiful moment. It was no secret that the two women had been feuding: their back-and-forth duels had provided much of the excitement for the week. It had been enough to push their husbands and the Coalition's council to the edge.

But as all watched, peace had finally come—these two women would now be able to lay aside their differences and bond over their common ground—motherhood.

Standing right in front of Rachel, Jasmine stared into the eyes of the woman she'd sent to jail. And she thought about how bad she'd felt about taking Rachel away from her children. She thought about how she'd repented for that.

But that woman had come back and taken this battle to a low that had nothing to do with the election. This had not been about making sure her husband won the presidency. This had only been about torturing her. This had only been about payback.

Rachel kept her smile sweet, innocent. But in her eyes, she taunted Jasmine.

And Jasmine took her dare.

It was quick.

It was efficient.

She cocked her right hand, and with the torque movement she'd learned in boxing class, she connected with Rachel's jaw; the cracking of Rachel's bones echoed through the silent room. The impact made Rachel stumble back, one step, two steps, three steps, until she fell flat on her back.

Knocked unconscious. At least for the moment.

R achel! Rachel!"

Rachel heard the voices, but they sounded like they were coming from far away. She squinted. Tried to get her bearings back. Slowly, she opened her eyes as the words grew louder. Why were these people screaming her name? Why was everyone standing around staring at her? She glanced around as she blinked back into focus. And what in the world was she doing on the floor?

"Are you okay?" Cecelia King knelt over her, lightly slapping her face.

"I . . . I'm fine," Rachel said, her hand immediately going to her jaw, which screamed with pain when she spoke. "What happened?" she asked as she tried to sit up.

Before anyone could answer, she looked over to see Hosea holding Jasmine back. The old lady that was always with them was also glaring at Rachel. Suddenly, everything came rushing to light.

She'd been coldcocked by this crazy trick.

"You hit me?" she yelled at Jasmine.

"I sure did," Jasmine spat. "And you're lucky that's all I did!" She was clutching her daughter. "How dare you take my child?"

"Mommy, I asked to go," Jacquie whimpered. "I'm sorry."

Rachel's first instinct was to get up and charge Jasmine like a raging bull. Rachel had changed, but not so much that she'd allow someone to knock her out and not retaliate.

"Oh, you have lost your mind," Rachel said, struggling to get up off the floor. She was just about to race over and rip that high-dollar weave out of Jasmine's hair when she noticed Cecelia helping her up. She looked around the suite. Every eye in the room was on her, including the police officers standing in the corner.

No, a catfight would only make them both look bad. Taking the high road would speak so much louder. Well, taking the high road and showing Jasmine what jail felt like.

"Officers," Rachel said, motioning toward the police, "I want this lady arrested for assault." She rubbed her sore jaw for dramatic effect. "You witnessed it. *Everyone* witnessed it and I want to press charges."

Hosea immediately turned to Rachel. "Rachel, that's not necessary."

"The hell it isn't! She hit me for no reason! I'm probably going to have to have surgery to repair my jaw. Come to think of it, not only do I want to press charges, but I'm going to sue you for damages as well!" she shot at Jasmine.

"Well, let me give you some more injuries to add to your lawsuit!" Jasmine said, charging toward her.

Hosea grabbed Jasmine and pulled her back. "Jasmine, calm down."

"Calm down! This woman deserves to have her throat slit for what she did! And I'm just the person for the job."

"Do you see this!" Rachel shouted to the officers as she stepped behind Cecelia. "Add terroristic threats to the charges!"

"Jasmine"—Hosea shook his wife—"Jacquie is safe and sound. There is no need to get out of control."

"Are you freakin' kidding me? This woman stole my child." Jasmine turned to the officers. "If anyone needs to be arrested, it should be her for kidnapping!"

"Kidnapping? I didn't kidnap anyone!"

By this point, tears were streaming down Jacquie's face. "Mommy, this wasn't like when the bad man had me. Auntie Rachel didn't kidnap me. I asked to go." Jacquie trembled as she spoke.

"She ain't your damn aunt!" Jasmine bellowed.

"Jasmine, you're scaring her." Hosea hugged his daughter tightly. "Sweetheart, it's fine. Mommy was just worried when she couldn't find you."

"I was playing with Nia." Jacquie sniffed. "She's my friend now."

"I would never hurt Jacqueline," Rachel protested. That much was true. Jacqueline had had a wonderful time. They'd popped popcorn and watched *The Princess and the Frog* until all three of them fell asleep. Of course, Lester had questioned why Jacquie was there, but Rachel had assured him that she'd wanted to come with Nia. "I told the chaperone that I was taking both girls because they were ready to go. I even left a note at the front desk," Rachel said innocently. She'd known Jasmine was going to blow a gasket, so she'd covered her bases last night and left a note to be delivered to the Bushes that Jacqueline was with her. She just didn't bother telling anyone that she'd asked that the note be given to the Bushes upon checkout.

Jasmine's nostrils flared as she glared at Rachel. Hosea gently patted his wife's arm. "See, honey, this was all a misunderstanding."

Jasmine snatched her arm away.

"Do you really think I would do anything to Jacqueline?" Rachel asked, feigning shock.

"I don't know what your crazy behind is capable of!" Jasmine said.

"Oh, we already know which one of us plays dirty," Rachel replied, her tone stiffening.

"Stop it!" Cecelia finally interjected. "The two of you just stop it! This is ridiculous." She glanced around the room at the twenty or so people enjoying the show. And with the commanding presence that seemed to accompany her every move, she stood tall, her voice firm. "The Coalition will not be reduced to these types of catfights." She focused her attention on Rachel. "I am sorry about your ordeal at the mall yesterday. But I was there and it was all a big misunderstanding." She turned to Jasmine. "Just like Jacquie's disappearance was a misunderstanding. The girl has told you it was her idea to go."

"But—" Jasmine began.

"No 'buts,'" Cecelia snapped. "This has gotten out of hand. We've never had this type of drama before," she couldn't help adding.

The officers sighed as if they had tired of the show. "Well, it looks like we're no longer needed," the taller of the officers said as he headed toward the door.

Rachel stepped in front of the officer to stop him. "No, you can't leave. I'm serious about pressing charges."

Jasmine spoke up as well. "And I want to press kidnapping charges, too."

Cecelia threw up her hands in exasperation. "No one is pressing any charges." She looked at the officers. "Thank you for your assistance, but everything is fine now."

Both Rachel and Jasmine looked like they wanted to protest, but the disgusted expression on Cecelia's face stopped them from saying anything.

As the officers and hotel security exited, Cecelia turned to the rest of the people in the room. "We have a busy day today." She shook her head like she was deep in thought. "And to be quite honest, I have some things to assess, so it would be best if everyone just returned to their rooms to get ready for the nominating meeting."

"Cecelia—"

Cecelia held up her hand to cut off Rachel. "Not now, Rachel. Just go back to your room."

Rachel didn't appreciate being treated like a child, but she didn't want to push her luck, so she swallowed and turned to Jasmine. "I really am sorry you were worried about your daughter." Rachel was actually sincere in her apology. She still couldn't stand Jasmine, but seeing her still tightly clutching her daughter, Rachel imagined how she would feel if she thought someone had kidnapped Nia. Especially if Nia had endured the tragedy that little Jacquie had gone through just a little more than two years ago.

Maybe she really had gone too far with this scheme.

"I never meant to scare any of you," Rachel added apologetically.

Jasmine took a step toward her. For a minute, Rachel thought she was going to plant another hook across her jaw, but Hosea was holding tightly to her right hand.

"As long as you are black and female, don't ever say another word to me," Jasmine said slowly and firmly. Then she grabbed her child tighter and walked out the door.

It didn't take much to scare Rachel, but the look in Jasmine's eyes let her know war had been declared. It was a good thing Lester was going to win because Cecelia had made it clear that she expected them to work together regardless of the outcome. And the way Jasmine just looked at her, it would've been hell working under her. Shoot, at this rate, there was no way they'd be able to ever work together at all.

Chapter
TWENTY-FOUR

It had taken two grown men to drag Jasmine away from her children. Well, not drag exactly, but Hosea and Reverend Bush had to spend long minutes convincing Jasmine that Jacqueline and Zaya would be safe while she was at the nominating session.

"They'll be here in the suite with Mrs. Sloss and Mae Frances," Hosea said over and over. "No one will be able to get to them."

"We'll even have lunch brought into the room," Reverend Bush told his daughter-in-law. "They won't leave until you get back."

Finally, Mae Frances pulled her aside and said, "Snap out of it, Jasmine Larson. Remember why you're here; we've put a lot into getting Preacher Man elected." So Jasmine smothered her children with good-bye kisses and told them that she wouldn't be away for long.

"I won't leave again, Mama," Jacqueline assured her. "Not even if Auntie Rachel and Nia try to come and get me."

"That ho ain't your auntie," Jasmine snapped, before she could even think about her words. But in the next second, she pulled her daughter close and covered her with more kisses, trying to wipe away the look of horror on Jacqueline's face.

Now, in her own suite, Jasmine paced back and forth, resisting the urge to call down to the children's suite once again. The moment Hosea had left her alone to take his shower, she'd begun making the calls, checking up on the children every couple of minutes.

My children are safe, my children are safe, she repeated the mantra in her mind. She felt like she was teetering on the edge of sanity, and any little thing just might push her over.

She grabbed the hotel phone once again, but the knock on the door stopped her from calling Mae Frances and Mrs. Sloss for the twelfth time.

She peeked through the peephole, stepped back, then sighed. She wasn't up for this, but this was the day of the nominations—he probably had some information that Hosea needed.

"Jasmine," Pastor Griffith said, entering the suite before she'd even invited him in. "I was just dropping by to check on you, make sure you're okay now."

She closed the door, folded her arms, and nodded. "I'm fine," she said, watching him as he sat on the sofa as if he planned to stay awhile. "Hosea's in the shower; I'll have him call you when he gets dressed."

Pastor Griffith unbuttoned his suit jacket and leaned back. "That's okay. I came to talk to *you;* I'm glad we have a few moments alone."

"I have to get dressed myself and—"

"This won't take long." He glanced at the other end of the sofa, as if he wanted her to sit down.

Jasmine sighed, but it was clear that the pastor was not leaving until he'd said what he'd come to say. She peeked into the bedroom, then closed the door so that Hosea would have privacy when he came out of the bathroom.

Sitting next to him, she waited for the pastor to speak. From the moment she'd met Pastor Griffith, Jasmine had been so intrigued. But that fascination had become suspicion and distrust over the last few days. Questions had started and now continued to nag her. Questions like: why was he so interested in this election? And his money . . . where was that coming from? He was the pastor of an average-size, thousand-member church. So, what was up with the seemingly endless supply of money?

But Jasmine asked him nothing, just waited for him to speak.

"I understand how you felt this morning—"

Jasmine held up her hand. "No." She shook her head. "No one knows how I felt." She shuddered. "How I still feel." She glanced at the phone once again. Maybe she should call . . .

But her thoughts were interrupted when Pastor Griffith leaned closer and rested his hand on top of hers. "No, really, I do know how you feel."

She glanced down at their hands, then raised her eyes to meet his before she slipped her hand away.

He backed off and chuckled as if something was funny. "Look, I'm sorry about what happened this morning, but I came to make sure that you haven't lost your focus . . . that you're still aware of what's at stake."

"And what is at stake?"

He tilted his head slightly, as if he knew there was more to her question. "Your husband's election," he said, as if that was obvious.

She couldn't hold her question in any longer. "What's in this for you, Pastor Griffith?"

"What do you mean for me? This is all about your husband being elected president of the Coalition."

Jasmine paused for a moment, wondering if he'd give her something more. Maybe give his intentions away with his body language. But he sat casually, with his legs crossed and his arm resting against the back of the sofa. "You seem to have quite a bit invested in this," she said.

"I do." He nodded. "Not only all the fund-raising I've done, but have you forgotten about that million dollars?"

She inhaled. "No . . . but we didn't ask you to do that."

"Well, if I hadn't, we wouldn't be having this meeting, because Hosea wouldn't have had a chance of winning after that lie that you told."

"It wasn't a lie!"

He raised his eyebrows. "Oh? You got a million dollars in the bank?"

She stood, crossed her arms, and pressed her lips together.

He stood and moved close to her, but Jasmine didn't back up.

"I just want you to remember," he whispered, "why we're here. We've put a lot into getting your husband elected."

Jasmine frowned. Where had she heard those exact words?

"So, I need you to know," he continued, "that there will be no more tricks, no more fights . . . no more lies. Leave Rachel Adams alone, now. We'll take it from here—you stay out of it."

"So what are you saying? You want me to sit down and shut up like a good little first lady?" she asked sarcastically.

"Yes."

His response and his smirk surprised her.

She asked, "And who's this 'we' that you're talking about? I know it's not my husband or my father-in-law."

He leaned his head back and laughed. "Please, your husband and your father-in-law are the least important people in this."

His words were shocking, his tone sinister, almost threatening. But she shook only on the inside. Unless it was about her children, Jasmine showed no fear to any man.

"So, have I made myself clear?" he asked.

Jasmine stayed in place, not moving, not acknowledging his words at all.

He chuckled. "I'll take that as a yes," he said as he moved toward the door. He'd only taken a couple of steps away when Jasmine stopped him.

Grabbing her purse from the table, she said, "No, we're not finished . . . not yet." She hadn't even bothered to put the money that he'd given her into her wallet; instead, she'd stuffed the bills into a side pocket.

Pulling them out now, she slapped the money into the palm of his hand. "This is what you gave me yesterday—less fifty dollars for the cab." She paused. "*Now* we're finished because you need to understand that my husband and I can't . . . be . . . bought."

Looking down at the money, he chuckled again before he tucked the bills into his jacket. "Can't be bought?" He shook his head as if her words were pathetic. "Lady Jasmine, haven't you been bought already?"

He strutted toward the door, and without turning back, he left her alone.

She stood frozen, his last words more shocking than everything he'd said before. In her mind, she replayed their conversation and she wondered which part had spooked her more.

And then it hit her!

What Pastor Griffith had said. *We've put a lot into getting your husband elected.*

She *had* heard that before.

This morning.

Mae Frances had told her the exact same thing, had used the exact same words.

Mae Frances, her best friend.

And now, Jasmine trembled more.

Chapter
TWENTY-FIVE

I really have to go shopping." Rachel glanced at the assortment of suits she'd laid out across their king-size bed. They were getting ready for the official nominating ceremony and the outfit Rachel had planned to wear just didn't seem fitting. She had splurged on a few suits at Macy's, shelling out almost two hundred dollars each. Yet none of them seemed as if they could hold up against Cecelia King or Jasmine Bush. Rachel wished that she had enough time to run over to the mall to find another suit to wear today. But not only was there not enough time, truthfully, she couldn't see paying five or six hundred dollars for an outfit anyway.

No, she'd have to make do with what she had. Rachel had just decided on a peach Tahari number when her cell phone rang. She smiled when she saw her brother's name pop up. Jonathan was five years older than her, yet they were still very close. Yes, like everyone else, she'd been shocked when he revealed that he was gay. Actually, he didn't reveal it—his boyfriend popped up at their mother's funeral, demanding to be acknowledged, and Jonathan had no choice but to come out of the closet. But when all was said and done, Rachel decided that Jonathan was still her brother and she'd love him no matter what. He could answer to God on the whole homosexual thing, but it wasn't her place to judge.

"Hey, Big Brother," she said, answering the phone.

"Hey, Little Sister. Are you okay? Dad told me about you getting arrested."

Rachel shook her head. She didn't want to get upset today, so she wasn't about to discuss that experience. "I'm fine. That was all a big misunderstanding. I'll fill you in on all the details later. I thought you were calling to congratulate me," she said, trying to change the subject.

"Congratulate?" He laughed. "Girl, the election isn't until later this week."

"I know, but you know we're gonna win."

"Then I would need to be congratulating my brother-in-law."

"I'm going to be the first lady, so I need to be congratulated as well."

"Man, I wish Mama was alive to see this. She wouldn't believe it," he said nostalgically.

"I barely believe it and I live it every day. But things change, people change," she said, laying out the jewelry she was going to wear with her outfit.

"Well, if I haven't told you, I'm proud of you."

"Thanks. How's my nephew?"

"Chase is fine. He's with Angela. I go pick him up this weekend." Chase was the son Jonathan had had with his high school sweetheart, back when he was in denial about his sexuality. He'd married Angela after graduating from college. She'd found out he was on the down-low and naturally had gone ballistic. But thankfully, they'd made peace for the sake of Chase, who was now nine years old.

"Who's that in the background?" Rachel asked when she heard a male voice calling out to Jonathan.

"That's Gerald. He's over here helping me pack."

Gerald was her brother's partner. Rachel didn't know a whole lot about him, except that he made her brother happy. Jonathan didn't like discussing his sexuality, so over the years they'd reached a comfortable place of nondiscussion.

"Pack for what?" Rachel dug in her suitcase and pulled out her BCBG pumps. Maybe if she accessorized her outfit, it would add to the classiness of it all.

"Our flight tomorrow," he said, like it was obvious.

"Where are you going?"

"Ummm . . . we're coming there."

Rachel's mouth dropped open as she froze, and her shoes fell out of her hand onto the floor.

"You're . . . coming to LA?"

"Yeah, our flight gets in at six twenty." He sounded confused.

"Ou . . . our?" she stammered.

Jonathan was quiet, then he slowly said, "Umm, yeah . . . You're the one told me to come."

"What?" It was her turn to be confused.

"You sent me a text, telling me you really wanted me and Gerald there for the election."

Rachel was speechless. As much as she loved her brother, there was no way in the world she'd ask him to show up at the American Baptist Coalition Conference with his *boyfriend*. She might've been understanding, but the members wouldn't be, and that would all but guarantee that Lester would lose this election.

"Jonathan, I didn't send a text."

"What?"

"I didn't send you a text," she repeated.

"Hold on." It sounded like he was fumbling with the phone. "Here it is right here. It's from your number. It says, 'Hey you, I know you are busy but Lester and I really would love to have you and Gerald here.' It was sent day before yesterday."

"I didn't send that," Rachel repeated.

"Well, if you didn't send it, who did?"

"I don't have a clue who—" She stopped. Only one person would do something that dirty. But how in the world had Jasmine gotten access to Rachel's phone? And how did she even know about Jonathan and Gerald? *The same way you know all of her business,* Rachel told herself. This witch was digging up dirt on her, too.

"Rachel, what's going on?" Jonathan said, snapping her back to the conversation.

"I didn't send the text. I don't know who would send it or why." She didn't want to tell him what was going on because

Jonathan was protective of her, and he would definitely be on the first flight out of Houston.

"So, you don't want me to come there?" he asked

"No!" Rachel said, too quickly, but then corrected herself. "I . . . I mean, I know you have to work."

She hated being like that with her brother, but Jonathan didn't deserve the wrath of people like Jasmine or any of the other holier-than-thou members of the ABC.

"Ohhhh," Jonathan said, realization setting in. "Look, sis, don't even sweat it."

Rachel could tell by the change in Jonathan's voice that he knew exactly why she didn't want him there.

"Jonathan—"

"Seriously, it's all good, really. It's like you said, I have to work. Not to mention that these last-minute tickets to LA were going to be an arm and a leg anyway."

The fact that he was willing to pay it just because he thought she wanted him there tugged at Rachel's heart.

"I'm sorry, Jon. I mean, you know, if *you* want to come, you can come." She made sure to stress the "you" part. She wanted to let her brother know that while he was welcome, bringing Gerald wouldn't be such a good idea.

Jonathan let out a small chuckle. "Don't worry about it. You know how I feel about church folk anyway." She knew that all too well. Some church folk had led a campaign to get him to "pray the gay away," so he now tended to stay away from church and worshipped in his own way.

"Besides," he continued, "I don't know what I was thinking anyway. You know it would kill your daddy for me to show up there with Gerald. So enjoy yourselves, and call me after the election and tell me how bad Lester beat that Rev. Bush."

That made her smile—and feel even worse. "I'm sorry, Jon."

"Don't be. Seriously, it's no big deal. You know I'm used to this kind of stuff."

"I love you, thanks for understanding," she said.

"I love you, too. Tell Lester good luck."

He hung up the phone and Rachel felt a mixture of sadness and relief. Then anger. Jasmine had tried to bring her down, but once again she'd dodged the bullet.

"Who was that?" Lester said, walking into the room.

Rachel shook off her budding anger and turned to her husband. "Jonathan. He was just calling to wish us luck."

"Oh." Lester held up a tie in each hand. "Which one?"

Rachel took both ties and held them up under her husband's neck. "Hmmm, Donald Trump or Sean John?"

She cocked her head to the side and studied both ties. Lester already looked amazing in his navy double-breasted suit and crisp white shirt. But she couldn't decide which tie would be the icing on the cake.

"I like this one," Lester said, pointing at the mustard-colored Sean John tie. Rachel frowned. Both men were rich, but Donald Trump was much more powerful and that's the look Rachel was going for, so she tossed the mustard tie and began tying the baby blue Trump tie around Lester's neck.

"Or maybe I'll just wear this one," he joked.

"There," Rachel said, tightening the knot. "Now you look presidential."

"Are you sure I look okay?" Lester asked, turning around to survey himself in the mirror.

"You look better than okay," Rachel said reassuringly. She stepped up behind him and smiled at their reflection. "You know I wouldn't let you go out of here looking anything less than spectacular."

He turned around and kissed her passionately. "Thank you, sweetheart. For everything."

"Hey, don't start nothing you can't finish." She laughed. They'd just finished an hour-long lovemaking session before Jonathan's phone call. Rachel hadn't really been in the mood for sex, but she'd had to literally seduce Lester to get his mind off the whole debacle of Jacqueline's disappearance. Needless to say, he hadn't been happy when Rachel returned to the room and filled him in on everything. And he'd been skeptical of her claim that she never intended to scare Jasmine. Tired of arguing, Rachel had used her womanly wiles, touching her husband in the places she knew he liked to be touched. Before she knew it, they were doing the passion dance all over the hotel suite.

Now Lester was clean, energized, and ready to receive his formal nomination.

"You think you can get dressed today?" he said, motioning toward her body.

"Yes, I had to get the kids situated," she said. "They're watching movies out front. The hotel babysitter is with them and she's making sure they stay out of trouble."

"Maybe we need her to come babysit you to make sure you stay out of trouble," he said with a sly smile.

"Haha, you got jokes." She stepped into her suit and headed toward the bathroom. "Now let me finish getting dressed so we can go claim our crown."

Chapter
TWENTY-SIX

Chatter filled the ballroom as they entered. Rachel wondered if folks were gossiping about all that had gone on between her and Jasmine. She shook off that thought. Today was all about Lester's formal nomination. After finding out about that text to Jonathan, as far as Rachel was concerned, she and Jasmine were even—that is, unless that skank had something else up her sleeve.

"There's your dad and Brenda," Lester said, pointing to a reserved section at the front of the room. "They're with the other members of the South region."

Rachel held her head high as she followed her husband to the front. Jasmine, Hosea, and what seemed like a whole entourage were seated in the reserved section directly across from them. Rachel couldn't help but notice the evil eye Jasmine was shooting her, but Rachel did her best to ignore her. Whatever she did, she was not going to let Jasmine ruin this moment for her.

The Coalition chairman sat at a long table at the front of the room. Cecelia and Reverend King sat to his right. Rachel had just spoken to her family and a few other people when the chairman called the meeting to order. They went through some formalities before getting to the part that Rachel had been waiting for all week.

"At this time, we'd like to officially certify the candidates for the presidency of the American Baptist Coalition. South region, please have your representative come up," he said.

Deacon Tisdale walked to a microphone that had been placed at the front of the audience. "Yes, Mr. Chairman. Marcus

Tisdale, Greater Matthew Baptist Church, Houston, Texas. Regional treasurer," he said, introducing himself. "The South region is honored to officially nominate Rev. Lester Adams as our candidate for presidency of the American Baptist Coalition."

Everyone on their side of the room began clapping loudly.

The chairman waited a few seconds for the applause to die down, then said, "Are there any objections?" He paused. "Hearing none, Rev. Lester Adams is officially certified. North region, please send up your representative."

A tall, lanky man rose and walked to the microphone. "Henry Ruffin, Faith Cathedral, Brooklyn, New York. Regional parliamentarian. The North region is happy to officially nominate Pastor Hosea Bush as our candidate for presidency of the American Baptist Coalition."

"Are there any objections?" the chairman asked as Henry returned to his seat. "Hearing none, Pastor Hosea Bush is officially certified. At this time we will take any nominations from the floor."

Rachel raised an eyebrow. The floor? What was that about? Her confusion must've been written all over her face because Deacon Tisdale leaned in and whispered, "It's just a formality. The bylaws say we have to do that but there's never been any, so it should just take a minute."

"Are there are any nominations from the floor?" The chairman paused, then repeated his question. "Are there any nominations from the floor?"

Suddenly, Reverend King loudly cleared his voice as he stood. "Excuse me, I know this is unprecedented, but I would like to nominate . . ." The room grew deathly silent as he turned and smiled at Cecelia. ". . . my wife, Cecelia King, to succeed me as president."

The room erupted in chatter. Rachel's mouth fell open. Cecelia was running for president? Rachel glanced over at Jasmine, who looked just as shocked as she did. In fact, Jasmine's whole entourage looked floored. And that Pastor Griffith looked the most disturbed. He was snarling; you would've thought he was the one running, not Hosea.

"Can they do that?" Rachel whispered to Lester.

"I have no idea," Lester replied.

"Please, may we have order," the chairman said, banging his gavel. The room settled down, but it was obvious the news had stunned everyone. "Now, I know this is highly unusual, but it is well within our bylaws. So, are there any objections to adding Cecelia King to the ballot?"

"I object!" That came from the crazy old lady who was always with Jasmine. Hosea quickly pulled her back down in her seat and flashed an apologetic look at the chairman. Rachel was actually glad that old coot had said something or else she would've objected herself.

"On what grounds are you objecting?" the chairman asked.

"On the grounds that she can't just up and decide she wants to be in the race!" the woman quipped.

Hosea tried to quiet her. Jasmine, meanwhile, sat stunned.

Reverend King held up a hand to quiet the chatter. "I'm sorry—Mae Frances, isn't it?" he asked the old woman. "My wife meets all of the qualifications. She only needs signatures from one-third of the general body supporting her nomination." He held up a manila folder. "Which we have right here."

Rachel was dumbfounded. How in the world did they get signatures? *When* in the world did they get signatures?

"But since you're not even a member of the American Baptist Coalition," Reverend King continued, glaring at Mae Frances, "you're probably not aware of our bylaws."

"Hmph," Mae Frances replied, a scowl setting in across her face.

"And in accordance with our bylaws," Reverend King continued, turning back to the chairman, "any nominee from the floor is allowed five minutes to speak. So, Mr. Chairman, at this time, I would like to yield the floor to Lady Cecelia King."

The room erupted in applause as a smug Cecelia stood, then graciously made her way to the podium. Rachel glared at her from her seat, but Cecelia refused to make eye contact. Rachel was definitely slipping. She hadn't seen this one coming. She'd been so focused on Jasmine that Cecelia had broadsided her with the stealth of a night prowler.

"Good evening, my fellow members of our illustrious organization," Cecelia began. "As my darling husband just said, I have five minutes to present my case to you, but honestly, I don't need the entire five minutes. I just need enough time to tell you that this decision did not come lightly. In fact, Rev. King and I were all too prepared to turn over the reins to someone we hoped would be worthy of continuing all of the good work that we've done. Unfortunately, these past few days have shown us that the individuals slated to carry the torch were simply not the worthy candidates we'd hoped for."

Rachel frowned. Was this heifer saying her husband wasn't worthy?

"No disrespect to Rev. Adams or Rev. Bush," Cecelia continued, finally looking their way, "who are fine, upstanding men who have effectively led their respective churches. But leading the ABC requires not only effective leadership, but the ability to keep your own personal house in order." She finally turned and looked right at Rachel. "And with the shenanigans of Rachel Adams"—she paused, then looked over at Jasmine— "and Jasmine Bush, well, it's no secret that your personal houses are in shambles."

Rachel couldn't believe this woman. After all of the butt-kissing she'd been doing, Cecelia had the audacity to stand up there and talk about her like that?

"Honestly, I had no intention of running, but after watching the catfights, the bickering, the underhanded and devious behavior of these two women, I said, 'Is this really who we want representing the ABC?'" She used both hands to dramatically point at Rachel and Jasmine. Rachel wanted to sink into her seat as several people turned and looked at her with disgust.

"We know that while the man would've been the head"— she turned and smiled at her husband—"the woman would've been the heart of the organization. I, for one, know that we have worked too hard, put too much into the success of this organization, to have it defiled by imperfect pasts, secrets and lies, and a total disregard for the sanctity of fellowship. Rev. King and I prayed long and hard about this and God laid it on my heart to throw my name into the ring."

"I want to lay something else on her, all right," Rachel mumbled, right before Lester nudged her to be quiet.

"You all know me. You know my background, my history, my work ethic. You know that I can work with anyone." She again looked at Jasmine and Rachel pathetically as she shook her head. "And you know that I won't at any time embarrass you or bring any negative light to the goals and the mission of the American Baptist Coalition. I hope that I can count on your vote. But I know what God has for me, is for me."

Several people stood and clapped. Like Rachel, Jasmine sat with her arms folded, glaring at Cecelia.

"Well, thank you, Lady Cecelia," the chairman said. "If there are no other objections, we'll officially certify Cecelia King as the write-in candidate for the ABC presidency."

Cecelia smiled and waved at the crowd like she'd already won the position. Rachel couldn't believe what she was seeing. Was Cecelia really that disgusted with Rachel and Jasmine that she didn't want either of their husbands to win? Or maybe this was something she'd been planning all along. Maybe she'd fully intended to run from the jump, but had just sat back and let Rachel and Jasmine cancel each other out. Rachel didn't know what to think. The only thing she did know was that she wouldn't rest until she figured out just what kind of game Cecelia King was playing, and then come up with a way to beat her at it.

Chapter
TWENTY-SEVEN

Everyone was talking, one over the other, as the Bush entourage packed into their hotel suite.

"I cannot believe this." Pastor Griffith had not stopped pacing for the entire ten minutes since they'd all rushed away from the pandemonium that had broken out from Cecelia's announcement.

Once the nominations were closed and the meeting was adjourned, the masses had charged to the front, almost stomping over Hosea and shoving past Lester to get to Cecelia and Reverend King.

Pastor Griffith had directed the Bush group to leave—and once again, they all escaped through the side door. Now here they sat—or paced—trying to digest this news.

Jasmine sat on the couch, between her husband and her father-in-law, still stunned as much as everyone else by the events of the meeting.

Cecelia King. It was a shocking but brilliant move, Jasmine had to admit. This was something that she would've done. And that's exactly why she should've seen it coming.

Jasmine knew never to trust any woman; that had been her life's mantra. But she'd been so busy trying to swat that fly-faced Rachel away that she'd been distracted, and now Cecelia was trying to step into what was supposed to be Jasmine's rightful place.

"What are you going to do about this?" The sharp tone of Mae Frances's voice brought Jasmine back into the hotel room. "You've got to do something."

"Don't you think that's what we're all working on?" Pastor Griffith snapped. He waved his hands toward the others in the room. Five men were pacing, just as he'd been doing, each one with a cell phone pressed to his ear. "Cecelia cannot do this; we have got to get Hosea elected."

Jasmine had no idea who the men were talking to, or what kind of deals they were trying to make, but they weren't her concern right now. Her eyes were on Mae Frances, her friend, and Pastor Griffith—the man who was beginning to feel more and more like an enemy. Both of them were operating like high-octane gas was pumping through their veins. Both were overly excited. Both were overly agitated. Like it was their election that was on the line.

Jasmine squinted as if that would help her see them better. Were Pastor Griffith and Mae Frances in cahoots? Did they have some kind of partnership that no one else knew about? And if they did, what did that mean for Hosea?

"I guess no one saw this coming," Reverend Bush said. But his voice was so gentle, so soothing, that Jasmine was sure her father-in-law was trying to diffuse some of the tension that had thickened the air.

"No," Pastor Griffith barked. "No one saw this because Cecelia never planned to do this. I know her and her husband well. This was not supposed to happen." He stopped moving long enough to stare Jasmine down. "But she had to step in because of what's been going on, and now this is what we're up against."

As Jasmine glared back at the pastor, Hosea reached for her hand. But she didn't need Hosea's protection on this. She hadn't done a thing wrong and she wasn't going to take the blame for Cecelia King's actions. Everything that she'd done, she'd done to help Hosea win. Everything she'd done had been effective—including the million-dollar gift that she'd given to the Coalition. And just about everything she'd done had been passed by Pastor Griffith, so why was he blaming her now?

And if he was talking about what she'd done to Rachel this morning, well, the truth was she hadn't beat down Rachel enough. There wasn't a woman on earth who wouldn't have taken that skeezer out and Jasmine's only regret was that Rachel had gotten up.

No, not a bit of this was her fault. Pastor Griffith could try to blame her if he wanted to, but they all needed to see what she saw. Cecelia and her husband had probably had this planned from day one. Jasmine was a world-champion schemer, and it took one to know one.

Two of the men stopped pacing and clicked off their cells almost at the same time.

"Okay." It was Pastor Penn who spoke first. "This looks like it can be saved. It's gonna be tough, but we can still win. Right now, Cecelia has the lead," he continued, "because the folks who want King out are evenly split between Adams and Hosea." Pastor Penn stopped and glanced over to the couch and Jasmine couldn't help but smile at the man.

Here Reverend Penn was, working so hard at getting the man who'd been nominated instead of him elected. Even his wife, Coco, had been cordial, and even sometimes sweet since they'd arrived in Los Angeles. Jasmine had been totally wrong about those two. The distrust she had for the Penns had been misplaced and should have been on the Kings the whole time.

Henry Ruffin, who had just officially nominated Hosea, said, "So, the fact is that the Adams people are going to be Adams's people. I don't think we should spend too much time going after them. But some of Hosea's folks did go with Cecelia. If we got half of them back, we'd win the election."

"So how do we do that?" Mae Frances asked, as if she were one of the boys.

As the men discussed strategy—everything from using scripture to denounce a woman running for the presidency to promoting the idea that Cecelia was really just a cover for her husband to keep his position—Jasmine sat back and massaged her temples.

Becoming first lady of the world was not as easy as she thought it was going to be. But still, she had faith. Not only was Hosea truly the best man for the job, she was the best one to be first lady. What were they going to do if Cecelia won the election— make Reverend King the first . . . what? The first man? And then there was Rachel as the first lady. Please! After really getting to know her, calling her ghetto would be insulting to all the people in the world who really were ghetto. Rachel was nothing more than a slut-bucket who had found a small-time country preacher, and then married up. Who would really want her as the face of the American Baptist Coalition? If the Adamses won, Jasmine was sure that the Coalition would lose half of its membership.

No, that was not going to happen. Jasmine had no doubt that once the votes were counted, Hosea Bush and his wife would be the new king and queen.

"Okay," Pastor Griffith growled to the men in the room. "We know what we have to do. Let's go hit the lobby. Start talking up Hosea to some of King's people." He looked down at Jasmine. "You better hope that we can still pull this out."

Jasmine's eyes got wide, but before she could stand so that she could tell him what she *really* hoped, Hosea jumped right up.

"Excuse me?" Hosea said, planting himself in front of Pastor Griffith. "That's my wife you're talking to." His voice was low, steady, and threatening.

"I know who she is." Pastor Griffith glared back at him. "And like I said, she better hope we can salvage this election."

Jasmine was ready to pounce, ready to stand by her man, but Reverend Bush put his hand on her shoulder, motioning her to stay seated. Instead, he stood next to his son.

The room was silent; no one dared to move. The tension was now off the Richter scale.

Mae Frances took a few steps toward the three men, but Reverend Bush held up his hand, stopping her. He spoke to Pastor Griffith. "Earl, I know you've worked hard and we all appreciate it, but let's keep this in perspective."

"I have the right perspective," he shouted. "Do you know what I have riding on this?"

Reverend Bush said, "I think it's the same thing that we all have riding, Earl. You're no different than the rest of us in here who have worked long hours, who have worked hard and want to win."

Reverend Bush's tone was soft, meant to calm, but it seemed to do little for Pastor Griffith. His eyes shifted between Hosea and his father as if he was trying to determine which one he wanted to take on.

Jasmine wondered if Pastor Griffith was really that much of a fool. Hadn't he heard about her husband? The gun-wielding pastor who'd been on trial for attempted murder because some man had dared to kidnap and abuse his daughter? The thing was, Hosea had no remorse—he would have gladly spent the rest of his days behind bars. Because it was all about family—his family, that he'd do anything to protect.

That included his wife.

Jasmine wasn't sure if it was the way Hosea stared Pastor Griffith down or the way Hosea started to shove off his jacket as if he didn't want to mess up his thousand-dollar suit. But Pastor Griffith finally took two steps back, shrugged his shoulders a couple of times as if he was loosening up . . . and then, he smiled.

"You're right, Samuel," he said to Reverend Bush. "It's just that we've all worked hard on this." Looking back at Hosea, he said, "I've worked hard to get you elected because I believe you're the right man for the job."

"And I appreciate that," Hosea said, though his voice was still hard. "But no one is going to disrespect my wife no matter who they are or what they've done."

Pastor Griffith nodded slightly, then glanced around Hosea to look at Jasmine. "I apologize, Lady Jasmine."

She nodded.

Then Hosea, being the gentleman that he always was, reached toward Pastor Griffith. The men shook hands and Reverend Bush patted both of them on their backs.

Jasmine watched her husband, his hand still in Pastor Griffith's hand, the two men nodding and smiling together.

Conflict diffused.

But though the tension began to seep out slowly, this little peace treaty did nothing for Jasmine. She still eyed Pastor Griffith with nothing but suspicion.

Then across the room, Mae Frances laughed.

Never trust any woman.

But Mae Frances wasn't just any woman . . . Mae Frances was her friend, right?

Jasmine wasn't sure anymore, but it was hard for her to believe that her friend had actually joined the ranks of her enemies. She didn't know how, but Jasmine had a feeling that she would soon find out whose side Mae Frances was really on.

Chapter
TWENTY-EIGHT

Rachel had never seen her father look so intense. He rubbed his salt-and-pepper beard and she could tell he was deep in thought.

"Dad, you don't need to get worked up about any of this," Rachel said. Although he'd been doing better healthwise, she didn't like seeing him stress out about anything. "I don't know why your doctor even let you come."

Reverend Simon Jackson shook his head. "I'm fine. I just don't have a good feeling about this," he said. "I know the Kings. They don't make impromptu decisions. They're up to something."

"Tell me about it," Rachel replied. She didn't know what their motives were, but the whole way this thing had gone down stunk and she knew the Kings had a plan up their sleeves.

They were gathered in her father's hotel suite. It looked like the entire Southern coalition was there. Her father, Lester, Deacon Tisdale, and several other men were seated around the long dining table.

"Did anyone see this coming?" one of the men asked.

"Not at all," Lester replied. He'd tried to play it cool for most of the week, but the look of shock on his face right now let Rachel know that he really wanted to win, and Cecelia might have just blown his chances.

"Personally, I just think it's a front so that Rev. King can keep running things." That declaration came from Deacon Tisdale. Rachel didn't know if she quite agreed with that, but she did believe this whole thing had been set up from the beginning.

Cecelia had tried to act like she just made this spur-of-the-moment decision because of her and Jasmine's fighting. If it bothered Cecelia that much, she would've pulled them aside prior to today. After all, she was there most of the time they had any kind of drama jump-off.

"So, what are we going to do?" Lester asked.

Simon shook his head. His brow was scrunched up, a nervous habit when he was trying to work things out in his head. "Well, I talked to someone on the board right after the meeting and he said the Kings gathered up signatures a couple of hours before the meeting. And he thinks they stand a good chance of giving us a run for our money. They could steal the undecided votes that were going to go to either Lester or Hosea. Couple those with any votes they get from the two sides, and they actually could win this thing."

Rachel stood up. She'd had enough of this strategizing and analyzing. Nobody here had any answers and she was the type of person who didn't believe in just sitting around talking. She wanted answers and she knew just where she could get them—straight from the source.

Rachel racked her brain trying to remember what Cecelia had said her room number was when she'd told Rachel to call. Then it hit her. Sixteen hundred! Like the White House's address. That had been Rachel's first thought when Cecelia mentioned it.

"I'll be back," Rachel announced. Yeah, she could call, but she wasn't going to give Cecelia a chance to hang up on her. She was going to march right up to Cecelia's room and ask her what kind of game she was playing. Rachel had tried to play nice and stay in that woman's good graces and it had all been for naught, so now what did she have to lose?

"Where are you going?" Lester asked.

"Gotta make a run. I'll be right back."

Lester just nodded and turned back to the men at the table.

Rachel stepped off the elevator on the executive level. Suite 1600 sat at the end of the hall. There was a housekeeping cart in front of the room. The door opened, and a petite dark-haired woman grabbed some more towels from the cart, then walked back inside.

Cecelia must not be in the room, Rachel thought. Surely housekeeping wouldn't be cleaning if she was. Rachel waited a minute, trying to decide her next move, when the door opened again. The woman made eye contact with Rachel, so she spoke.

"Good afternoon."

"Bueno," the woman said.

"Umm, I'm looking for Cecelia."

The woman grinned widely as she nodded. *"Sí."*

"See what?" Rachel asked, confused. "Is she in there?"

The woman just nodded like she had no idea what Rachel was saying.

Rachel narrowed her eyes at the woman. "Do you speak English?"

"Inglés?" the woman said, shaking her head. "Ah, no *inglés.*"

Rachel exhaled in frustration when the woman said, *"He terminado ahora."*

"Excuse me?" Rachel said.

The woman stepped aside and moved the cart out of the way. "All done," the woman said in broken English as she held the door open.

Rachel stood for a moment, unsure of what to do. She didn't want to break into Cecelia's room. But technically, this wasn't breaking in. The cleaning lady was inviting her in. Maybe this was God's way of opening the door so she could get to the bottom of what was going on. But what would she be looking for in Cecelia's room?

Answers.

That little nagging voice that always got her in trouble grew louder. *Just get in, look around, see what you can find, then get out. Five minutes.*

But if she got caught in there, it would be all over. Cecelia would hang her. Lester would kill her. And Jasmine would have a field day.

You won't get caught. Five minutes.

Rachel found herself smiling at the woman as she said, "*Gracias*. I'm very tired and want to lie down."

The woman nodded, that I-have-no-idea-what-you're-saying grin still on her face as she moved aside and let Rachel pass.

The door slammed and Rachel jumped. Her heart was racing. What in the world was she doing?

You're fighting back. You're not going to let this woman play you. You're not stealing anything, so it's okay. You're just looking for answers.

Rachel took a deep breath, then looked around the suite. It was definitely fit for a president. The chocolate furniture was modern and classy. There was a fifty-two-inch television screen on the wall with a brick fireplace underneath. A plush copper-colored rug sat in the middle of the floor, a long mahogany dining table sat in the corner. The place was immaculate, with the exception of some papers on the marble bar. Rachel wanted to duck in and check out Cecelia's clothes, but she reminded herself that she didn't have time for that.

She headed over to the bar and started sifting through the papers. They were definitely Coalition-related, but it all looked like a bunch of gibberish to Rachel. Rachel had just flipped to the third page when she heard Cecelia's high-pitched laugh, then a fumbling at the door.

Rachel panicked as her eyes darted across the room. Her first instinct was to hide in the bathroom, but what if Cecelia had to use it? Without much time to think, she ducked into the hall closet and began a silent prayer.

Please, God. Don't let me get caught. I'm sorry I came in here. If You get me out of here, I'll never do anything like this again.

The door opened and Cecelia came in, chatting with someone. Rachel kept praying. What if they were in the room to stay? What would she do then?

"I just can't get over you," the other voice said. "That was simply priceless." Rachel recognized the voice, but she couldn't place where she'd heard it.

Cecelia laughed again. "I told you, just let me handle it. And to think my darling husband doubted that I could do it. But we are poised, once again, to merge with the National Baptist Coalition, which will make us the most powerful religious organization in the world next to the Catholic Church. And I plan to be at the helm when that merger happens."

"Well, it didn't hurt that you had those two psychopaths ready to go to war. They're all but ensuring you win this thing."

"Amen to that," Cecelia replied. "I mean, really, they did all the work. By the way, thanks for passing that information about Jasmine on to Rachel."

It was the other woman's turn to laugh. "Oh, you did all of the work, but it was my pleasure to be the messenger."

Rachel's mouth dropped open. So it *was* a plan. And she and Jasmine had played right into it. And what information had the woman passed on to her?

"But, I swear, my husband wanted to use the information to bring Pastor Bush down," the woman continued. "You know he should've been the Northern nominee."

"Well, Coco, I'm glad that you convinced Rev. Penn that we had to let it play out this way. I appreciate both of you coming to me and offering your assistance. I have to admit, I was a little hesitant about sharing my plan," Cecelia said. "This is a big deal because the bishop and I had been working with Earl on this merger for a long time, but it fell through before."

Earl? Who's Earl? Rachel asked herself.

Cecelia continued like she was in confessional, "But this time, the bishop and I cut out all the other folks and put this together ourselves, and we weren't sure who we could trust. But I'm a good read of people, and something told me I could trust you. And I was smart enough to know I couldn't do this alone."

"You can always trust us," Coco said.

"I know that. And you let Rev. Penn know I will keep my promise to find him a great position once I'm elected."

That's who the voice belonged to! Coco Penn had been the woman who had given Rachel the information on Jasmine being a stripper. Coco acted like she was just a concerned Coalition member wanting to help Lester get elected, and Rachel had fallen for the whole act—no questions asked.

"I just wished you could've gotten Rachel's brother to waltz up in here with his gay lover." Cecelia released a hearty laugh. "That would've been hilarious. Can you imagine the looks on our members' faces?"

Coco laughed with her. "I know, right? To have him call while I was trying to reach Alize was divine intervention. Thanks to your dossier, I knew all the players in this game."

"I'm just glad you were smart enough to think to send that text."

Rachel was livid. Coco had been the one to send the text to Jonathan? All so Cecelia could humiliate Rachel's family? And now they were sitting here bragging like it was some kind of lovefest? She couldn't believe she'd been played for a fool. Both she and Jasmine had.

Jasmine.

As much as Rachel despised her, Jasmine needed to know what was going on. Sure, Rachel could try to work this out on her own, but the vote was in two days. She had to come up with a plan, figure out a way to bring Cecelia down. And right about now, Jasmine was the only person who could help her make that happen.

Rachel wanted to win this election more than anything she'd ever wanted in her life. But after what she just heard, if she had to lose, she definitely didn't want to lose to Cecelia King's crooked behind. And if that meant swallowing her pride and working with Jasmine, well, she'd just have to do that.

She just had to figure out how to get out of this damn closet first.

Peace and quiet. That's what Jasmine craved. And that was the only reason why she hadn't yet left the suite to go see her children. She knew they were safe—locked behind the doors of their hotel room. She'd finally calmed down enough to know in her heart that Jacqueline had not been kidnapped. Evil had not barged into their lives again . . . just stupidity . . . and silly games . . . and Rachel Adams.

But as much as she still fumed about Rachel taking Jacqueline, her mind was now more consumed with thoughts of Pastor Griffith . . . and Mae Frances.

Standing at the floor-to-ceiling windows that gave her a royal view of downtown Los Angeles, Jasmine replayed every word, every gesture, every conversation she'd had with Pastor Griffith. Clearly, this wasn't an ordinary election for him. He acted as if he expected a far greater reward than just the pride of having his candidate elected as the first Northern pastor of the Coalition in sixty years. What was he going to get out of this? Was he going to ask Hosea to appoint him to some high-powered position? No, it couldn't be that. If that's what he wanted, all he had to do was ask.

This was a mystery that she had to solve, that she had to figure out before Hosea laid his hand on the Bible and took the oath to uphold the principles of the Coalition as the new president.

A knock on the door banished those thoughts. Although she turned toward the double-door entryway, Jasmine stayed in place. Surely, the person on the other side was looking for

Hosea. And if she didn't answer, they would discover soon enough that he'd left for the emergency strategy meeting that Pastor Griffith had arranged. She'd just stay quiet so that she could have these few minutes of solitude.

But the person outside had other plans. The knock came again, more urgently this time, and with a sigh, Jasmine strolled toward the door. But when she opened it, her jaw just about hit the floor.

"I need to speak with you," Rachel said, breathing heavily, as if she'd just run a race.

So many thoughts flashed through Jasmine's mind. And the thought that was safest—for both her *and* Rachel—she put into action. Jasmine pushed the door, determined to close it, but Rachel set her body as a blockade, forcing Jasmine to just stand there.

"Please," Rachel said. "This is important." She glanced over her shoulder as if someone was following her.

"You have lost every single dang-gone brain cell that you've ever had if you think I'm going to let you in here."

"Trust and believe I don't want to be here either, but you need to hear what I have to say," Rachel hissed.

Jasmine shook her head. One thing she could say about this fool was that Rachel had guts. After what she'd pulled, she had the nerve to come to her suite, alone and unarmed.

Slowly, Jasmine's lips spread into a sly smile. If Rachel wanted to come in, she'd let her in. It was Rachel's choice, it would be Rachel's funeral.

She stepped aside, so that Rachel could enter, closed the door, then with an extra flourish made sure that Rachel noticed that she'd locked the door behind her.

"Are we alone?" Rachel asked as she took a quick glance around the suite. But then she paused and let her eyes wander around again, slower this time. "This is just like Cecelia's room," she whispered when her eyes rested on the flat-panel TV.

Jasmine folded her arms. "Yes, she's right next door. Remember the day we arrived and Cecelia got me this room because you canceled my reservations?"

Rachel hesitated a little too long before she protested, "I didn't do that."

Jasmine held up her hand. "Spare me. Just tell me what you want. And while you're at it, tell me why I shouldn't beat you down again for what you did to me and my daughter."

Rachel took a step back as if she wasn't about to let Jasmine land another surprise right hook. "Look," she said, "I know you don't like me—"

Jasmine laughed. "Can you spell 'understatement'?"

"And I don't like you either," Rachel said, ignoring Jasmine's sarcasm. "But you need to know that you and I have been played big-time. Cecelia set us up."

The smirk faded from Jasmine's face. "What are you talking about?"

Rachel looked toward the couch as if she wanted the two of them to sit down and talk, but when she glanced back at Jasmine, she knew that wasn't going to happen. She was just going to have to bring Jasmine the facts standing up.

Rachel blew out a short breath. "I just overheard Cecelia talking to Coco Penn."

Coco Penn? Reverend Penn's porn-star wife? Why would Coco be talking to Cecelia?

Rachel continued, "Besides calling us psychopaths, she arranged this entire week. She set up everything so that we'd look bad and she'd come out smelling like the new president!"

Jasmine twisted her lips, absolutely sure that this was just another trick by this trick. But for what? What was Rachel really up to?

"Okay, you don't believe me," Rachel said. "Well, see if you think I made this up." She recounted for Jasmine everything she heard, word for word.

Sometimes, Jasmine's eyes narrowed, and then a moment later, they'd widen. Rachel just talked, not pausing, not even, it seemed, to take a breath.

"So, that's it," Rachel said, finishing up. "She knew we would fight it out, then split the vote. She planned it all."

"And she planned for you to take my child?"

Not even a second passed and Rachel responded, "Did she plan for you to set me up for shoplifting?"

It was the "touché" that Rachel saw in Jasmine's eyes that let her know that at least Jasmine had heard her, at least Jasmine believed her, but she wanted it to really sink in. "Think about it. Every time something jumped off between us, Cecelia was always there, right?"

Jasmine thought for a moment, then nodded.

Rachel said, "And really, when you look back, she never tried to smooth things over with us. She just kept jumping from your side to my side, then back to your side, adding fuel to the fire." She paused, giving Jasmine more time to think about it. "She wanted us to fight."

Jasmine shook her head slightly as if she was remembering it all. "Wow!"

"We've got to do something about this," Rachel implored. "The two of us . . . we need to get her back."

Slowly, Jasmine sauntered to the sofa. She sat down, and clasped her hands together—as if she was in deep thought or deep prayer. After a few moments, Rachel joined her on the couch.

"So, where did you overhear all of this?"

Rachel blinked. "I overheard, you know, them. Downstairs, you know, in the restaurant."

Jasmine frowned; she'd told enough lies to know what Rachel's stuttering meant. "You need to tell me what's really going on or you can just walk right out that door."

Rachel took a breath. "Okay, I was in her room . . . and then, she came in with Coco . . . and then, I hid in the closet, and then I dashed out when they went outside on the balcony."

Jasmine shook her head, as if the thought of that was just ridiculous.

Rachel rolled her eyes. "Yeah, right. As if you haven't hidden in somebody's closet before."

The truth of those words jolted Jasmine a bit. How had this girl pegged her so right? Jasmine *had* found herself hiding in closets, underneath beds, behind couches . . . once, she'd even found herself in the trunk of some man's car. That's what happened when married men were your drug of choice. So she couldn't look down on Rachel, and somehow, Rachel knew that.

I guess it takes one to know one.

"So," Rachel began, "you can either sit here and judge me and Cecelia wins, or we can stop her from winning together."

"All right," Jasmine said, "though we don't have a lot of time to stop her. The election is——"

"The day after tomorrow," Rachel finished. "I know that, but I don't care. I'm not about to let Cecelia get away with what she's done to us."

"Okay, genius, what do you propose?"

Rachel sucked her teeth. "Look, if you're gonna be nasty about this, and keep calling me names, then we can just forget it and I'll do this all by myself." Rachel stood up. "I don't even know why I came to you. I should've just brought you *and* Cecelia down. Lester is gonna win anyway and——"

Would you just shut up? is what Jasmine said in her mind. But aloud, she apologized. "Okay, I'm sorry. I shouldn't have called you a genius. Forgive me."

Rachel's eyes narrowed. "That's right," she said as if she was the one who was now in control. "So, if you want to work with me, I'm cool, but I'm not about to sit here and be insulted."

Insulted? I just called you a genius, fool! Jasmine had no idea how she kept her laughter inside. "Whatever you say."

"Good! So, this is what I was thinking," Rachel began as she sat back down. "All we have to do is a little digging, find some stuff on Cecelia, and bring her down with it."

"How do you know we'll find anything?"

"Everybody has something that they don't want anyone else to know," Rachel said, as if she was remembering her own secrets about her family.

Jasmine nodded. "That's true. So, we're going to do this together, right?"

"Right!"

"To bring Cecelia down, right?"

"Right!"

"So that Hosea will win, right?"

"Hell, I mean, heck nah! I ain't making no deal like that."

So their feud hadn't ended. Rachel still wanted her husband to win. Well, that was never going to happen.

"What I mean," Jasmine started over, "is that we should just play it out . . . let whoever is going to win this, win it. We won't interfere in that process—between Hosea and Lester—at all."

Rachel shrugged. "That's how I wanted it to be all along."

Jasmine gave her a stop-lying sideways glance.

"What?" Rachel said. "You're the one who started it—leaving me out of the first ladies' meeting you had and then making me read that made-up bio . . ."

Jasmine chuckled. It was amazing to watch the brain of a goose at work. Rachel had totally forgotten how she'd canceled the limousine and the hotel room, and then had her daughter spill a cup of punch on Jacqueline so that Jasmine would have to leave the reception—and that was just the first day!

But Jasmine reminded Rachel of none of those things. They'd both taken shots, they'd both landed some great punches, though Jasmine knew that she was way ahead if points were to be given.

Still, if they were that good apart, how much damage could they do to Cecelia together? She would be the brains, Rachel would be her sidekick, they would make something happen.

"Okay, I'm in." Jasmine stood and extended her hand.

Rachel left her hanging at first, studying Jasmine's hand as if she wanted to make sure Jasmine wasn't hiding a snake up her sleeve.

After a couple of seconds, Rachel stood up and shook Jasmine's hand . . . right at the same moment as Hosea entered the suite.

"What's going on here?" Hosea said slowly as he stared at Jasmine and Rachel standing in the exact spot where he and Pastor Griffith had called their truce just a couple of hours before.

"Nothing, baby." Jasmine strutted to her husband and kissed his cheek. "Rachel just came by to——"

"To apologize," Rachel interjected. "I'm so sorry, Pastor Bush, for the misunderstanding with Jacqueline. Honestly, I would have never done anything to hurt her and she had a great time hanging out with Nia."

He smiled——a little. "Jacquie told us that. But"——he looked at his wife as if he couldn't believe this scene——"I'm glad you and Jasmine have worked it all out."

"Yup, we have," Jasmine said, and the two women pasted strained smiles on their faces.

Hosea looked from one to the other——as if he wasn't sure what to believe. But then, as if he'd decided that he preferred peace, he nodded.

"Thank you for coming by." Then, to Jasmine, he said, "I'm going into the bedroom to make a few calls."

"Okay, we're finishing up here."

He smiled again at Rachel before he left the two women alone.

"Are you going to say anything to him?" Rachel whispered.

"No." Jasmine shook her head. "Hosea believes that God should just work this whole thing out."

"Lester believes the same thing, girl," Rachel said, then snapped her mouth shut as she noticed her snafu. Did she just call Jasmine "girl," as in friend?

Naw! they both said to themselves. The two of them would never be friends.

To make sure that Rachel understood that, as she opened the door, Jasmine said, "Well, it looks like we're living proof that the enemy of my enemy is my friend."

Rachel frowned, as if Jasmine were speaking another language.

Jasmine just nodded her good-bye, not even thinking about explaining that old proverb to Rachel. As she closed the door behind the woman whose fingers she'd wanted to break when they'd shaken hands a minute ago, another cliché passed through her mind——keep your friends close, keep your enemies closer.

And that's exactly what she was going to do. Keep Rachel close. Keep Rachel close enough and busy enough that she wouldn't even realize what was going on.

Then, tomorrow night, she would make her move. She would bring Cecelia *and* Rachel down.

And Jasmine already knew exactly what she was going to do.

Chapter
THIRTY

Less than twenty-four hours ago, if someone had told Rachel Jackson Adams that she would be huddled at a table, in cahoots with her nemesis, she would've told them they were crazy.

That's why you should never say never.

Because not only was she working with that highfalutin skeezer, it had been her idea. But the one thing Rachel hated more than a conniving tramp was a backstabbing, conniving tramp. And Cecelia King was queen of the backstabbers.

At the end of the day, Rachel knew Lester could beat Hosea. Cecelia, on the other hand, might be a challenge. So at this point, it was the lesser of two evils. That's not to say Rachel wouldn't continue to take Jasmine down, but she could do that on her own. Taking Cecelia down was going to require some help.

"So, how'd you dig up all this stuff so fast?" Jasmine asked, flipping through the papers Rachel had laid in front of her. They were meeting in Jasmine's suite, something she'd been wary about, since it was right next to Cecelia's. But Jasmine had insisted it was the best way to avoid any interruptions.

"You just found out about Cecelia yesterday," Jasmine continued. She looked shocked at the sheer magnitude of what Rachel had dug up. There had to be at least two hundred pieces of paper.

"Let's just say I'm pretty resourceful." Rachel flashed a proud smile. "I know how to find out what I need."

A beat passed, Jasmine, no doubt, recalling all the dirt Rachel had dug up on her.

"So, why didn't you put those investigative talents to good use?" Jasmine asked snidely.

"I have," Rachel said, defensively pointing to the stack.

Jasmine shook her head as she flipped a piece of paper and scanned the page. "No, I mean like college or something," she said nonchalantly. "How someone can just be content with a high school diploma is beyond me."

No, this chick wasn't trying to take a dig at her. Rachel took a deep breath to keep herself from getting heated. She knew Jasmine had an MBA in finance but Rachel had a PhD in real life, so she wasn't impressed.

"If you must know, I did go to community college for a semester, it just wasn't for me. I had two kids, so it was hard to balance it, not to mention the fact that my family wasn't wealthy." She put her finger to her temple like she was thinking. "Oh, wait, neither was yours. That's why you took to the pole—" The way Jasmine was glaring at her stopped her midsentence. Rachel paused, then said, "I'm sorry. That was uncalled for." She hated apologizing to this woman, but they didn't have time to be fighting. So if that meant she'd have to be the bigger woman, she would be.

Rachel turned her attention back to the papers. "Let's just stay focused on our mission." She picked up a few sheets and started flipping. "I'm not even sure what all is here, but I pulled some stuff, then I had my private investigator, um, I mean my friend, pull up some stuff and fax it to me as well. I even had Melinda from the TV station run the Kings through this special database called LexisNexis, which compiles just about everything there is to know about someone. Government and investigative agencies use it a lot. I just figured we could go through everything and see if we can find anything we could use."

Jasmine turned up her nose as she scanned the papers. "Ummph, it looks like just a bunch of articles singing the praises of the Kings and all they've done for the ABC. What is that supposed to do?"

Rachel bit her bottom lip. She wanted to slap all of this

negativity out of this woman. They didn't have time for her to be shooting down everything Rachel was doing. She was such a hater, she couldn't even give Rachel props for all that she'd done so quickly.

"Yes, there are articles," Rachel said calmly, "but we don't know what all is in them. No one is that squeaky-clean, so there has to be something there. Plus, there's some background info on the Kings and a bunch of other stuff."

Jasmine looked like she wanted to say something sarcastic. Instead, she just said, "I still don't understand what we're supposed to do with all of this stuff. And even if we find anything, how are we gonna confirm it, then let everyone know by the election tomorrow?"

Rachel threw her papers down. This heffa was working her nerves. "Do you have a better idea? Because seems like to me you walked into this meeting empty-handed."

"Well, I . . . I made some calls, too," Jasmine stuttered.

Rachel leaned back in her seat and folded her arms across her chest. "Okay. What did you find out?"

"Well," she said slowly, "I'm waiting on some people to call me back."

Rachel let out a small laugh. The way Jasmine cut her eyes, Rachel could tell she didn't appreciate the humor of the moment. Rachel almost told this bootleg Barbara Bush about herself. She was trying to act like she was all that, but when it came down to it, she was as fake as that Yaki 1B ponytail on her head.

Still, with only one day left before the election, Rachel needed Jasmine, so she kept her thoughts to herself.

"Well, until your people call you back, this is all we have to go on," Rachel said, not bothering to hide the edge in her voice. She jabbed the papers. "My point in bringing all of this was so that we could go through it and hopefully find something we could use."

"Fine," Jasmine huffed, and started studying the paper in front of her.

They sat in silence, reading the documents for more than

twenty minutes. Then Rachel found something that struck her. She read it again and her mouth fell open.

"What?" Jasmine asked, noticing her expression.

"Look at this," Rachel said, turning a paper around for Jasmine to see. "The Kings quietly settled a civil lawsuit against an unnamed woman who charged that Cecelia had her beat up for having an affair with Rev. King."

"What?" Jasmine exclaimed.

"Dang," Rachel said, turning the page over, "it doesn't give any more details."

"I don't believe Cecelia would have someone beat up," Jasmine said.

"Did you believe she would smile in your face and stab you in your back?"

Jasmine looked pensive as Rachel continued, "Does Cecelia look like someone who would let you have an affair with her man and get away with it?"

"No, but—"

"But nothing. This is the ammunition we need." She waved the paper. "If Cecelia wasn't guilty, why in the world would she settle out of court? I know I've only known her a few days, but I do know she wouldn't take this all the way to court if there wasn't some truth to it. We just let everybody know about this, and bam, she can hang up her chances."

"No," Jasmine protested. "First of all, they can say they settled to avoid a costly trial or something like that, and they end up looking like the victim. Secondly . . . The. Election. Is. Tomorrow."

Rachel let out a frustrated sigh. She hated to admit that Jasmine was right. The lawsuit wasn't an angle they had time to explore and there were so many ways the Kings could wiggle out of that one. Plus, revealing this would just seem like more dirt-digging, and that could backfire on them.

"So what do you suggest?" Rachel asked.

"I don't know," Jasmine replied. "But I'm starting to wonder if there's even anything to be found."

This was getting ridiculous. Rachel leaned forward on the table. "Jasmine, let's keep it real, we don't particularly care for each other."

"That's the understatement of the year," Jasmine mumbled.

Rachel ignored her and continued talking. "But think of the things you did to try and sabotage me."

Jasmine raised an eyebrow.

"Okay, the things *we* did to sabotage each other," Rachel admitted. "But if we'll go to such lengths for a position we *want,* imagine what Cecelia would do to hang on to something she *has.*"

Jasmine looked doubtful. "Okay, I'll give you that because I don't really trust *any* woman," she said, emphasizing "any." Rachel wanted to tell her that the feeling was mutual but she let Jasmine continue talking.

"But if Cecelia had this planned all along, we need to find out why. My instinct tells me there's something more to this story," Jasmine said.

That's because a liar knows a liar, Rachel wanted to say. Instead, she said, "I've been going through these papers all night. And I haven't been able to find anything we can use. I mean, I thought this merger information was something, but it turned out to be nothing."

"What merger information?"

"You know I told you she was talking about merging with the National Baptist Coalition." Rachel had shared that bit of information with Jasmine, but she had been so focused on Cecelia's backstabbing that she hadn't thought much about it.

Rachel dug through the papers until she found the one she was looking for. She slid it across the table to Jasmine. "This. Apparently, Reverend King and two other men—a Pastor Griffith, and Reverend Lyons—were working a deal to merge the ABC with the National Baptist Coalition. I don't know what that means, but since Cecelia mentioned it, this caught my attention."

A look Rachel couldn't make out passed across Jasmine's face.

"You think that's something?" Rachel asked.

Jasmine just kept staring at the paper.

"I mean, I know the two groups have this big rivalry, so it's surprising that they would agree to come together," Rachel continued. "So between that, Cecelia talking about it, and both Lester not knowing anything about a merger, and they're real active in the ABC, I thought there might be something to this. Now that I think about it, my dad said it sounded like a secret deal." She stopped talking because Jasmine hadn't taken her eyes off the paper. "Jasmine?"

"Oh," Jasmine said, shaking out of her trance, "there may be something to this."

"The more I think about it, the more I think there is. The National Baptist Coalition isn't as big as our group, but it's still huge and they have some major political clout."

"And if the two groups merge, the result would be phenomenal."

"Making the ABC even more powerful than it already is?" Rachel added.

"Exactly," Jasmine said.

Rachel's eyes danced as images of being an even more powerful first lady filled her head.

"That has to be why Cecelia wants this," Rachel muttered.

"I'm sure it is," Jasmine replied, sounding more and more sure. "And I'll bet she wants to keep the merger news under wraps until she's elected."

"She won't be elected," Rachel quickly said. *Lester will,* she wanted to add, but she left it at that.

"But why is Earl Griffith involved in this?" Jasmine said, more to herself than to Rachel.

Rachel's eyes widened. Earl! That was the name Cecelia had used yesterday. "Earl Griffith is your Pastor Griffith?"

Jasmine shook her head, like she didn't want to focus on that. "We need to be worried about Cecelia. She thinks she's slick," Jasmine said. "The one complaint Cecelia and her husband get all the time is that people say they have too much power. She knows that telling everyone about the merger ahead of time might bring that issue back up. That's why they're keeping it a secret. But I guarantee you, that's why she wants the position."

They sat for a moment, processing this discovery. The members of the ABC wouldn't take kindly to any secret deals, but she and Jasmine had to tread carefully. Cecelia was a smart woman, so they had to figure out a strategy to use this information against her.

Rachel glanced across the table at Jasmine. She looked like her mind was churning. Rachel hated to admit it, but together, she had no doubt she and Jasmine Bush would come up with a plan to bring Cecelia down.

Chapter
THIRTY-ONE

The two women paced from one end of the suite to the other, their heads down, their thoughts focused. There had to be a way to use this information.

Rachel said, "Well, we could go to our husbands and tell them what's going on."

But before the words were completely out of Rachel's mouth, Jasmine was shaking her head. "You already told me that Lester is just like Hosea. They would want to investigate this, and like you said, we don't have that kind of time."

Rachel nodded. "Yeah, you're right."

As Jasmine paced, though, her thoughts were beyond Cecelia. Yes, she wanted to bring that backstabbing, RuPaul-looking, slime-eel down, but it was Earl Griffith's name in that article that troubled her the most.

Rachel said, "You know, it's the three-way race that's the problem. If one of our husbands dropped out, the other would get all the votes and clobber Cecelia."

"So, Lester's prepared to do that?" Jasmine smirked.

"In your dreams."

Jasmine chuckled—if she wasn't her enemy, Rachel might have made a good friend.

A knock interrupted Jasmine's thoughts and she'd barely opened the door before Mae Frances barged in, already talking.

"Jasmine Larson, there's just one day left to win this——" Mae Frances stopped so suddenly, Jasmine thought she'd topple over. Her glance moved from Jasmine to Rachel. Back and forth.

When her eyes settled on Rachel, Mae Frances growled, "What's she doing here?"

"She . . . came to apologize. About, you know"—Jasmine waved her hand—"the whole Jacquie thing."

"The whole Jacquie thing?" It must've been all the lies that Mae Frances had told in her life that made her shake her head. "What's really going on?"

In the past, Jasmine would've had Mae Frances right beside her, helping her handle this business—especially the part about Pastor Griffith. But it *was* the part about Griffith that made her keep her mouth shut.

"We're just talking, Mae Frances," Jasmine said, directing her back to the door. "Trying to settle things because we think that even with Cecelia in the race, one of our husbands is going to win. We're just finding a way to be cordial."

Her friend wasn't having it. "This is too important to be mixing with the enemy."

Behind her, Jasmine heard Rachel grunt, but she kept her eyes on Mae Frances. Right now, Rachel felt more like a friend than Mae Frances did, but there was no way that she could say that. Just like there was no way that she would get rid of Mae Frances if she didn't toss her some kind of bone.

So, she winked, then mouthed, "I'll call you later."

"Oh," Mae Frances mouthed back, and winked herself before she left the two alone.

"Who is that old hag anyway?" Rachel asked.

Through lips that barely moved, Jasmine said, "She's a good friend," trying not to let Rachel see how offended she was by that comment.

"Really?" Rachel said as if she found that hard to believe. "Why does she walk around wearing that old rabbit coat?"

"It's a mink!" The words burst from Jasmine. She'd let Rachel get away with the hag comment, but that was it. Until she knew for sure, Mae Frances was still on her side. That meant that she herself was the only one who could talk about her friend that way. "And," Jasmine added, "I wouldn't make too much fun of her if I was you."

Rachel laughed. "As if she could do anything to me."

"Do you have a brother who's gay and one who's on drugs?"

Rachel's eyes opened wide as her mouth snapped shut.

"Exactly!" Jasmine said. "All of that—and a whole lot more about you—came from Mae Frances. You think *you* have someone who can dig up dirt? *No one* is better than Mae Frances."

After a few seconds, Rachel said, "She found out all of that about my family?"

Jasmine nodded. "And like I said, even more."

"Well, maybe we should use her to bring down Cecelia."

Jasmine had to pause and look at Rachel again. Just a little while ago, she'd made a dig about Rachel's education, but there was no way you could hate on Rachel Adams. She was focused, and willing to do anything—even work with her and Mae Frances—to win.

"So"—Rachel cut through her thoughts—"you think your friend can help us?"

"No," Jasmine said. "She'll . . ." She paused to think of a good lie. "She'll tell Hosea."

Rachel fell onto the sofa. "Then what in the world are we going to do now?"

"What about *your* friend?" Jasmine asked, the thought just coming to her.

Rachel frowned.

"Your TV reporter friend. Did you tell her about this?"

"No, not really. I just asked her to look up the Kings to see what she could find."

"So, you didn't tell her about the story?"

"No . . ." Rachel sat up straight on the sofa. "I didn't even know it was a story until a few minutes ago. That's what I have to do!" She jumped up and grabbed her cell from her purse.

While she dialed, Jasmine thought about the plan. Yes, if they could get Rachel's friend to report on this story, even without all the information, it could be enough to get a few people to move their votes away from Cecelia. It would be all innuendo, of course. But reporters didn't need all the facts . . .

the reporter would just ask a few questions, get Cecelia off guard, and bam!

Yes, that would work. Because most of the Coalition would be against a merger.

So, that would bring Cecelia down for sure.

Now all Jasmine had to do was make sure that those people who left Cecelia didn't vote for Lester, either. And she knew exactly how she was going to do that.

"Okay," Rachel said, tucking her phone back into her bag. "I left her a message. This is absolutely perfect because Cecelia is a press hog; she'll be happy to talk to Melinda again. And when Melinda asks her about the merger . . ." Rachel pumped her fist in the air. "This is it. I just pray she calls me back in time."

With that handled, Jasmine needed to get Rachel out of her suite so that she could get working on the part of the plan that would take Rachel down at the same time.

But it seemed as if Rachel was as anxious to get away as Jasmine was to get rid of her.

"I'm going to go and . . . um . . . wait for Melinda to call," Rachel said, rushing to the door. "And I'll . . . um . . . call your room when I hear back from her."

"Okay," Jasmine said, opening the door for Rachel, then closing it just as quickly behind her.

Good! If that reporter was as good as she was the other morning, that was one down. Now for the Adams family part of the plan.

Jasmine would need the hotel's business office for that.

Jasmine glanced over the flyers once again.

It hadn't taken too long to complete this—less than an hour, actually. It was her own exposé and now everyone in the Coalition was going to know the truth about everyone in her competition's family.

The top of the flyer introduced the happy couple—a mug shot of Rachel (from back in the day) and one of Lester (from his false arrest). The pictures added authenticity to the facts that followed: Rachel's arrest, followed by the litany of tricks she'd pulled to try to win back her baby daddy. That was followed by the information about Lester's arrest. Then came the supporting cast: one brother so strung out on drugs that gang members and drug dealers often showed up at Zion Hill (because his father used to be the pastor) with guns and knives, threatening death to church members because of the money that Rachel's brother owed. Then there was the other brother who had married, fathered a child, but kept a gay lover on the side the whole time.

Of course, the stories were so exaggerated they were *almost* false. But one thing that Jasmine had learned this week was that the saints of the American Baptist Coalition loved themselves some good drama. It didn't matter if it was true or not—just as long as it delivered enough for them to talk about.

Stuffing the flyers into a manila envelope, Jasmine knew that she'd finished the easiest part; the most difficult was yet to come. She had to slip these six-hundred-plus flyers under the doors of all the guest rooms—after hours, of course. She had no idea how she was going to get out of their suite, and even less of an idea of how long it was going to take her. But it had to be done. Tonight. It was all over tomorrow.

Tomorrow! The morning couldn't come fast enough for Jasmine. She was tired, dead tired of all of this work—the back-and-forth between her and Rachel. Bringing down Lester Adams was a full-time job because Rachel had been a formidable opponent.

But was it worth it? Beyond definitely! Hosea was going to be the new president. Tomorrow at this time, they would all be celebrating—she and Hosea, Reverend Bush, Mae Frances . . . and Pastor Griffith.

She sat back and stared at the now-dark computer screen. Pastor Griffith, the dealmaker.

She pushed her nagging thoughts about that article aside. After all, the mission had been accomplished. If Rachel reached

Melinda, Cecelia would be out of the race, and with what she held in her hand, Hosea would be victorious.

Would the merger still go through with Hosea as the president? That would make him (and her) even more powerful—and that was a good thing, right? But if the merger was so good, why was it being done in secret?

That was it! That was the question that had been gnawing at Jasmine from the moment she read the article. The secrecy—why? She guessed see could understand Cecelia's motivation for running—it was all about power. But what kind of power would Pastor Griffith have? And if he'd put this together with Cecelia, why hadn't he backed her from the start?

For that matter, why hadn't he run for office himself?

Jasmine tossed aside the flyers. The day was getting late and she was supposed to be having dinner with Hosea and some of the others from the North. But there were things that she had to know. She swiped her credit card to add time so that she could use the Internet.

And then she got to work.

Melinda had turned out to be a blessing. Rachel had been concerned that the reporter would grow weary of her, but Melinda had returned Rachel's call in less than an hour. And once Rachel had filled her in on everything, she had been more than willing to help—again.

"Thank you so much for agreeing to come back out. I know I have worried the mess out of you this week," Rachel said. "But you just don't know how grateful I am."

"Well, I told you I owe you, and to call on me anytime."

"Yeah, but I'm sure you didn't think that call would come over and over." Rachel chuckled.

"It really is no problem. Actually, you're doing me a favor because there's nothing like some juicy item to lead the five o'clock news."

"And there's nothing juicier than some good ol' church drama."

"You ain't never lied." Their laughter died down and Melinda spoke again. "So, look, I'm just gonna call Cecelia myself so she doesn't think something is up. I'll give her some spiel about needing to redo the interview."

"Yeah, and if you tell her you're going live right before the election, she'll eat that up. You just can't let her know you've talked to me. She might get suspicious."

"Trust me, I've got this under control."

"Okay, but, Melinda, don't make the organization look too bad, all right? You know I'm about to be first lady."

Melinda let out a laugh. "I got you. As long as you promise I get the scoop if any drama does jump off at any time."

"The exclusive scoop!"

"Great!" Melinda exclaimed. "So, I'll see you tomorrow. Pray we don't have any breaking news that I get called away to."

"What?" A flash of panic swept over her. Melinda had to show up. They had to follow through with this plan—it was the only shot they had at bringing Cecelia down.

"Calm down," Melinda said. "We have a full staff, so it shouldn't be an issue. I'll be there."

"Whew, okay. I'll see you then."

Rachel had just pressed the end button on her cell phone when she heard, "What in the world are you up to now?"

She spun around to face Lester. She had been so caught up in her conversation that she hadn't heard him enter the suite.

"Are you eavesdropping on me now?" she asked.

Lester loosened his tie as he walked over and kissed her on the cheek. "No, I'm not. I just walked in to hear you using your conspiratorial voice."

"I don't have a conspiratorial voice."

He chuckled. "Okay, darling. I'm sure that was the pizza man."

Rachel didn't have time for a lengthy debate with her husband. She'd handled Cecelia, but she still had to contend with Jasmine. Sure, they were working together, and while she actually made a great ally, she didn't trust Jasmine one bit. Jasmine thought she was some young, dumb country hick. (For the life of her she couldn't understand why people considered Texans country. She'd never in her life owned a pair of cowboy boots!) Rachel might not have been educated, but she dang sure was smart. And she knew all the "Kumbaya" coming-together mess was just a front. At the end of the day, Jasmine wanted to win as bad as she did, and that wasn't about to change just because Cecelia had stepped in the ring.

The game was still survival of the fittest. And Rachel was the queen of the jungle.

That meant she needed a plan B, for after she implemented plan A.

"And I'm taking the kids and moving to China."

"Huh?" Rachel said, snapping her attention back to her husband.

He pointed an accusatory finger at her. "That right there is how I know you're up to something. I've been talking to you for five minutes and you haven't heard a word I said."

"Babe, I'm sorry. I'm just nervous about tomorrow, and thinking about Cecelia."

"Well, don't be nervous and definitely don't think about Cecelia."

"Did you guys ever figure out what she was up to?" How Rachel wanted to tell Lester what they'd uncovered. But Jasmine was right, he wouldn't do anything about it. In fact, he'd say something to Hosea, who would probably say something to the Kings. And right about now, Rachel wasn't trying to tip her hand.

"No, I think she just wants the position. I don't buy that whole 'this was a last-minute decision.' I think she's lying about that."

"Ya think?"

"Regardless, I still am not going to stress over it. In Cecelia's own words, what God has for me is for me." He turned and walked toward the bedroom.

Rachel made a choking motion in his direction. After they won this thing, she was going to work on that we-are-the-world, can't-we-all-just-get-along mentality. He was definitely going to need some backbone, some aggression, if he planned on leading one of the most powerful religious organizations in the country.

She reminded herself of the pending merger. "Make that one of the most powerful religious organizations in the *world*," she mumbled.

"What did you say?" Lester called out from the bedroom.

"Oh, I just said I'm going to go get the kids from that children's event so we can have a lovely dinner as a family.

Tomorrow, our lives will change drastically and it's going to be hectic from then on."

Lester stuck his head out the bedroom door. "Let's not get ahead of ourselves, darling."

"Oh, we got this, baby," she said sweetly. Cecelia was taken care of. As for Jasmine, well, Rachel had one last trick up her sleeve for that one. She wouldn't use it unless she absolutely had to. Rachel actually hoped that she didn't have to use it. But Loretta Jackson hadn't raised no fools, so just in case Jasmine wanted to pull some type of last-minute dirty trick, Rachel was ready. And if Jasmine did double-cross her, she'd definitely leave LA wishing that she'd never met Rachel Jackson Adams.

Chapter
THIRTY-THREE

Jasmine was shaking, even as she closed her eyes and prayed.

It hadn't taken her long to find out what Pastor Griffith was up to. She had her answer. It had been hidden deep inside the Internet, but the secret couldn't stay concealed from her. She could thank the training that she'd gotten when she'd worked at her godbrother Malik's nightclub. There were always investors who were eager to partner with the hottest nightclub in Manhattan, Rio. Of course, their private investigators did most of the work, but Jasmine and Malik always checked out the potential investors first.

That's when she'd learned to use the Internet to uncover the truth. And that's what she'd uncovered today.

Jasmine knew she didn't have the whole story, but she had enough. And honestly, she didn't want any more. What she had was frightening all by itself.

But the scariest part of all was that the woman she'd called her friend, the one whom her children loved as their grandmother, could be involved in this, too.

That's why Jasmine couldn't stop shaking, even as she stood outside her children's hotel suite. Because what was going to happen if Mae Frances was in the center of this?

Before Jasmine could knock, the door opened.

"I thought I heard someone out here," Mae Frances mumbled. "It's about time you got down here, Jasmine Larson. What were you doing up there with Rachel Adams?" She sounded as if her feelings were hurt. As if she couldn't believe she'd been left out.

Jasmine peeked through the suite. "Where are Zaya and Jacquie?" she asked, ignoring Mae Frances's question.

"Mrs. Sloss took them down to the children's center. Jacquie wanted to play with some of the kids she'd met."

Jasmine's heart skipped a beat, but only for a moment. After that scare with Rachel, she knew that Mrs. Sloss wouldn't let either child out of her sight. Her children were fine, they were safe. Now she had to take care of her husband.

She hadn't been sure where she would handle this with Mae Frances; there was no place to hide in the hotel. Even in the business center, she'd been careful, choosing the computer that was in the farthest corner. But for talking, they needed privacy. And there weren't many places that would give them that. Certainly, none of the public areas were an option. And Jasmine couldn't take Mae Frances back to her suite because Hosea could walk in at any moment—with Pastor Griffith.

So, having the children gone with Mrs. Sloss was a blessing.

Jasmine faced Mae Frances and was surprised to see the woman standing with her arms crossed and her face set in a scowl, as if she was the one who had something to be mad about.

Mae Frances said, "So, do you want to tell me what you were doing with Rachel Adams?"

"Are you my friend?"

Mae Frances frowned. "What?"

"You heard me!" Jasmine exclaimed, her voice louder now. "Are you my friend?"

It must have been the question, her tone and the volume, that made Mae Frances drop her arms and peer into Jasmine's eyes. "What are you talking about, Jasmine Larson?" Her voice was whisper-soft and filled with confusion.

Jasmine took a step closer. "I'm asking you a question—are you really my friend?"

Mae Frances blinked. "I'm more than that. I love you like I'd given birth to you myself."

Jasmine sucked in a breath. Over the years, Mae Frances had

said that often—and every time, Jasmine believed her. Even now her words felt the same as they had before.

That's why all that she'd seen, all that she'd heard, and what she'd just discovered didn't make sense.

"I don't know if I can trust you," Jasmine said.

"Where in the hell is this coming from?" Mae Frances's hands cut through the air with each syllable.

Jasmine was almost ready to tell her . . . but not yet. "Why do you want Hosea to be the president of the ABC?"

"What? Jasmine Larson, what is this about?"

"Just answer me, Mae Frances! Please!"

"I . . . I want him to be the president because that's what you want. You told me that you *had* to be first lady, and has there ever been a time when I didn't help you?" She paused. "Whenever you ask me for anything, if I am able, I will give it to you; I will make it happen for you."

There it was—the truth. And Jasmine knew that . . . from that place deep in her heart. Hadn't Mae Frances proven her love over and over again?

Or maybe that's just what Jasmine wanted to believe, what she needed to believe.

Either way, she was exhausted, and she settled onto the couch.

"What is this about, Jasmine Larson?" Mae Frances asked as she sat next to Jasmine.

It was time to see which side Mae Frances was on. "What do you know about Pastor Griffith?"

"Earl?"

"Yes. What do you know about him?"

Mae Frances paused as if she had to give that some thought. "Well . . . I met him years ago; he was a new pastor visiting New York for a convention. We stayed in touch over the years."

"How did you meet him?"

"Jeremiah Wright introduced us."

Jasmine nodded; the mention of that pastor's name helped her to feel better about the decision to trust her friend. "Did you know Reverend Wright threw Pastor Griffith out of his church years ago?"

"What? No! Earl said that he left to start his own church."

"He did. And he took quite a few of Reverend Wright's members with him. But according to what I've read, that didn't matter to Reverend Wright. He just wanted to get rid of Griffith—for improprieties. It looks like Reverend Wright tried his best to keep it out of the news for the sake of his church, but Pastor Griffith was taking money from athletes and other celebrities and helping them to launder money through the church."

"Are you kidding me?" Mae Frances pressed her hand against her mouth as if she were trying to hold her shock inside.

"It's true," Jasmine said. For the last few hours, exhaustion had held her hostage, not letting go. But now the aches of her weariness dissipated. Adrenaline surged through her, and she stood and she paced and she told the story.

"Pastor Griffith would take a ten-million-dollar check from someone, have them call it a tithe so that they could write the entire amount off, and then flush five million back to them in cash. And there were other schemes, too—money laundering for drug dealers."

"Oh, my God!" Mae Frances sat, stilled by the shock. "So . . . what does this mean?"

"It seems that his church is now under federal investigation for these same practices. He's been able to keep the story quiet because he keeps telling officials that he'll cooperate." Jasmine took a breath. "What I think is that he's looking for another place to put all of this money. He's betting that no one would look at the Coalition, especially if the ABC merged with the National Baptist Coalition."

Mae Frances shook her head. "You're losing me. What merger?"

Jasmine filled Mae Frances in on everything that Rachel had told her—about overhearing Cecelia with Coco, about what Lester Adams said about no one wanting the merger, and lastly about the article she'd read. "It was that article that I couldn't get out of my mind. About the merger and Pastor Griffith's connection to Cecelia," she said. "It was that article that made me search for more."

"And that's when you found out about the investigation?"

Jasmine nodded.

"But the merger, you said he was in it with Cecelia?"

"Yeah," Jasmine sighed. "That's the part I can't quite figure out. If he was in on the merger with Cecelia, why didn't he just back her?"

Mae Frances shook her head. "I don't know. Maybe he thought it would just be better with Hosea at the helm."

"Maybe." Jasmine nodded. "Maybe he felt that with someone like Hosea, the authorities would never look at the Coalition, especially if it had merged and was twice the size."

Mae Frances said, "They might have even chosen Hosea specifically."

"Exactly."

"A high-profile preacher who always does the right thing. No one would look at him. But if the law did come . . ."

Jasmine stopped walking, stood in front of Mae Frances, and nodded. "Hosea would be the one in charge of the Coalition. He'd be the one responsible. He'd be all up in this. And if he didn't do what Pastor Griffith and the Killer B's told him to do—"

"Wait!" Mae Frances held up her hands. "The Killer B's?" Her eyes were wide at the mention of one of the most notorious gangs in the country.

Jasmine nodded. "This whole investigation began because of the Killer B's and Pastor Griffith's connection to them."

"Oh, my God." Mae Frances shook her head. "I just can't believe this, Jasmine Larson."

Jasmine said, "I think that's where Pastor Griffith got all of the money. For the North and even the million that he used to cover me. I think much of the money is drug money."

Mae Frances pushed herself from the couch. "I've got to check this out."

"No." Jasmine grabbed her arm. She was shaking with fear. "You can't say anything to Pastor Griffith," she pleaded. "If only half of this is true, it's enough to—"

"I'm not going to call him, Jasmine Larson." Mae Frances

snatched her arm away. "Give me some credit." She walked toward the phone. "I need to make a call, though."

"To whom?"

"Jeremiah Wright."

Jasmine nodded. She could handle that; she felt safe with the call going to him.

It took Mae Frances a couple of calls to get through, but as Jasmine watched her talk to the reverend and then his son, she knew she'd been right. What she'd discovered was just the tip of what could be a disaster.

Though the phone was still pressed to her ear, Mae Frances fell onto the bed as if the burden of the shocking revelations was just too heavy to handle. When she yelped another "Oh, my God," Jasmine slowly took out the flyers that she'd made about Lester and Rachel from the envelope.

She began to rip them in half.

There was no way she was going to let Hosea win this election. The problem was, she couldn't go to him with this information, though. Hosea wouldn't be afraid; he would just tell Pastor Griffith that there wouldn't be any illegal activities going on while he was president of the Coalition.

No, Hosea wouldn't have any fear at all, and he'd tell Pastor Griffith that he wasn't scared.

That was okay. Hosea didn't have to be afraid; Jasmine had enough fear . . . and enough good sense not to mess with this, enough for the both of them.

As Mae Frances kept talking, Jasmine kept tearing the flyers . . . one by one, two by two, three by there. And she thought of new flyers that she had to make.

She only had a few hours to make it happen, but she was sure by the time morning broke, and the new flyers were read in the light of day, there would be very few who would vote for Hosea Bush as the president of the American Baptist Coalition. Merger or no merger.

And that was exactly the way Jasmine wanted it.

Chapter
THIRTY-FOUR

Now she knew how Michelle Obama felt on that brisk November day back in 2008. Rachel felt a mix of queasiness, anxiety, and eager anticipation. In just a few hours, the votes would be cast and she would officially become the first lady of the American Baptist Coalition.

But first, there was one other order of business.

I'm in front of the ballroom. CK on her way down. The text from Melinda had put the game plan into motion. Rachel kissed her kids, who sat in the living room of the suite watching *SpongeBob SquarePants*. They were oblivious to the fact that their lives were about to change forever. And Rachel liked it that way. She wanted her kids to have the best in life. Granted, she grew up in a pretty middle-class household, but she wanted her own family to know a life she only dreamed about.

And she was about to give it to them.

"Be good for the sitter, kids," Rachel said, heading toward the door, where Lester was impatiently waiting. "When we get back, we're gonna have a big celebration."

"What we celebratin'?" Nia asked.

"Daddy's getting a new job," Rachel said.

"Rachel . . ." Lester began.

Rachel stroked her daughter's hair. "Daddy is modest about his new position, but Mommy has enough excitement for us all."

"What's 'modest'?" Nia asked.

"You so dumb," Jordan said, not looking up from his PS2.

"No, I'm not, and I bet you don't know either."

"Okay, stop that fighting." Rachel shot them both warning glances. "If the sitter tells me there's been any fighting when I get back, you're in big trouble. Understand?"

"Yes, ma'am." Nia nodded.

Jordan just grunted. Brooklyn and Lewis were engrossed in a Fisher-Price piano.

"Sweetie, are you ready? It was your idea to get down there early," Lester said.

Rachel nodded as she scooted toward the door. Lester thought they were getting downstairs a little ahead of schedule just to get situated. But Rachel wanted to make sure they were front and center for the show.

By the time they made it downstairs, the show had already begun. Melinda was at the back of the ballroom, looking over some notes. Scott, the photographer, was behind the camera. Another lean, lanky man was pulling cords and cables across the floor. Cecelia was coming down from the stage and heading toward Melinda.

"Hey, why didn't you tell me we were getting some more media coverage?" Lester asked as they walked in.

Rachel feigned surprise. She didn't respond because she didn't want to outright lie to Lester any more than she had. "Wow, that's Melinda. Let me go say hello."

Rachel left her husband's side, but took her time getting over to Melinda. She wanted to give Cecelia enough time to get within earshot.

"Hey, Rachel," Melinda said as both Rachel and Cecelia approached. "Mrs. King."

"Hello, Melinda," Cecelia said, not bothering to acknowledge Rachel. The blatant diss was a slap in the face, and had she not known what was about to go down, she probably would've been angry.

"What are you doing here?" Rachel asked, leaning in to hug her.

"Oh, the tape with Cecelia's interview messed up. I would've called you, but I've been swamped. I just figured I'd see you here and—"

"Hey, sorry to cut you off, but we're thirty seconds out," Scott said.

"Sorry, Rachel," Melinda said, moving into place. "We're actually going live, so I'll just chat with you later."

"Yes, she'll chat with you later," Cecelia said with a haughty tone.

"Well, is it okay if we stand back and watch?" Rachel asked. She wasn't going to let Cecelia get under her skin. Payback was just seconds away.

"Yeah, but I need you to stand back and stay quiet," Scott said as he waved back Rachel and several other people who'd gathered around to watch.

Cecelia stepped into place with an air like she was about to be interviewed by Oprah.

"Standby, and three, two." Scott pointed a finger at Melinda.

"Good evening, Colleen. We are live at the American Baptist Coalition Conference," Melinda began. Cecelia stood confidently, just out of frame. Rachel wanted to rejoice at how the entire ballroom had literally gone quiet so that they could hear.

"The ABC is one of the largest religious organizations in the country. And it appears that they're about to get even bigger. NewsChannel Four has learned about a secret deal that the ABC is working that will merge this group with the National Baptist Coalition." Gasps filled the ballroom. Melinda turned to Cecelia, who stood in stunned disbelief. "With me now is Cecelia King, the current first lady of the ABC, who with her husband, Rev. Andre King, is responsible for this merger. Mrs. King, how does it feel to know that your group is about to become one of the most powerful in the country?" Melinda pointed the microphone at Cecelia.

"I . . . ah . . . I . . . where in the world did you get your information from?" Cecelia said, trying to pull it together.

"There has been a very public rivalry between the two groups, so it's big news that the two of you are coming together. Particularly in light of the fact that the NBC recently filed for bankruptcy and is accused of misappropriation of funds."

"Again, where did you get that information from?"

"Is it true or not?"

Cecelia's eyes darted over the room. Every person inside was staring at her, waiting for her answer. "Well, yes, but—" She could barely finish her sentence as chatter filled the room.

"I take it from the reaction here that many in your organization didn't know about this merger?" Melinda said.

"We sure didn't!" someone yelled from the front.

"We'll merge with them over my dead body!"

"What's going on? Are you really trying to merge us with those crooks?"

The photographer made wild gestures behind the camera, trying to get everyone to settle down.

"I—I thought this interview was about my plans for the ABC," Cecelia stammered. No longer was she the poised, sophisticated woman who could woo anyone. Now she looked like a teenage girl who'd been busted with a boy in her room.

"It is," Melinda said. "We're trying to find out if you plan to acquire the NBC's debt. What about all of the charges against the organization? Or was this a way for you to defraud the creditors the group owes as some people are alleging?"

"What?" Cecelia's face was aghast. "I never!"

"And you never will!" somebody shouted.

"Why are the details of the merger not being made public? Is there something you're trying to hide?"

"I resent your implications."

Melinda continued, "And is it true that you and your husband negotiated as part of the merger that the salary of the president of both organizations would be combined, making the president of the ABC the highest-paid president of any religious organization, at four hundred fifty thousand dollars a year?"

"What?" several people yelled as noise filled the room again.

Cecelia took a deep breath, then gritted her teeth. "I resent you waltzing up in here, trying to ambush me."

"I'm just asking simple questions—things our viewers want to know," Melinda said innocently.

"Really, I don't understand why anyone outside the ABC should care," Cecelia replied with arrogance.

"You don't?" Melinda said. "You're a tax-exempt organization. If you become the biggest religious organization, that's millions of dollars in taxes you'll be denying the American people."

Cecelia huffed. "Young lady, I'm going to ask you and your photographer to leave our meeting."

"But you were okay with us being here a few minutes ago."

"That's before . . ." Cecelia stopped talking as she realized all of the people in the room were staring at her. "This interview is over!" She turned and stormed away.

Melinda turned back to the camera. "Well, as you see, Cecelia King didn't want to answer our questions. But that doesn't mean we're going to stop asking. We'll stay on top of this story and keep you updated. Back to you."

Scott flipped his camera off and people began bombarding Melinda with questions. Rachel didn't want to stand around, just in case people wondered if she had something to do with the ambush. Lester was already eyeing her suspiciously, as if he knew she was involved.

Rachel didn't give him time to say anything as she turned to make her way to her seat to wait for the meeting to begin. Cecelia had made a hasty exit. Hopefully, she wouldn't return. But if she did, Rachel was confident that interview had cast enough doubt to steal Cecelia's thunder.

Jasmine stood in front of the bathroom mirror and yawned. All she wanted to do was go back to bed and get the sleep that had eluded her all night. But that was not possible—she had to be downstairs with Hosea in just a few minutes. It was time for the Coalition to vote for president.

"Darlin'." Hosea banged on the door. "Are you almost ready? We're late."

"I'm coming," Jasmine said, though she didn't make a move, at first. After a few moments passed, she slowly walked into the lavatory area, closed the door behind her, lowered the lid on the toilet, and sat down.

The hem of her knit skirt rose slightly as she crossed her legs and glanced at her watch, wondering how much more time she could waste. Hosea wasn't going to stand for this much longer. Any second now, he'd be busting into the main part of the bathroom, demanding to know what was taking her so long.

But she needed the minutes to tick by because the more time she spent up here in their suite, the less time there would be for anyone to reveal to Hosea what she had done.

She covered her mouth as she yawned again, the evidence of just how tired she was. It had taken so much longer than she thought for her and Mae Frances to slip all of those flyers under the doors last night, but every moment had been worth it. As far as she was concerned, she was working to save her husband and children's lives. At least, that's how she looked at it by the time Mae Frances had finished talking to Reverend Wright last night . . .

Mae Frances had hardly been able to speak when she hung up the phone, but finally, she'd conveyed to Jasmine all that the reverend had told her. Reverend Wright did not know about Pastor Griffith's involvement with Hosea's election; he'd made that call to Hosea's boss, suggesting that Hosea run because Mae Frances had called him and he was such a fan of the Bush men.

"But he said for us to stay away from Earl." Mae Frances had almost cried when she'd told Jasmine that. "He said that there are definite connections between Earl and that gang and many believe he's not only laundering money, but dealing drugs."

Jasmine had sat down right next to Mae Frances. Together, they stared ahead, envisioning what their lives would be like if Hosea won the election.

"Jeremiah said that it would make sense for Earl to want this," Mae Frances continued with the bad news. "To get the gang involved in something bigger than his church—it would be easier to hide money. But he wasn't aware of the merger being back on. He said there had been a rumor that Earl was working with the Kings on trying to move the merger forward a couple of years ago, but because so many on both sides were against it, it was all so hush-hush. And Jeremiah was very surprised to hear that talks of the merger were back on."

"Are the Kings involved with Pastor Griffith and the gang?"

Mae Frances shook her head. "Jeremiah didn't know anything about that. He's not sure where Cecelia and her husband fit in, but he doubts that they would be involved in this. He said the Kings are all about power; they're money hungry, but he doesn't believe they would get caught up in anything too far out there—like drugs and money laundering."

"So." Jasmine squinted as if she was trying to think this through. "Maybe these are two separate things. We're trying to connect the dots, but maybe there's no puzzle."

Mae Frances nodded. "Maybe it's just about the Kings wanting the merger and Earl wanting a place to hide what he's doing. Maybe the Kings are not caught up in that at all."

"No," Jasmine sighed. "It looks like it's just Hosea who's caught up."

Mae Frances had taken Jasmine's hand. "Jeremiah said that if I have any proof of anything, I need to take it to Hosea and Sam——"

"No way," Jasmine said before Mae Frances could even finish. "I know my husband and father-in-law, and they'll try to fight it. They'll move forward with this election, they'll fight to win, and then they'll dare Pastor Griffith to mess with the Coalition. But I think it's too late, anyway. I think Griffith has probably already promised people things. And they won't care for a second how much of a stand-up guy my husband is."

Mae Frances nodded.

"I don't want Jacquie and Zaya anywhere near that gang. You've heard the stories," Jasmine said, leaving out how the gang was known for not even caring about women and children.

"But what are you going to do? This morning, Earl said that Preacher Man was edging ahead. He's always had the lead, but the way they've been working, even with Cecelia in the race, Hosea will win by a good margin."

Jasmine nodded, not surprised.

Mae Frances sighed. "You know why Hosea is so far ahead, right?" She didn't give Jasmine a chance to respond. "It's because of everything we did to make Rachel Adams look like a fool. Those people don't want her as the first lady—they don't want her as the face of the Coalition. They think she's young and dumb."

"She's not dumb," Jasmine said. "Trust that." She inhaled. "Rachel will be able to handle herself. She *almost* handled me."

"But she didn't, and we're going to win this thing. And then, Preacher Man will be caught up with . . ."

Jasmine had saved one flyer—just to show Mae Frances what her plan had been. "This was going to be my last shot before the election tomorrow," she told her friend. "This would have taken down the Adamses."

Mae Frances studied the flyer and the tears that were in her eyes a moment ago were replaced by a smile that Jasmine hadn't seen in a while. "Jasmine Larson," she said, "I've taught you well." But then her despair returned. "But this will guarantee that Preacher Man will win!"

Jasmine took the flyer from Mae Frances's grasp and did to it what she'd done with the others—she tore it in half and then in half again. "No one is going to see this. Instead we're going to make up a new one." Jasmine closed her eyes as if that was the only way she'd be able to tell Mae Frances what she had to do. "This time, the flyer will be all about me. And my days as a stripper . . . and . . . all the other things I used to do at that club."

There was a moment of silence before Mae Frances asked, "Are you sure?"

Slowly, her eyes fluttered open. "I have to. I have to make sure that Lester Adams wins. I have to protect Hosea."

So, that's what they'd done. After Jasmine had lied to Hosea, telling him that she was staying in the children's suite because Zaya wasn't feeling well, she and Mae Frances had made new flyers that exaggerated the story of Jasmine Cox, the stripper and high-priced call girl. And though she'd never been in jail, the flyer cited arrest after arrest, scandal after scandal. Then they'd printed up three hundred copies (because the center had run out of paper) and waited until after midnight to get them to as many rooms as they could. They'd had a good amount of flyers left over, but Mae Frances had destroyed them all.

There was no trace of their deception, no link between them and the flyers. And as Jasmine had laid her head on the pillow at just after four in the morning, her prayer had been that she'd done enough.

And in just about an hour, she would find out.

"Jasmine!"

Just as she expected, Hosea had barged into the bathroom.

"Are you okay in there?" he asked.

She stood, and even though the lid was still down, she flushed the toilet. Then she pressed her hand against her stomach and opened the door.

"I'm sorry, babe," she said, keeping her voice at a whisper. "My stomach is a little unsettled."

The annoyance that was on his face melted and he pulled her into his arms. "Darlin', you're just nervous."

"Yeah, I guess I am."

"Don't sweat this. It's going to work out the way God wants it to."

Jasmine nodded and Hosea clasped her hand inside his and led her into the bedroom. She grabbed her purse, took a final glance in the mirror, and prayed that God's plan and hers were exactly the same.

Jasmine was still holding Hosea's hand as they walked toward the ballroom. She tried to prepare herself for the glances and the whispers that she was sure would come her way; she just wasn't prepared for what she would say to Hosea.

Before she and Hosea even turned the corner, thoughts of the flyers that she prayed would seal Hosea's fate flew out of her mind. The hallway in front of the ballroom was packed with people, shouting. And in the narrow space of the hallway, their voices bounced off the walls, making it sound almost like a riot.

And in the center of the commotion was Rachel's friend Melinda. She was being bombarded with questions by members of the Coalition.

"How did you find out about the Kings' plans?"

"Who else is involved with this?"

"Can you do a full exposé to make sure nothing like this happens?"

From the questions that were being thrown at her, Jasmine knew that Melinda had done her job well. Now she was sorry that she had missed the show, but she'd had no choice. At least her reporting had taken away any attention that anyone had on the flyers.

Jasmine and Hosea pressed their way through the crowd, but inside the ballroom, the confusion continued. The aisles were filled with members, talking over one another, surprise on everyone's face. Onstage, Reverend Capers, the sergeant at arms, was trying to call the meeting to order, but no one seemed to be paying attention to the pounding of the gavel.

"I wonder what's going on?" Hosea whispered to Jasmine.

She shrugged, as if she didn't know, but at the same time, she scanned the space for the Kings, though it was hard to see anyone through the hundreds that filled the room. She did see Rachel, though, sitting in the front row, all prim and proper, with her eyes on Reverend Capers. It was as if Rachel was totally oblivious to all that was going on.

For the first time in hours, Jasmine smiled. Rachel created chaos, and then sat back and let it all unfold. If she didn't hate her so much, she just might like her.

Hosea led Jasmine down the center aisle, and few looked their way. The members were caught up with the merger; right now, they had little thought of the flyer that had appeared in their rooms this morning.

At the front, Hosea turned one way to greet Lester. She turned the other way and looked right into the face of Pastor Griffith.

"Good morning," he said, all smiles, all confidence.

It was hard for her to greet him back. Now that she knew what this man was all about and who he really was, she not only didn't want to have anything to do with him, she didn't want to talk to him.

But she had to act as if everything was the same. He was, after all, affiliated with the Killer B's. So she smiled, she nodded, and then she sat down and folded her hands in her lap.

With just a slight motion of her head, she turned the other way and glanced at Rachel, who was already looking at her. Rachel nodded, sending her a message. Jasmine nodded back, message received. They'd worked together for just twenty-four hours and it looked like they had brought Cecelia King and her husband down.

Hosea slipped into the seat next to her and unbuttoned his jacket. "You are not going to believe what happened," he said.

Her heart began to pound. Had Lester told Hosea about the flyers? Had she or Mae Frances made the mistake of putting one under the Adamses' door? Or had someone from their side showed it to Lester?

It had been so confusing last night. Mae Frances had been able to get a roster of who was staying in what room. But it was so much to digest and they had been tired . . . had they made a mistake?

"Cecelia King was just ambushed by a television reporter," Hosea said. "That's who's in the hallway. Turns out the Kings were trying to merge the ABC with the NBC and that's why Cecelia entered the race."

"Really?" Jasmine feigned surprise as her heartbeat slowed down to normal.

But she didn't get to say anything else. Reverend Capers was finally able to bring order to the room, and the Coalition members settled into their seats.

"We will now bring this meeting to order," the reverend said as he slammed the gavel against the podium.

Jasmine could barely breathe as another pastor went to the stage and led them in prayer. She didn't listen to the pastor's words, though; she had her own petition that she wanted God to hear.

After that, the conference parliamentarian took the stage and explained the voting process.

Finally, the parliamentarian said, "And now, as we prepare to vote, we would like to have the candidates go to the holding room. First, we have Lester Adams and his lovely wife, Rachel."

The Adamses stood, waved to the crowd, and the Coalition members responded with applause.

"Next," Reverend Capers continued, "Hosea Bush, and the beautiful Lady Jasmine."

As Hosea stood, he took Jasmine's hand and they both waved to the crowd. But this time, the applause was mixed with hisses and whispers.

Hosea frowned a bit, but led Jasmine through the side door. "I wonder what that was about?" he asked once they were outside.

Once again, Jasmine shrugged, as if she didn't know. But now that she was away from all of those people, she didn't want to think about what she'd done, she didn't want to think about what the members now thought of her and Hosea. All she wanted to do was get to that holding room, take her husband's hands, and pray until all the votes were in and tallied.

Chapter
THIRTY-SIX

The Kings weren't in the room, but Hosea and Jasmine were. They sat at a corner table, their heads bowed in prayer. Hosea's father stood in the other corner, his own head down as if he was praying, too. For a moment, Rachel wondered why the senior Reverend Bush was not in the other room voting—but then she remembered, the Bushes had not been members of the ABC. Reverend Bush couldn't vote.

When the Bushes finished praying, Rachel stood to go over and talk to Jasmine. She wasn't in the room during the interview and Rachel was anxious to tell her how well it had gone. But Jasmine's odd expression stopped her in her tracks.

She didn't seem as excited as Rachel. She looked scared. Nervous. Worried. Maybe she was about to pull a trick out of the bag. Rachel hoped that wasn't the case because this last little bit of info she had on Jasmine, she was hoping she wouldn't have to use. Despite all her bourgieness, Jasmine seemed like she could be cool. In fact, she kinda reminded Rachel of herself—in about thirty years.

That's why she was hoping Jasmine didn't stab her in her back, because then she'd have to play this last card, and it wouldn't be pretty.

Rachel studied Jasmine from across the room. She was in some serious thought. Suddenly it dawned on Rachel. Of course Jasmine was worried. Cecelia might no longer be a problem, but Jasmine knew Hosea was about to lose to Lester. Naturally, she had cause for concern.

Rachel shrugged. *Oh, well, guess we won't be friends, after all,* she thought as she sat back down next to Lester, who had his head buried in a Bible. Jasmine was probably going to return to her old funky self after Hosea lost.

"I wish I had your confidence," Lester said, looking up to see Rachel sitting nonchalantly at the table.

"I told you, sweetheart, you got this."

"But Hosea . . ." Lester whispered.

"Is a good man. I'll give him that, but you're working with tradition. Sixty years, that's how long it's been since a Northerner was elected president. That's not about to change now. Not to mention the fact that you're the young breath of fresh air this organization needs. Those people in that room know that."

Before Lester could reply, the conference parliamentarian stuck his head in the holding room. "They're ready. The votes are tallied."

Nervous anticipation finally set in. Rachel placed her hand on her stomach to quell her nerves. This was it. She glanced over at the Bushes again. Dang, she really had Jasmine scared. If she hadn't started to kinda like Jasmine, she would've delighted in her fear.

Back in the auditorium, Rachel followed her husband to their seats. A couple of people gave her suspicious glares. Those were probably just Cecelia's people thinking she had something to do with the TV ambush.

Rachel kept her head high as she took her seat. Cecelia and Reverend King were the last to enter the room. Cecelia looked like she'd been crying. Her eyes were puffy and slightly red. No doubt she'd spent the last thirty minutes trying to pull herself together.

When Cecelia passed Rachel, she stopped and glared. If looks could kill, Rachel would definitely be six feet under. Rachel shrugged innocently, shook her head like she was so disappointed.

"Please, everyone, take your seats," the conference chairwoman said. "We need to get this meeting started." She sounded flustered, like the drama from the merger news had taken its toll.

The merger. That's all everyone had been talking about since Melinda packed up and left. Most people were livid. Rachel had wanted to stay and hear what everyone had to say, but they'd been ushered to the holding room. She did hear a few people demand answers from Reverend King, but he'd ducked out a side door without talking.

Now he was back, walking hand in hand with his wife to the front. The Kings took their seats as the chairwoman called the meeting to order.

Rachel took a deep breath and patted her husband's hand. He could act like the outcome of the election didn't matter all he wanted, but she could tell he wanted this.

"Is Lester all right?" Simon leaned in and asked.

Rachel smiled at her father. "He's fine. Just nervous."

"I'm okay," Lester repeated. "Just ready for this to be over with."

"We're almost home, baby."

Rachel took a deep breath as the chairwoman began.

"Ladies and gentlemen, the votes have been tallied and it is my honor to announce the new president of the American Baptist Coalition."

Rachel squeezed her husband's arm. *Wait for it, wait for it . . .*

"With a final tally of 275, 240, and 117, I present to you, your new president . . . Rev. Lester Adams!"

Rachel couldn't help it—she let out a squeal as she jumped to her feet. Lester sat stunned, like he couldn't believe it. Several people immediately came over and congratulated him, including Hosea and the man who had introduced himself as Hosea's father earlier in the week. Rachel didn't expect to see Jasmine, but she was right by her husband's side as well. Only Jasmine no longer looked worried. Or nervous. In fact, Rachel couldn't be sure . . . but Jasmine almost looked . . . relieved.

The private charter hovered above the clouds at thirty thousand feet, and for the first time in a week, Jasmine felt at peace.

Hosea rested his hand on hers right before he said, "Darlin', you sure you're not disappointed?"

She faced her husband and looked into his eyes. It wasn't until Lester Adams's name was announced that she realized how much she'd given up—for herself, for her family, but especially for Hosea. She'd felt his disappointment, but her husband was full of grace in his defeat, convinced that the results were the will of the Lord.

"I'm a little disappointed," she said. "But I'm like you. For once, I left all of this up to God."

He leaned across the oversize leather seat and rubbed his lips against her cheek. "I'm going to check on the kids," he said as he stood and sauntered toward the back of the plane.

She sighed as she twisted back to the window, and the beauty of the highest parts of the sky.

This picturesque view reminded her of her first plane trip, when she was just ten years old. She'd never looked down upon clouds before and she was convinced that she was in heaven, God's home. And if she pressed her face hard against the window, she'd probably get a glimpse of Him.

She hadn't seen God that day, but she couldn't count the number of times she'd seen Him in the years that had followed. And He'd been with her today, for sure—Lester Adams had been elected, exactly the way she planned it.

It had been bittersweet to hear Lester's name announced as the new president of the Coalition, but Jasmine took special pride in the fact that there was no one on earth who could bring her down—they'd only lost the election because she'd given it away. But no one, except for Mae Frances, would ever know that. No one, could . . . especially not Pastor Griffith.

Jasmine felt the seat next to her recline, and she turned to face her husband. But her smile vanished right away.

"It's hard to believe we lost," Pastor Griffith said.

Jasmine could feel the pressure of her heart push against her chest—not pounding yet, but almost there. "Yeah," she said, doing her best to keep her voice steady.

After Lester's name had been announced, Jasmine had done everything she could to stay far away from the pastor. She'd caught him staring at her, time after time—as they left the hotel and packed into the limousine, then at the airport as they all checked in—but she'd always turned away as if she didn't notice him. But she had been able to feel his gaze. And he never stopped.

She'd done a great job ducking and dodging till now. But Jasmine knew that she couldn't run forever, and on this plane, there was no place to hide.

Pastor Griffith shook his head. "It doesn't make sense to me. When we counted the votes last night, right before we went to bed, Hosea was a shoo-in."

Jasmine shrugged. "I guess people changed their minds. You know how it is with a secret ballot; people say one thing, and then they do something totally different," she said, thinking that she had to give him some sort of explanation.

"It could be that, or it could've been this." Before he pulled the paper completely from his pocket, Jasmine knew what it was. And now her heart did hammer against her chest.

How did he get that? Since they'd put out these flyers last night, Jasmine couldn't stop wondering if they had been careful enough. They had stayed far away from anyone who was too close to the Northern team. Though she always knew there was a good chance that the flyers could come back, she had prayed that they didn't end up with Hosea . . . or Pastor Griffith.

But here it was, and here he was.

It must've been the shock that was stuck on her face that made him say, "So . . . you didn't know anything about this?"

"No!" She snatched it from his hand for the added effect. "Why would I? And where did you get this from anyway?"

"Seems like there were a whole lot of people in the Coalition who got one of these."

As he talked, Jasmine turned the paper over and looked at the other side that listed all of the arrests that she had made up.

He said, "The funny thing is, not everyone got one."

It took her a moment to think of something to say. "Well, thank God for that," she breathed as if she were relieved. "Because every word on this paper is a complete lie!" She stared at the flyer as if she still couldn't believe what she was seeing.

In a way, she couldn't. She was sure that once they'd left the hotel, she was totally free. Though after the election, some had looked at her with a sideward glance, no one had said anything to Hosea because the attention was mostly on Lester.

For that, Jasmine had been grateful. She didn't want the evidence of what she'd done to end up in her husband's face.

But then she relaxed—whether Hosea saw it or Pastor Griffith had it, who would believe that she had made up these flyers and had done this to herself? Rachel would get the blame for this, for sure. And that made Jasmine almost smile.

Almost—but she didn't. Because Pastor Griffith was still right there.

"You know"—he snatched the paper from her hand, then held it away so that Jasmine wouldn't be able to get it back—"I have a theory."

He paused, as if he wanted her to ask what it was, but Jasmine said nothing. She didn't want to prolong this conversation.

When she stayed silent, he continued, "I think someone who didn't want Hosea to win slipped these under the doors last night."

You think? "Well, that's obvious," she said. "It had to be someone from the Adams team."

He nodded, as if he was thinking about her words. "Or . . . it could have been someone from ours."

Jasmine wondered if she was going to die right there. What would he do if he knew for sure how those flyers had ended up in the hotel?

All Jasmine could think about were the Killer B's. But she couldn't lose it now. She'd gone through all of this to save her family; she had to make sure it played out all the way to the exact end that she wanted. And what she wanted was for her family to be back in New York, safe and away from this madness.

She twisted in her seat so that her whole body faced him. "Now, why would someone from our team do that?" she asked. Not only was she wearing her game face, but she had on her game attitude. She spoke as if she thought his words were foolish.

He shrugged. "Maybe *she* didn't want Hosea to win."

Jasmine raised an eyebrow. "She? I know you're not thinking it was me?" She folded her arms as if she was indignant. But really, that was just to make sure that he didn't see her shaking.

With a slight smile, he nodded. "Yeah, I was wondering if it was you."

She chuckled. "Please! Why would I do that?"

He shook his head slightly. "That's the part that I can't figure out."

"Well, let me help you out, because obviously you don't know me very well. But Jasmine Bush does whatever she has to do to win. 'Losing' is not a word that's in my vocabulary."

"Yeah, that's what I thought."

"And think about it, Pastor Griffith—you were the one who told me to stop interfering with trying to get my husband elected. Remember that? Remember the shoplifting setup and everything else?"

He nodded. "Yeah, you played hard. You were one of the reasons why we wanted your husband as the Northern nominee. We really did think that you'd be the perfect first lady."

Oh, God! Had they planned to have her all up in their mess, too?

"Well, whatever, I certainly wouldn't make up a flyer like that"—she pointed—"with all those lies."

He tilted his head slightly, and nodded as if he was thinking about her words. "Well, who could it be?"

She thought for a moment. "Did you know that the Penns were working with Cecelia?"

He frowned. "What are you talking about?"

"Rachel Adams told me that Coco Penn was working with the Kings to bring me down." And then Jasmine repeated the parts of the conversation that Rachel had overheard with Cecelia and Coco—leaving out, of course, the sections about the merger and his name.

"When did Rachel tell you this?" he asked.

Jasmine paused for a moment. "This morning, in the holding room," she lied, wanting him to think that it had been too late for them to do anything about this information. "Rachel wanted me to know that there was a *snake* amongst us."

He stared at her when she said "snake." And she stared right back as if she knew that he was a snake, too.

"Why would Rachel Adams want to tell you anything?"

Jasmine shrugged. "I guess that was just another way for her to gloat about Lester winning."

"Doesn't sound like gloating to me."

"Well, you know, she's not very bright."

He nodded. "That's an interesting theory, Jasmine."

"You have yours and I have mine."

"We had big plans for your husband."

"I'm sure you did."

He sighed. "There are a lot of people who are going to spend a lot of time wondering what happened," he said. "People who really believed in Hosea Bush."

"We're all sorry about the results."

"And we put in quite a bit of money . . . remember that million dollars?"

She was so pissed at herself for that now. The Child Find Centers—Jacqueline's Hope—would be started, probably with drug money. "Hosea and I will find a way to pay you back. Or we can cancel the centers altogether and give you back that million now."

He waved his hand. "No need for that. We're just gonna have to figure out what to do next."

In the week that had passed since they'd landed in Los Angeles, Jasmine had experienced every emotion: joy, pain, shock, despair . . . and finally, fear. Now she swallowed it all and said to Pastor Griffith, "Whatever you were going to do with a president from the North, you can just do it with a president from the South."

He tilted his head as if he was trying to get a better look at her. As if he was trying to see if they were talking the same talk, on same page. But after a few seconds, without another word, he tucked the flyer back into his jacket, stood up, and disappeared down the aisle.

She wanted to call him back, she wanted to ask for that flyer, but now that he was gone, she could breathe. Let him keep it— what was he going to do with it anyway?

Whatever you were going to do with a president from the North, you can just do it with a president from the South.

She hadn't planned to throw Rachel and Lester under the bus like that, but the truth was, Lester Adams had won. Anything that had to do with the Coalition was his problem now, and that included Pastor Earl Griffith.

And like she'd told Mae Frances last night, Rachel Adams could handle it. Jasmine didn't know what Lester could handle; he seemed pretty weak to her. But his wife? Rachel could surely handle anything.

Hosea slipped into his seat.

"I saw Pastor Griffith talking to you," he said. "He's really disappointed . . . even more than I am."

For a moment, Jasmine thought about telling Hosea everything. But she knew that she couldn't. Because even though he'd lost the election, he would still try to do something about it. He would still be that stand-up guy who thought he could fix everything.

No, Hosea Bush could never know anything about what she'd found out this week at the American Baptist Coalition convention.

Jasmine curled her fingers around Hosea's and brought his hand up to her lips. "I am so glad to be going home."

"Really?"

She nodded. "I just want to get back to our normal life."

Hosea laughed. " 'Normal' and 'Jasmine Bush' in the same sentence? I didn't think that was possible."

"I guess you don't really know me. So let me introduce myself. My name is Jasmine Cox Larson Bush, the first lady of City of Lights at Riverside Church."

He shook his head. "It's not the first lady of the ABC, is it?"

"Nope," she said. "But I'm the first lady to the best man on earth. And that means I'm exactly who I'm supposed to be."

When Hosea leaned over and kissed her with a passion that they'd only shared a few times this week, Jasmine knew that her words were the truth.

Sinners and Saints

Both Rachel Jackson Adams and Jasmine Larson Bush stand by their men—both of whom are pastors. But when their husbands are each nominated for the role of president of the American Baptist Coalition, the largest organization of African American churches, the kid gloves come off. Rachel and Jasmine each want her own husband to win—solely for the betterment of the ABC, of course. To become the most important first lady in America, the ladies will have to figure out what they're willing to sacrifice. Neither is quite a saint, but will they have to become sinners to make it to the top?

For Discussion

1. *Sinners and Saints* opens with Jasmine's promise to God. Do you think that Jasmine keeps her promise throughout the course of the story? Why or why not?

2. Jasmine feels bored with the routine of her life with Hosea (p. 4). How do you think this boredom influences her strong pursuit of the ABC's first lady title?

3. Rachel Jackson Adams imagines her love for her husband as agape love (p. 7). Look up the meaning of the word *agape* in a dictionary or the meaning of *agape love* on the Internet. Do you think this sentiment is true for Rachel and Lester, based on their interactions with each other throughout *Sinners and Saints*? Is agape love a good description of any of the relationships in the book?

4. Mae Frances seems like a fairy godmother to Jasmine. Do you think their friendship is beneficial for Jasmine? How about for Mae Frances? How did you perceive Mae Frances's role over the course of the ABC conference?

5. Rachel reminds Lester that "faith without works is dead" (p. 22). And Hosea is described as walking in his faith, while Jasmine works in hers (p. 33). What do you think of this idea of faith? Do you think you can be faithful without deeds? Are the first ladies faithful in their actions? What about the pastors?

6. Rachel's plan to sabotage Jasmine's arrival is cut short when current first lady Cecelia offers Jasmine's family half of their

floor. What did her generosity make you think of Cecelia? Were you proven correct or incorrect?

7. There is a strong divide between Jasmine and Rachel, and it's exacerbated by their backgrounds (country versus city, North versus South, etc.). Rachel takes pride in looking good for less, while Jasmine enjoys her designer brands. With which mind-set did you empathize? Do you love a bargain or an indulgence? How does the North/South divide impact their mind-sets? What could the ladies learn from each other about their different hometowns?

8. At different points in the novel, both Jasmine and Rachel find themselves humiliated in public. Do you think each of the women handled it well? Did one outshine the other in a mortifying moment? What's the best way that you've found to deal with embarrassment?

9. How are Lester and Hosea similar? Are their relationships with their respective wives markedly different, or do they interact in comparable ways? How do each of the pastors relate to God through word? Did you find yourself rooting for one or the other in their race to be president of the ABC?

10. What did you think of Cecelia's shifting alliances? Does she seem to truly favor one of the pastors (and his wife) more than the other? How would you characterize this woman, who has so much sway within the ABC?

11. At what point in their rivalry do you think Jasmine and Rachel cross a line? Which revelation or accusation or insinuation was the point at which you would have stood up and said, "Enough!" Have you ever taken a rivalry too far? What made you realize it was time to stop the conflict?

12. Discuss the ending of *Sinners and Saints*. How do you think Jasmine and Rachel's interactions will change now that the outcome of the presidential race has been decided? Will it change at all? What do you predict for the next novel starring these two powerful women?

13. *Sinners and Saints* is written by two authors—Victoria Christopher Murray and ReShonda Tate Billingsley. Did you notice any indication of the two authors? If so, how did this affect your reading of *Sinners and Saints*? If you have read any of their previous novels, did you pick up on any similarities in the writing?

A Conversation with
Victoria Christopher Murray and
ReShonda Tate Billingsley

How did the idea to write a book together come about? Did you two coordinate it, or was it suggested to you?

Well, that's a common thread that we both heard when we were out on our individual tours. Everyone would say, "Jasmine and Rachel should meet up." At first, we just laughed it off, but then when people started debating who would win in a Rachel-Jasmine battle, it seemed inevitable that these ladies would meet.

What was it like working together, letting two such beloved heroines interact? What was the writing process like? Did you plot it out together or hand off the manuscript, playing off each other's ideas?

This was the most fun either of us have ever had writing a book. We tried to lay out a general outline (which of course, changed along the way) but for the most part we fed off each other's creativity. In fact, reading each other's chapters only fueled our fire. We found ourselves trying to one-up each other after every chapter.

*How did you decide to set **Sinners and Saints** in Los Angeles? Was it the only place you thought to put the convention, or did you toy with the idea of holding it in one of the heroines' hometowns? How do you feel the neutral ground plays into the story?*

From the start we wanted a neutral location. Since Jasmine was living in New York and Rachel was living in Houston, we felt Los Angeles would be the ideal spot for the conference to take place.

What is it about the first ladies that lead them to make promises first—giving $1 million, knowing Regina West— and worry about fulfilling those pledges later? Did you intend for the characters to act similarly in this way?

Both Jasmine and Rachel's downfall is they sometimes act first and think later. At the spur of the moment, neither woman wants to be outdone, which is why they go overboard with their pledges and promises of what they can accomplish. We never planned for them to act similarly. We just let our characters be who they are, and their similarities showed.

Victoria, how do you write characters from different generations so seamlessly? Do you have an easier time with characters of one age, or is it equally challenging to get all the voices right, regardless of the characters' ages?

That's interesting; I've never paid attention to the differences in my characters' ages, though I work very hard making sure that each of my characters has an authentic voice. I'm not sure age has as much to do with it as does the content of their character. Whichever character, I just try to stay true to who they are— that takes in everything including their ages.

Both Jasmine and Rachel have to grapple with their pasts in order to do what's right for their families and churches. Do you think that their checkered lives give them more depth than more perfectly behaved characters? Do you empathize more with their sinful or their saintly sides?

Rachel and Jasmine are actually fan favorites for a reason—they are flawed characters who in their hearts want to do right, but can't ever seem to stay on the righteous path. That's why their sinful sides seem to garner the most empathy. That's also something women from all walks of life can relate to.

ReShonda, you often write about a whole cast of women. Is it easier to write a story centered around one main female character, or do you prefer to write ensemble pieces? Tell us about the difference between writing these two different types of novels.

I actually don't have a preference. I simply enjoy getting into the minds of my female characters. When I'm centering a story on more than one main character, I have to be more focused to make sure each of them has their own unique voice. But I actually like the challenge of doing that.

You both have fantastically crafted websites that offer ways to get in touch with you via the site, Twitter, and Facebook. What is the most common feedback you get from readers? Have you ever incorporated that feedback in your writing? How connected do you feel to your fans?

We both always joke about how accessible we are to readers. We both try to answer all of our e-mail; we interact with readers on Facebook and Twitter. What we hear the most is how much readers enjoy the books. We also hear a lot from people who want us to come to their area and do book signings.

Who are the sinners and who are the saints? With which character do each of you empathize with the most?

Hmmm, good one. Well, we definitely know Rachel and Jasmine are nowhere near sainthood! (Although if you were to ask them, they'd both probably claim they were the saints.) Both Lester and Hosea are as close to saints as you'll get in this book. If anyone deserves empathy, it's those two men, because their wives are truly out of control!

Finally, what can you tell us about your next book together? What's in store for Rachel and Jasmine, and when can readers expect to get their hands on the next installment?

What's so great about this project is that when we started, we had no idea who would win the election. Actually, we were nearing the end of the book, and we still had no idea. Then, when the events unfolded as they did, we knew the door was opening for book number two. You know, even though the battle may have been won, the war is far from over. Now that a new president is installed, these two women will have to work together, and deal with some danger that they find themselves embroiled in. We can't wait for readers to check out that book as well!

Enhance Your Book Club

1. Have your own vote! Make a ballot box (or just use a hat), and have everyone write down on a slip of paper the name of the pastor they would have voted for if they were at the ABC election. Tally the votes and see who comes out on top!

2. The pastors and first ladies each use scripture and prayer to help them through the hard times. Have a Bible on hand and give all participants the opportunity to share their favorite scripture passage, prayer, or personal motto. What kinds of help do you need throughout the day?

3. If members of your book club are not Baptist, visit a Baptist church. If members are Baptist, visit another Christian denomination for Sunday services. After the celebration, talk with one another about the differences and similarities between the church services you've experienced.

Don't miss the second installment in

Victoria Christopher Murray

and

ReShonda Tate Billingsley's

electrifying collaboration...

COMING FROM GALLERY BOOKS IN 2013!

In the meantime, catch up with your favorite heroines in these thrilling titles, available now at SimonandSchuster.com!

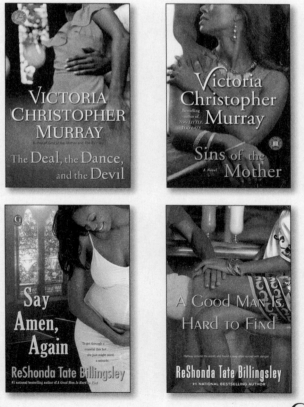